Virt[...]
Real Punishment.

TOM CLANCY'S NET FORCE™

Don't miss any of these exciting adventures
starring the teens of Net Force . . .

VIRTUAL VANDALS

The Net Force Explorers go head-to-head with a group of
teenage pranksters on-line—and find out firsthand that virtual bullets can kill you!

THE DEADLIEST GAME

The virtual Dominion of Sarxos is the most popular war
game on the Net. But someone is taking the game too
seriously . . .

ONE IS THE LONELIEST NUMBER

The Net Force Explorers have exiled Roddy—who sabo-
taged one program too many. But Roddy's created a new
"playroom" to blow them away . . .

THE ULTIMATE ESCAPE

Net Force Explorer pilot Julio Cortez and his family are
being held hostage. And if the proper authorities refuse to
help, it'll be Net Force Explorers to the rescue!

THE GREAT RACE

A virtual space race against teams from other countries will be a blast for the Net Force Explorers. But someone will go to any extreme to sabotage the race—even murder . . .

END GAME

An exclusive resort is suffering net thefts, and Net Force Explorer Megan O'Malley is ready to take the thief down. But the criminal has a plan—to put her out of commission—*permanently* . . .

CYBERSPY

A "wearable computer" permits a mysterious hacker access to a person's most private thoughts. It's up to Net Force Explorer David Gray to convince his friends of the danger—before secrets are revealed to unknown spies.

TOM CLANCY'S
NET FORCE™

SHADOW OF HONOR

CREATED BY

Tom Clancy and Steve Pieczenik

BERKLEY JAM BOOKS, NEW YORK

TOM CLANCY'S NET FORCE: SHADOW OF HONOR

A Berkley Jam Book / published by arrangement with
Netco Partners

PRINTING HISTORY
Berkley Jam edition / February 2000

The Penguin Putnam Inc. World Wide Web site address is
http://www.penguinputnam.com

ISBN: 0-425-17303-8

BERKLEY JAM BOOKS®
Berkley Jam Books are published by The Berkley Publishing Group,
a division of Penguin Putnam Inc.,
375 Hudson Street, New York, New York 10014.
BERKLEY JAM and its logo
are trademarks belonging to Penguin Putnam Inc.

PRINTED IN THE UNITED STATES OF AMERICA

10 9 8 7 6 5 4 3 2 1

We'd like to thank the following people, without whom this book would not have been possible: Mel Odom, for help in rounding out the manuscript; Martin H. Greenberg, Larry Segriff, Denise Little, and John Helfers at Tekno Books; Mitchell Rubenstein and Laurie Silvers at BIG Entertainment; Tom Colgan of Penguin Putnam Inc.; Robert Youdelman, Esquire; and Tom Mallon, Esquire; and Robert Gottlieb of the William Morris Agency, agent and friend. We much appreciated the help.

Prologue

Solomon Wiest glided through the halls of Bradford Academy, excitement lengthening his stride. The freshly waxed floors gleamed in the morning sunlight streaming through the tall windows and carried a faint peach scent.

He bypassed the classrooms in the hallways. Those were locked down and wouldn't be opened until the teachers arrived. Despite the exclusivity of the Academy's student roster, there had been occasional cases of vandalism and theft that had prompted the decision to close the classrooms until supervision was present.

The library and the gym, however, remained open between six in the morning and ten in the evenings on weekends. Not everyone enrolled at Bradford had memberships in health clubs where they could work out, or state-of-the-art computer-link chairs for accessing the Net in their homes. So the Academy provided those facilities on weekends and even during the summers. It kept things fair for the students whose families didn't have the bucks for that kind of stuff.

"Hey, Sol. You're up early again."

Solomon barely restrained himself from jumping out of his skin. Although he was no stranger to spending weekends at Bradford, his agenda for today carried a certain amount of tension with it. He turned and spotted Benny Towers, one of the night maintenance staff, pushing a cleaning cart out of the school nurse's office.

"Hi, Benny." Solomon smiled brightly. He was good with that smile and knew it. He might not wear all the latest clothing fashions, might not fit in with the jock crowd, but he knew how to work that smile.

Of medium height, he was thick-chested and broad-shouldered, with long arms that had earned him several ape-boy taunts in grade school. But he was big enough no one wanted to go toe-to-toe with him over the point very often. He kept his dark hair razored off so he'd only have to deal with it every couple weeks or so. His mother insisted it left him looking moon-faced and thought he should let his hair grow out. He'd ignored the advice. His mother hadn't had a significant impact on his life since the day his father had betrayed them both.

"Extra credit or punishment this time?" Benny asked in his raspy voice. He was a thin old rake of a man with wispy white hair. The dark gray maintenance uniform had never fit him well, making him look like he'd gotten lost in it somehow.

"Punishment."

Benny cackled with glee and shook his head. "What did you do this time? More hijinks, or arguing with the teacher again?"

"They really hate it when I win," Solomon said.

Benny laughed again. "I know they do, boy, I know they do."

Solomon had won those arguments even if the teachers and the administration hadn't admitted it. When he walked into class, he was prepared. He had a reputation that made sure the teacher was, too.

Bradford Academy was an affluent educational facility with an impressive curriculum. It catered to the children of politicians, diplomats, business entrepreneurs, and military officers.

Solomon was none of those. The only child in a single-parent family, he'd gotten into Bradford on the strength of his academic excellence. Verbal combat with his teachers was, originally, his way to prove to the other students that he was more than their equal in scholastic aptitude. After three years of attending the school, his arguments were now more of a hobby, something to break the daily monotony. He had nothing left to prove.

"But it's not punishment for me," Solomon said. "This time I'm going to be doling it out."

Benny laughed again and shook his head. "You sure are a stubborn kid. Remind me of me when I was your age."

Except I won't ever be a janitor when I grow up, Solomon promised himself. He kept the smile in place and didn't let any of his thoughts show. He was good at that, too. Nobody knew what he was thinking or feeling unless he wanted them to. And that wasn't often.

"I've got to make another round," Benny said. "You have a good day, young rebel."

"You, too." Solomon waved and headed down the hall to the library.

The room was huge. Only a few books remained on the shelves, more keepsakes than anything else. The school's vast library was located in veeyar on the Net. Computer-link chairs occupied most of the available space.

He took one in a back corner of the library. As he sat down and prepared to enter the Net, he always felt vulnerable here in the library, not totally in charge of his environment. He didn't like that. He enjoyed surfing the Net much more in the quiet of his home, where he could be sure he would be unobserved and undisturbed by anyone.

His mother was rarely home. When she wasn't working, she was off socializing with her friends. They didn't care for Solomon and he returned the favor. He often thought that if it wasn't for the support check his mother got from the government for him she wouldn't have him around at all.

They had a computer-link chair at home only because Solomon had worked summers and weekends and sometimes even during the school year to pay for it. Saving up had been hard after his mother had found out he had a job, and trying to maintain grades high enough to keep him qualified for the academic scholarship to Bradford while he was working hadn't been a smooth ride, either.

But the computer-link chair at home didn't have the smooth

interfaces of the ones at the academy. And if he was going to be successful today, he needed the superior quality offered by the equipment here.

He sat in the chair, one of the extra-comfort models for logging-on long-term, feeling the cushions automatically adjust for his size and stature. He placed his legs on the footpads and his arms in the troughs provided for them.

Leaning his head back into the headrest put the subdermal neural implant circuitry in his neck in line with the chair's receptors. There was a click and a hum as the headrest lined up his implants with the chair's laser beam. He felt a slight shock as the computer took control of his senses, blocking out everything from the outside world except what he'd programmed it to let through. Those filters were currently set to a fairly high sensitivity—he wanted to know if anyone got too close to him in the real world.

He was now in virtual reality, sitting in a room that existed only as a programmed entity, but which felt as solid and real to him as anything in the physical world. He was in the academy's generic veeyar entryway, an exact duplicate of the school's library, the one he'd left behind, along with his body, when he'd entered virtual reality. But he'd changed dramatically. While in veeyar, he didn't keep the body that had caused him so much grief growing up. He used a proxy he'd programmed himself, a computer-generated image created to his exact specifications.

In virtual reality Solomon was tall and powerfully built, his body half flesh and half cyborg. Dark skin overlapped the silvery sheen of his metal parts. In the physical world such an amalgam of man and machine wasn't possible, even with all the advances made in medicine in the twenty-first century. In veeyar anything was possible.

The school's operating system was simple. The computer reconstructed the library, right down to the chair he was sitting in. But in veeyar there was a console in front of him with various icons to choose from. One was for phone connections, several were files of his class assignments—both completed and pending—and some represented class notes posted by his various teachers. The largest number of icons symbolized direct links to the Bradford Academy's databases in the sciences, languages, and arts. Finally there was the icon that would connect him to the worldwide Net.

He touched that icon, his heart thumping rhythmically in his cyber-flesh body, and connected to the South African embassy's public relations office in Washington, DC.

He'd studied the embassy and found out that, although they kept a flesh-and-blood staff available during the weekends, they tended to let the automated system handle almost everything.

Breathing easily, but every sense aflame as he thought about what he was going to do, Solomon regarded the new series of icons that appeared before him. When he reached the section regarding the history of the country, he selected that menu.

Immediately the veeyar changed around him. He stood in a barren room furnished with only a large viewing screen floating in the air.

"Please identify the time period you wish to research," a cultured feminine voice invited. "You will be allowed to make further choices once the chronology is defined."

The embassy's security system read his personal identification number. He felt the probe crawling along the outside of his skull, searching for his identity.

He'd anticipated this. One of the special utilities he'd programmed for the hack fed the security system's ID program the false PIN he'd created. He knew it wouldn't hold long, but it didn't have to. The South African systems were way behind anything in use in the United States. Even though the South African War had been officially over for ten years, some feeling of hostility remained between the two countries. The USA and South Africa's present governing body hadn't exactly been on the same side during the war.

As a result, although the South African government had resumed diplomatic relations with the USA, they refused to use computer security programs from there. The country's decision-makers worried those programs would be compromised, somehow. So they were consequently light-years behind the top-of-the-line security programs developed in the last few years. Solomon didn't doubt someone really good could break into the South African computers on a regular basis without getting caught.

And Solomon was really good. He didn't have all the programs and utilities available to a group like Net Force, who could pretty much go where they wanted anywhere on the Net. But then, with the antiquated system he was raiding, he didn't think top-flight utilities would be necessary. He could make do with what he had.

With his ID utility engaged, Solomon selected the time frame he wanted, then pulled up the school's menu again. It appeared before him, a palette in electric blue that didn't interfere with the embassy's programs.

Touching the phone icon, he gave it the emergency number he'd memorized and accessed the embassy's alarm systems. It had taken a fair bit of hacking to find out the embassy's emergency numbers, even though some of them had to be easily available to South African citizens traveling in the USA. But the ones commonly listed went through a sorting server and so were not useful for his current purpose.

Solomon had found the direct number and he used it now. The embassy's emergency menu appeared in front of him. It took the form of a pale gray obelisk with icons carved into it. Mythological figures from ancient South African history were engraved around the edges, reflecting the current government's interest in those things.

He studied the icons briefly. Then he pushed the one that would trigger the embassy fire alarm. The icon flared, then threw out a huge ruby oval that sped away to cover the entire virtual building.

Immediately the computer systems started downloading all the information stored in the embassy, logging onto the Net and shooting it in burst transmission to the computer systems in Mandelatown—formerly known as Bloemfontein, and now South Africa's current capital.

The embassy's system quit probing his defenses, giving up its search for Solomon's identity immediately as more prioritized programs took over. A whirling hurricane of activity flashed through the PR room, copying and transmitting every bit of data open to it back to South Africa.

Solomon ran forward and threw himself into copy program upload. Out of control for a moment, knowing he was at the mercy of the emergency dump-and-save programs, he forced himself to breathe and to remain calm. It helped knowing he could log out of the Net at any time, but he also knew he might not be able to get back into this area again.

Everybody learned from having their systems crashed. And usually the same method wouldn't work twice. Although, on occasion, Solomon had found that it did. Sometimes this was because a trap had been set. The traps had been interesting, too.

Part of the embassy's dump-and-save program worked to archive information, compressing it and making it easier to deal with. The compression program would also make Solomon's presence easier to detect. He activated a second utility, one that grafted on a command line to download an outside accessible database open to the South African embassy.

If the archival process was allowed to take place, the programmers would locate him and boot him from the system. He grinned. But they wouldn't be able to archive the entire United States Library of Congress easily.

Shooting through the Net, Solomon was barely aware of the neon colors that marked various major corporate and government Web-nodes that filled the virtual landscape around him. Sites of all shapes and sizes, all connected by the Net, whizzed by below, above, and around him. He arrived in Mandelatown while the South African programmers were struggling to figure out what had hit their systems.

The Library of Congress had virtual tons of files.

The room he was dumped into appeared to have been carved from a giant obsidian stone, all gleaming black surfaces. It was large, filled with huge stacks of shiny steel vaults that represented the different files on site. The sorter program archiving the arriving data was represented by a hydra-headed humanoid with deep blue skin. Its mouths opened up, swallowing whole datastreams.

Solomon opened his third utility and fed it into the sorter, staying tagged onto the datastream that held the historical information he was after. He knew the South Africans would have buried the data deeply, but he was counting on the theory that they wouldn't have gotten rid of it.

There was a moment of blackness when the sorter shunted him off into another part of the computer system. He reappeared in still another obsidian room filled with the huge steel vaults. Neon colors played against the various surfaces, winking red, gold, green, and purple.

The third utility was a strainer program, a search engine he'd designed to look for the documents he wanted. Thin monofilament cables sprouted from Solomon's chest, representing the strainer program. The green-glowing monofilament cables whipped and roved, opening various vaults.

"Halt! Identify yourself!"

Solomon glanced around the stacks and saw the system security program speeding toward him. It looked like a representation of an older version of Norton's Tools, a boxy cube of dark sapphire metal with ruby laser sensors sweeping constantly around it to give it the appearance of a spider. It closed in on him quickly.

"Feek!" Solomon yelled, wishing there were some way to speed the strainer program up. If the sys/ops sec found him, he'd be purged from the system, possibly even identified.

Then one of the monofilament tendrils from his chest glowed even brighter green, letting him know it had found the requested documents. Solomon ran to the indicated stack with the security utility following close on his heels.

Activating the retrieval program he held at the ready, Solomon felt climbing spikes shoot out from his hands and feet. He slammed them into the tower representation of the storage area, then climbed up to the open vault. When he reached it, he stabbed a hand in, shaking dozens of monofilament wires out of his fists, wires that greedily attached themselves to the files he wanted, downloading information into the school system back at Bradford.

As the security program closed on him, sweeping two of its lasers toward him, Solomon felt the molasses-slow pull of an ident-scan hooking him. Finished with the download, he logged off before the scan could finish.

Solomon opened his eyes back in the computer-link chair. He was covered in perspiration from the anxiety levels he'd been hitting. Not that they posed a real physical danger to him, but it still felt as if he'd been running a marathon.

Automatically he downloaded the information he'd hacked onto a two-inch square datascrip and wiped the source files from the school's computer, then popped the datacube out into his hand. Shaking a bit, he climbed out of the chair and went into the hallway for a drink. The clock on the wall showed it was 6:37 A.M.

The hack hadn't even taken two minutes.

He smiled, pleased. *Nobody does it better.* He whistled a theme from a famous old spy movie on his way back to the computer-link chair.

When he logged on again, he went to the veeyar operating system he used at home. Stepping through a door that appeared in the virtual library, he entered a familiar laboratory filled with exotic-looking devices. A number of people fired specially modified machine guns into test dummies, burned more of the dummies with flame-throwers, and worked on a new baby blue Viper sports car.

"Hello, Double-oh One."

"Hello, sir," Solomon replied as he crossed the big room to an available workstation with the holovid capabilities he needed. Actually the workstation was a representation of the programs he needed to work on the documents he'd hacked.

The inventor was an incredibly old white-haired man in a too-big white lab coat. He looked campily cartoonish. He was modeled on a movie character that had created a holovid replacement of himself when his body had finally given out. In the holos the inventor had uploaded his mind onto the British spy agency's computers, created the holovid replacement, and gone right on equipping the world's most famous spy with the world's most exotic weapons.

Solomon had picked the Double-oh One designation for his character. If he had a choice, he didn't want to be anything less than number one.

As a personal veeyar operating system, Solomon loved it. He was never alone, yet he was never bothered, either. Activity constantly went on around him, providing a soothing atmosphere for his hyperkinetic mind. He sat at the workstation and opened up the files he'd swiped.

Footage of the South African War that had raged through that area from 2010 to 2014 filled the holo projector space in front of him. Solomon fast-forwarded through the material, switching from urban assault scenes to special ops battles in the bush, finally locating the documents he wanted.

"What have we got today, Double-oh One?" the inventor asked, standing behind Solomon with his hands behind his back and staring over Solomon's shoulder.

"Spy stuff," Solomon answered. "Secret documents kept bur-

ied for ten years by the South African government. Lies, pro-
paganda, and the tail wagging the dog."

"Good show, Double-oh One," the inventor enthused. "Will
you be needing anything we have here?"

"The car," Solomon said. "I want to go for a drive later."

"We'll have it ready."

Solomon worked on the holovid and found one of the files
he needed most. A man's face filled the holovid space. He was
dark-haired and in his middle forties, with a clean jawline and
ice-blue eyes. His colonel's insignia gleamed on his shirt collar.

"Identify," Solomon prompted.

"Moore," the computer responded. "Robert Andrew. Colonel, United States Marine Corps. Assignment: South Africa,
Black Ops. Classification: Top Secret."

"Direct hit!" Solomon said softly. He scanned through the
file, realizing what he'd hoped to find took even more twists
and turns than he'd thought. The real story wouldn't do after
all.

Thinking quickly, his vision already in his mind, he opened
a menu for editing tools on the holovid. It didn't matter how
it had started out. By Monday morning class time, the piece
would be everything he needed it to be.

He smiled in anticipation and bent himself to his labors.
There was nothing like revenge.

1

Andy Moore walked carefully through the urban decay left over from a nuclear holocaust. Bloodred clouds marred the pale blue sky, interrupted by broken, blackened buildings with green mossy growths attached to them.

Earthquakes and gas-main explosions had ripped the streets between the crumbling buildings and left islands of concrete and pavement tilted in all directions. The noonday sun's heat burned down fiercely, but the wind held an arctic chill and the stink of salty sea.

He proceeded cautiously through the rubble, his senses alert, his ice-blue eyes raking the potential battlefield. He pushed his unruly blond hair out of the way. Lanky and quick, he moved with a natural athlete's grace. He wore skintight commando gear, complete with rations, a canteen, and a one-man tent to keep him safe from the caustic acid rains.

He was used to carrying packs and moving quietly, thanks to camping trips and the training course and refreshers he'd taken to be a member of the Net Force Explorers. As an Explorer, his training had been nearly as exhausting, demanding, and detailed as a Marine recruit's. Andy had excelled in the physical departments.

The chunk of pavement he stepped onto teetered for a moment. He waited till it found a balance point again and the echoes of rock grating against rock faded from the street.

He knew he wasn't alone. He felt hostile eyes gazing at him.

When the sensation touched him, he couldn't help smiling in anticipation. He tapped the ear-throat headset he wore and opened the channel. "So what do you think, Matt?"

Only empty static sounded in the button speaker pushed just inside his ear canal.

"Matt?" Andy spoke a little louder, and an apprehensive knot formed in his stomach. He thumped the pencil-thin mike in front of his mouth with his forefinger and heard the noises relayed through the speaker. The pick-up was working fine. *Oh man,* he thought, *I knew splitting up was a bad idea. But nooooo . . . Matt thought we could cover more ground, get the area mapped sooner.*

He glanced down at the nav-comp strapped to his left wrist. The display screen pulsed gray-green snow instead of the flat-film sim it should have been receiving from the satellite over-head. Leftover electromagnetic pulse signatures interfered with the operation in pockets throughout the city. This was one of the spots. There was no sign of Matt Hunter. It was as if his friend had vanished off the face of the planet.

Rock grated to the left.

Andy spun, throwing his right arm out. Crosshairs suddenly formed in his vision, marking off the field of fire for the weapon mounted on his right wrist. The Tangler was short and blocky, four inches tall with an oval mouth nearly that wide. Its weight slowed his reactions a little. It was designed to fire when he squeezed his closed fist.

The dilapidated remains of a two-story comic book shop sandwiched between a department store and a carpet outlet drew his attention. The sign—bearing the name CAPED JUSTICE and a picture of a super-heroine wearing an armored bikini, gloves, boots, and a cape—hung crookedly above the shattered door. Gleaming glass shards filled the huge picture window where comic magazines fluttered in the breeze.

With Hooper involved, Andy thought, *it's got to be the comic shop. That fits his sense of humor.* Cautiously he stepped through the debris of broken pavement and rusty steel rebar support rods warped out of their original shape.

He dropped into position beside the doorway, using it as a

shield. Constant training in dozens of veeyar game scenarios gave him reflexes that had kept him "alive" throughout hundreds of sim-battles. He spun around the door frame, the Tangler extended before him.

Nothing moved in the long shadows filling the room. Rats twisted and ran through the debris scattered across the floor where comics, books, and magazines had been reduced to so much chewed confetti. Wind whistled eerily through the broken windows, making the vacant building seem even emptier.

Andy took a deep, shaky breath. *Okay, so Hooper's got a lot of imagination.* Andy tried to push past it, but the creepy feeling stayed with him. *And I thought Matt was going to be the one freaked out by this.*

The grating sounded again, coming from upstairs.

"Matt?" Andy called over the headset. He aimed the Tangler at the darkened stairway and started forward again. Had Matt been taken captive?

Only a few steps into the room Andy knew he'd screwed up. Broken rock slithered behind the shattered display counters behind him to his left. He turned, knowing from the quick slaps against the pavement that he was going to be too late.

The zombie charged at him with full, lumbering speed. She wore an armored bikini and cape, just like the woman who'd been featured on the store sign, but the resemblance ended there. Raggedy blond hair clung to a face so barren of flesh the skull showed through. Yellowed eyes sat deep in shadowed sockets. And the too-tight mouth was pulled back in a hungry death's rictus. She screamed, an ululating wail that filled the building's interior.

Taken off-guard, Andy froze. He wasn't sure if it was the scream or the looks; certainly he hadn't quite expected either. The zombie was almost on top of him when Matt stepped in front of Andy and pushed him out of the way.

Andy stumbled back, brought the Tangler up, and closed his fist. But the back of his knees struck a block of pavement, and he went down flat on his back.

Matt's Tangler fired first, spewing a wadded net that wrapped around the shrieking zombie and blew her backward. The net flared out as she flew through the air. When she struck the wall on the other side of the room, the net stuck, securing the zombie.

She howled and tried to tear free, but the net was indestructible. The strands glowed lemon yellow, running with electricity from top to bottom. When the circuit reached the bottom, the zombie and the net turned into lavender dust that poured in streams to the floor.

Matt turned to Andy, smiling and shaking his head. "Another minute and it would have been game-over for you, buddy."

Andy slapped the Tangler mounted on his wrist. "I think it misfired or something."

"Nope," Matt said easily, his brown eyes scanning the room. "You choked."

"Oh, now that's real ego-sensitive of you." Andy pushed himself up.

Tall and athletic, his brown hair neatly in place, Matt grinned. "If I'd let it get you here, maybe I'd have been more sensitive outside veeyar."

Andy got the definite impression that wouldn't have been so. His own competitive nature brought out the same in his friends when they were playing. Matt might have cut someone else some slack, but he wasn't going to take the edge off for Andy.

"Right," Andy said.

"Of course," Matt offered, "I could have let you take your lumps here, then let Hooper get his licks in when he found out how easily you went down."

"No, thanks. I agreed to test this game sim for him, not to be a target for verbal darts." Andy had figured it would be fun. Hooper Lange wasn't just a good basketball player, he was an excellent game programmer. Andy had participated in several of the scenarios Hooper had dreamed up.

"Let's go. I think there are more of them upstairs." Matt took the lead, staying to one side of the debris-strewn steps as he went up.

Andy followed, keeping his Tangler ready. The second story was incredibly dark compared to the lighted expanse of the lower room. Crates filled the open space.

"Hooper's lighting is off in this area," Matt stated quietly.

"Yeah," Andy agreed. "He's going for that Goth tone, trying to creep people out."

Matt smiled at him. "Is it working?"

"No," Andy lied. "Is it working on you?"

"Personally, I think these things are juvenile." Matt led the way deeper into the room.

"Hey," Andy said, "you happen to be treading on a favorite pastime of mine. You just need a particular mind-set to really get into the shooters."

Shooters were what games like the present sim were called, based on the same kind of PC and console games that had been so huge thirty years ago. Most people who gamed these days liked more developed role-playing worlds like Sarxos, but a lot of interest remained in the down-and-dirty quickness of the shooters for instant relaxation.

"You mean twitch games," Matt corrected good-naturedly. "You're trained by the game to twitch quickly and take out whatever's threatening you. Or an opponent. Guys with short attention spans really get into these."

"Are you trying to say something here?"

Matt never got the chance to get in another dig because three zombies exploded from behind stacks of crates ahead of them. One of them threw a metal barrel that caught Matt on the chest, knocking him back. The zombies wasted no time in getting into rush mode.

Coolly Andy stepped in front of Matt and leveled the Tangler. He aimed and squeezed his fist three times in quick succession. The glowing nets flew across the distance, pulled the zombies back, and reduced them to lavender ash.

"Twitch, twitch, twitch," Andy said, feeling good about having a chance to show off his skill. He blew imaginary smoke from the Tangler's barrel.

Matt shoved the metal barrel off his chest. In real life the attack would have put him in the emergency room, but in veeyar it was only a minor distraction. "This is not my kind of game."

"Yeah, but you have to admit, it's kind of fun hanging zombies out to dry."

Matt tried to hide a grin but couldn't. "There's a certain . . . primitive . . . satisfaction."

"I know. I think Hooper's on to something here."

"If he finishes it."

Andy nodded. Hooper had a tendency to let his attention drift, starting new projects before he finished current ones. Veeyar contributed to that, allowing him to put away a huge amount of work behind one convenient icon, then start all over somewhere else.

"His spatial's off on this room, too," Matt commented.

Andy looked around the room. It was true; the upper room was a lot bigger than the lower one. "Yeah, but Hooper does that a lot. He reads a lot of Heinlein. There was a guy in one of the stories that had a house bigger on the inside than it was on the outside. I guess it left an impression on him."

Taking over the lead, Andy moved quickly, sweeping the Tangler over any potential zombie hiding places. Even if Matt preferred flight sims in veeyar to straight shoot-'em-ups, there wasn't anyone else Andy'd rather have at his side in a tough spot. They worked well together. Where Matt was sometimes deliberate and calculating in finding solutions to game problems, Andy's own innate impulsiveness and restlessness, as well as his unconventional thinking, solved as many game situations as Matt's careful planning.

A shrill buzzer echoed through the warehouse-sized room.

"That's the warning bell," Matt said. "Class in five minutes."

Andy nodded reluctantly. Class was something he could do without today. He called out for the game console and it appeared in the air in front of him. He ignored two zombies that broke free of the shadows and pressed the icons for Save and Exit.

"So how's the strategic analysis class coming?" Matt asked as the game environment melted around them.

"Boring," Andy answered truthfully. "Mass regurgitation of things that have already happened."

"I thought it covered wars and battles," Matt said. "That sounded interesting."

"Translation," Andy said, "history with an attitude. You should have taken this class."

"Couldn't fit it in. I'm taking physics this hour. Any problems with Solomon?"

Andy glanced at Matt and tried to look innocent. The rivalry he had going with Solomon Weist was something of a legend at Bradford. "No. Should there be?"

"Actually," Matt answered as his image blurred and fell apart, "I'd hoped you two had chilled your jets. Catch you later?"

"Later," Andy agreed. "Thanks for helping me spec out this game." He logged off.

Blinking up at the fluorescent lights on the ceiling, Andy sat up in the computer-link chair in strategic analysis, feeling the gentle buzz of disconnection. He popped the datascrip with Hooper's game out of the computer, put it in a plastic protector, and dropped it into his pocket.

More zombies, he thought as he gazed around the classroom. Only a few of the chairs held other students. The others were out in the hallway waiting till the last bell or on their way from an earlier class. *That's what I need instead of lectures, reports, and erudite speculation.*

Then a flash of guilt touched him. Dr. Eugene Dobbs, the instructor, had pulled some strings to get Andy into the class. Andy was a B student at best according to his scores, and not really on the list to take specialized classes. But Dr. Dobbs knew Andy wasn't living up to his full potential as a student. He'd even told Andy that before he'd allowed him into the class, citing it as the deciding factor that made him go to bat for Andy.

Personally, Andy would have liked school a lot better if he'd been allowed to choose his own classes. If he could find something he was really interested in. That was the biggest problem.

The only thing he knew for certain about his future was that he wanted to be part of Net Force when he got old enough. And he knew a class like strategic analysis, taught by a professor with the credentials that Dr. Dobbs carried, would look good on his college applications. And, given his grades, anything that helped get him into a good college got him closer to getting into Net Force.

Andy just didn't like waiting. He wanted to actually get out and do something now.

Figuring he had a chance to beat the bell, Andy pushed up from the computer-link chair and jogged out to the hall for a drink of water. He waited in line briefly at the water fountain, got a drink, and walked slowly back toward class.

"Hey, Andy. Got your report ready for today?"

He turned and spotted Megan O'Malley. She was one of his favorite people, and—like him—a Net Force Explorer. "Hey,

Megan," he replied. "As a matter of fact, I actually do have my report ready. Why?"

Megan O'Malley blew a wisp of her short brown hair from her face. Her hazel eyes gleamed a bit in the hall's fluorescent lights. She was dressed casually in jeans and a knitted yellow sweater. And carrying a book bag. She was a die-hard reader and often preferred to read an actual book instead of spending time on-line.

Andy blamed it on the fact that Megan's mom was a *Washington Post* reporter and her dad was a mystery writer. But he couldn't imagine the agony of sitting in one place holding a book and reading it for hours. He preferred the interactive experiences available on the Net.

"I'm asking about your report," Megan said, "because there were some people in class who had bets on whether you'd have a report or an excuse."

Andy didn't get offended. In fact, he took a certain amount of pride in the pool. It was a joke. Maybe not his joke, but it wouldn't have existed without him. "Did you bet?"

She hesitated a moment, then nodded. "Yep."

"Win or lose?"

She grinned. "Lost."

"Sorry." Andy laughed at her.

"So what made you get the report in on time?"

"Dr. Dobbs."

Megan nodded. "I heard he gave you a pep talk before you signed up for the class."

"Big-time."

"Well, don't feel too bad about the pool," she told him.

Andy raised his eyebrows. As class clown, he'd learned to do a lot with facial expressions and body language.

"There's another pool," she said. "I could recoup my losses."

"What's this one?"

Megan gave him a frank gaze. "Whether the report's any good or not."

"Ouch," Andy said. "That's bitter. And which way did you—"

"Uh-uh."

Andy shook his head. The hallway had nearly cleared out, most of the students vanishing into their respective rooms. He hadn't seen Solomon Weist and was beginning to think the boy was going to be a no-show.

Then a cultured voice spoke in a put-on British accent. "I say, do I detect the stench of swine in the air?"

Anger surged through Andy, jerking him around. He hated the air of smug superiority Solomon could produce when he wanted to. He gazed at Solomon, who stood by the door just out of arm's reach and didn't look at him. Solomon's comment had drawn the attention of nearby students, infuriating Andy even more.

2

"Oh," Solomon continued, looking directly at Andy now and continuing in the fake accent. "It's you. Perhaps you failed to clean your shoes properly before attending our honorable establishment. I suppose it's hard to notice that barnyard aroma when you're standing in it all day."

Andy felt the hot flame of embarrassment across his face and hated not being able to control it. Everyone who really knew him also knew that his mother was a veterinarian and had her own clinic in Alexandria, Virginia, where they lived. She'd raised him by herself after his father's death, and he often helped her in the clinic before and after class. That morning he hadn't, but Solomon's suggestion still set his teeth on edge.

"You could leave your shoes out in the hall," Solomon suggested. "Or allow the horticulture class to scrape them off and continue the recycling process."

Andy stepped toward him. Solomon didn't move away. He was bigger and heavier, and obviously not feeling threatened at all.

Unbelievably, Megan stepped in front of Andy, blocking his way. She was extremely athletic and very good in martial arts, and Andy knew she wouldn't be easy to get by.

"Blow it off, Andy," Megan advised. "He's just trouble you don't need."

"And, I promise you, more trouble than you can handle," Solomon added, grinning broadly.

"Megan," Andy said, "*please* move." Part of him couldn't believe Solomon had actually been so direct with him. They'd avoided each other over the weeks since the strategic analysis class had begun.

"No." Megan said.

Andy held his anger in check with difficulty. The emotion often seemed to swirl inside him, just below the surface. Sometimes it was frustration caused by Solomon and others like him. But sometimes it was emotion left over from losing his father in the South African War. His mom had helped him see that.

A swift rebuttal was already on Andy's lips. Solomon was a big target. His father had been career military in the U.S. Army till he'd gotten dishonorably discharged for black marketeering. When most kids at the Bradford Academy wanted to deflate Solomon's ego, they generally attacked him through his dad's criminal record.

That was when most of Solomon's verbal altercations turned physical.

Even as mad as he was, and despite the long-term grudge between them, Andy had never stooped low enough to say anything about Solomon's dad. He never would. That was off-limits as far as Andy was concerned. But he wasn't above going after the other boy with a well-placed fist.

"Megan," he said again.

She still didn't move.

"Mr. Moore, Mr. Weist," an authoritative voice cracked, "stand down this minute!"

Andy pushed out a tight breath, never taking his eyes off Solomon. Andy knew that Solomon had thrown sucker punches in the past when he had the opportunity. Winning was everything to Solomon.

"Yes, sir," Andy said, stepping back and letting his arms hang at his sides in the at-ease posture he'd learned in the Net Force Explorers.

Dr. Eugene Dobbs stopped in front of the door. He was a little overweight under his tan suit and wore thick black-framed glasses, but there was no softness about him. Short blond hair showing a little gray at the temples framed his clean-shaven face.

Solomon hadn't moved.

"Mr. Weist," Dr. Dobbs warned, "you'll comply summarily or I'll slam your fanny into the vice principal's office. Is that understood?"

Before turning to teaching, Dr. Dobbs had spent time in the military as an officer and later in the diplomatic corps. Andy had never gotten the full scoop on that because the files were locked away as classified material. But Dobbs could clearly handle himself. Andy had nothing but respect for the man.

"Fine," Solomon grumbled, making one last effort to stare Andy down. He turned away from Andy and walked into the classroom.

Dr. Dobbs ushered Megan and Andy into the room with a wave of his hand. He didn't say anything further about the incident. He was undoubtedly already aware of the animosity that existed between the two boys.

The final bell shattered the stillness out in the hall. Cold fingernails ran up Andy's spine as the teacher took his place at the podium in front of the class. Andy plugged his class schedule datascrip into the computer-link chair. Despite his intention not to, he glanced at Solomon, who, like him, had taken a seat at the back of the class.

Solomon just wiggled his eyebrows tauntingly and smiled broadly, like he had a secret he wasn't sharing with anyone.

Megan normally sat near the front, but she chose to sit beside Andy today. "Is he worth the demerits you'll get if you fight with him?"

Andy let a tense breath out between his teeth. "Almost." But he shifted his attention back to Dr. Dobbs.

"If you'll all join me in the classroom veeyar, we'll get on with the reports." Dr. Dobbs left the podium and went to the computer-link chair behind his desk.

Andy leaned back and felt the implants buzz. In the next moment he was in the classroom veeyar, an exact duplicate of the physical classroom.

Dr. Dobbs stood in front of them again, ramrod straight beside the podium. "As I recall, yesterday we'd just gotten to Megan O'Malley's presentation when class ended. Miss O'Malley, are you prepared?"

"Yes, sir," Megan said. "My subject is the benefits of the Spanish-American War."

"Or, as it's more fondly known, the conquest and subjugation of the last Spanish holdings in the New World by the American military," Solomon interjected.

Andy fought a battle with his temper. Solomon was really asking for it today.

"Mr. Weist," Dr. Dobbs said, "you will kindly refrain from making comments until after each presentation."

Solomon flipped him a salute.

Andy knew Solomon hated appearing in veeyar as himself instead of a proxy. Everyone at Bradford Academy knew about the cyberhybrid body Solomon liked to use. But Solomon was pretty much stuck looking like himself while at school. The only classes Andy had ever taken where proxies were allowed were art, drama, and speech. And then only occasionally.

"The Cuban War for independence broke out in 1895," Megan said. Immediately the classroom veeyar picked up on the changes she'd cued into her report. The classroom vanished, replaced by a port city filled with white buildings and homes roofed in red and maroon tiles. Tall ships occupied berths and anchorages along the wooden docks, their masts creating an ungainly forest in the harbor. Most of the ships flew Spanish flags.

Andy stood on one of the low, grassy hills overlooking Havana. He smelled the sea and heard bird cries in the trees behind him. Men's voices, the splash of oars, the *thwap* of ship's rigging slapping masts, and the infrequent thump of barges bumping into freighter hulls rolled in from the docks. *Megan really did her homework on this one,* Andy thought. He even felt the Caribbean sun burning down on him.

"The War for Independence was a continuation of the Cuban revolt against Spanish rule." Megan took the lead and the rest of the class followed. The programming was deceptive, though, time-compressing their journey. In minutes they were deep in the heart of Havana, walking through the streets without being noticed by the sim-inhabitants. "The revolt lasted from 1868 to 1878. Spain smashed down all resistance. Spain's commanding officer, General Valeriano Weyler *y* Nicolau, created prison camps in all the major cities and locked up the rebels."

Megan led them to a prison encampment in the city, and the

veeyar responded by changing the scenery around them. Barbed wire walled off the prisoners from the rest of the citizens. Uniformed Spanish soldiers stood guard.

"People in these prison camps died from starvation and disease," Megan said, leading them through the barbed-wire fence. The class passed through the barrier like ghosts, untouched by the barbed strands.

Andy gazed around at the death and disease around them and felt slightly sick. People lay on the ground and in the shade offered by ramshackle sheds. The prisoners' eyes were hollow and hopeless.

"I apologize for the graphic footage," Megan said, "but there was no way to downplay this and truly show how horrible it was. At least, that's how I felt."

"Any of you who are having problems with this," Dr. Dobbs said, "can log off now. I'll call you back in."

Andy glanced around but didn't see anyone disappear from veeyar. Strategic analysis class had drawn from the best of the best at the Bradford Academy. For a moment, he took pride in the fact that he was there. Then he remembered Solomon had made the cut, too—by his grades.

Megan continued with her presentation.

As he watched the day turn into night, Andy followed Megan onto the United States warship that had been deployed to Cuba to protect American citizens in the country. In the middle of the night, the U.S.S. *Maine* exploded out in the harbor with them on board.

The pyrotechnics were great, Andy decided, but it was still sobering when Megan explained how the 260 men killed had died that day. The class took part in the mad scramble through the smoke-filled ship as it went down. They barely got out. They swam through the harbor and regrouped on shore, feeling the cold wind bite into them.

"Spain claimed that a boiler or ammunition magazine onboard the *Maine* blew up," Megan said. It became day again in the veeyar and all their clothes dried. "The United States was certain an underwater mine had been put on the hull. Two months and four days later, on April nineteenth, the U.S. recognized Cuban independence. On the twenty-fifth of April President William McKinley declared that war with Spain had started four days earlier."

"Yeah," Solomon said, "and you know William Randolph Hearst caused a lot of trouble when he printed the Spanish ambassador's letter to his friend in Havana stating that he didn't know what McKinley's intentions were."

"True," Megan said. "Enrique Dupuy de Lome's letter was printed on the front page of Hearst's newspaper, the *Journal*, and Joseph Pulitzer's *World* shortly before the explosion aboard the *Maine*. There were some people who raised serious questions about where the letter came from."

"Hearst printed sensationalism back then," Solomon said. "Not news. There's some argument to be made that he helped start the war."

"Mr. Weist," Dr. Dobbs said irritably.

Solomon looked exasperated but managed to keep himself quiet.

Andy was swept through military recruitment in Spain as well as the United States as Megan continued her presentation. He was amused at Solomon's repeated—and failed—attempts to gain center stage, and at the same time totally blown away by the work Megan had done. He knew he was looking at an A-plus report. His own, he figured, would net him a passing grade, and that was fine. But now that he saw what Megan had done, he wished he'd done his own a little differently.

She guided the class through the rest of the war. They stood aboard a ship in the Spanish fleet as well as one in Commodore George Dewey's Asiatic Squadron during the sea battle of Manila Bay. They were aboard the *Merrimac* when it went down in Santiago Harbor, sunk by Spanish guns before the American forces could block the harbor.

They marched with the American troops that landed near Santiago, then crossed through the jungles to Las Guasimas, drenched in sweat, apprehensive at every noise or movement. From Las Guasimas, they marched to El Caney, where Megan introduced them to the ridges called San Juan Hill and Kettle Hill.

In a final flurry of excitement they attacked with Lieutenant Colonel Theodore Roosevelt and his Rough Riders. Though they ducked for cover, the white smoke from their out-of-date guns plumed up to reveal where the American forces' positions were. Andy and the other students were pinned down by enemy fire. Then Roosevelt rallied the Rough Riders as well as men from other units. They rushed up the broken terrain through the fog of burned cannon and rifle powder and claimed the victory at San Juan Hill.

Andy's imagination was totally captivated by the presentation. Even though they were in veeyar and nothing could happen to them, adrenaline was cooking through his system. Several of the students, Andy included, joined in the brief revelry of the American forces.

Tagging his own interface, Andy uploaded the report into his datascrip. He'd have to know it for the test anyway, but he wanted to run through it again and get a chance to examine more closely some of the other events Megan had touched on. His interest was sparked in spite of himself, and he wished he'd been this interested when he'd done his report on the Roman occupation of the British Isles.

Megan finished up with a brief display of the sea battle that took place between the retreating navy of Admiral Cervera and Commodore Schley's squadron. The American Navy destroyed the Spanish fleet in four hours. On July 17 the Spanish surrendered, Puerto Rico was captured soon after, and the official ending of the war came on August 12.

"The Spanish-American War provided several major benefits for the United States," Megan summarized. "Most obviously, the country gained the Philippines, Guam, and Puerto Rico. The war also pulled American fighting forces together. The Civil War had split the North and the South, and this was the first time both sides fought together since the War of 1812."

Andy watched the final montage of footage rolling around the class. He followed Megan's lead as the scenes changed, showing snippets of the changes as she mentioned them.

"The American Navy grew stronger," Megan said. "The Panama Canal was built to link the Atlantic and Pacific Oceans. Dr. Walter Reed, whose name is on the medical center here in Washington, found the cause and cure for yellow fever with the help of a Cuban doctor, Carlos J. Finlay. And the United States was at last recognized as a world power by the rest of the world's nations."

The veeyar stuttered, then returned to the classroom appearance.

"Very good, Megan," Dr. Dobbs said. "You covered a fair bit a material there. I'm sure the rest of you will find several questions regarding the Spanish-American War on our next test."

Groans went up from the student body.

Dr. Dobbs grinned and shook his head. "That's why you do the uploads, people. Who's next?" He looked out at them expectantly.

Knowing nobody would want to raise his or her hand to go next and follow Megan's lead, Andy started to volunteer, wanting only to get it over with. He was as ready as he intended to be. But before he could raise his hand, Dr. Dobbs said, "Okay, Solomon, since you were so eager to add to Megan's report, you can go next."

"Of course. I'd be happy to," Solomon said.

Startled, Andy glanced over at the other side of the class. *Okay, now I definitely smell a dead rat,* he thought. *Solomon would never voluntarily follow a report like that unless he figured he had a real mindblower.*

"We're only going back eleven years," Solomon said, "but you're going to enjoy this."

The way he said that put Andy's teeth on edge.

The veeyar classroom altered to a panoramic view of a night-shrouded bush scene. Thin tendrils of black clouds broke the yellow half-moon. In the darkness the harsh noise of metal striking metal echoed over the countryside. Helicopter rotors beat the air, rushing through the sky.

Andy stood with the rest of the class in a stand of trees. He watched as British commandos wearing combat black and camouflage paint rushed by their position, totally oblivious to them. A sick feeling twisted in Andy's stomach when he realized where they had to be. It explained Solomon's behavior today— why he'd suddenly gone out of his way to bait Andy.

"The year is 2014, and we're in the final days of the South African War in this scenario," Solomon said.

Megan and a few of the others turned to look at Andy. He kept his "stone" face on, the one he'd learned to wear when he didn't want anyone getting inside his thoughts.

A helicopter dropped through the air overhead and swung toward the British commandos' positions. Either South African ground forces had called in their positions, or the helo pilot had picked them up on FLIR. Andy caught just a glimpse of the forward-looking infrared radar under the Huey's belly, then its twin side-mounted rocket launchers lit up the night.

Rockets thumped into the ground, knocking down trees, brush, and men. The carnage was appalling. Craters smoldered all around, abscesses filled with gray smoke and glowing orange embers and surrounded by the torn bodies of the dead.

The heated backblast from the explosives washed over Andy. He tried not to let any of it touch him, but he couldn't help remembering all those scenarios he'd dreamed up after his mom told him how his dad had died. Later, she'd given him the Congressional Medal of Honor his dad had been posthumously awarded. It was still in a drawer in his desk at home. He hadn't looked at it in years.

The helicopter buzzed by only a few feet overhead. Cherry-red tracer rounds cut into the jungle. Return fire struck sparks from the helo's metal skin and rotors.

"End program." Dr. Dobbs's voice cut through the onslaught of explosions and heavy machine-gun fire. Immediately the scene disappeared and they returned to the classroom. "Mr. Weist, I presume you have a report to make."

"Yes, sir," Solomon said, looking innocent.

"*Without* all the dramatization."

"Megan had battle scenes in her report," Solomon stated sullenly.

"She also had a point."

"So do I."

"State it."

Andy was grateful the veeyar had ended. He hadn't known getting exposed to the war was going to bother him so much. But he suspected Solomon had made his subject selection with that in mind.

Solomon cleared his throat and prepared to give his best pitch. The fact that he was taking Dr. Dobbs's interruption politely without whining about his right to present the report spoke volumes to Andy, letting him know whatever Solomon's plans were, they were huge. And one thing seemed certain. Solomon did *not* intend for Andy to enjoy this report.

3

"I mentioned Hearst's publication of the de Lome letter during Megan's report," Solomon said, "to illustrate what I wanted to say in this presentation."

"Serving your own interests instead of listening to Megan's material," Dr. Dobbs said.

Solomon blinked owlishly.

Andy grinned. *You're busted!*

Keeping control of the anger that showed on his round face, Solomon continued, "I wanted to point out that the country that wins a war gets to rewrite events that happened. History is in the hands of the winners."

"I'm less than intrigued," Dr. Dobbs said, "but I'll allow you some leeway."

"Can we go back to my report?"

Dr. Dobbs waited briefly, enough time to remind Solomon whose class they were in. "I don't want any more material that graphic shown."

"Those engagements underscore the whole report," Solomon said. "You allowed Megan to take us through a death camp where people were starving."

"It lent weight and a presence to her piece. It showed us what the Cubans were fighting against," the professor said.

"Your selections so far appear to have been chosen gratuitously."

Solomon's face turned the color of a blood blister. Andy silently cheered, barely keeping himself from adding insult to injury. The only thing that stopped him was the realization that Dr. Dobbs might get deflected from the dressing-down he was giving Solomon.

Frowning, Solomon said, "Okay, I'll get rid of any scenes you might find objectionable."

"The next one," Dr. Dobbs promised, "and I close down the whole report and we move on. You'll get an unsatisfactory grade on your report."

Andy knew that hit Solomon where he lived. Grades were important to Solomon. He fought for them and usually won.

"Fine." Dr. Dobbs relinquished control of the scenario, and Solomon took the class back to South Africa.

Andy blinked. He was in the jungle again and it was still night. A small village of straw-roofed huts on stilts occupied a clearing in the brush. A lazy stream glimmered silver in the moonlight. Campfires threw shadows and light over four South African tanks parked under the trees.

"This is a small village north of Mandelatown," Solomon said. "It never really had a name until the United Nations called it Site Forty-three."

Andy's mouth dried. His father had died at Mandelatown—far from this spot, but he still didn't feel relaxed. Nothing about Solomon was relaxing.

"Some of you may remember that a biological weapon was detonated at Site Forty-three and caused the deaths of over five thousand people, mostly civilians," Solomon continued.

Andy prepared himself, figuring Solomon would show that as well. He was familiar with the story because he'd read about the designer plague when he'd been researching stories about his father. But that had been back when he'd been trying to understand what had caused his father to go to Africa and die instead of staying home with his wife and son. Now Andy was past caring. At least, most of the time he was.

Dr. Dobbs shifted slightly, making it clear to everyone that if Solomon pulled out footage of the plague victims the show was over.

Solomon grimaced, and the footage around them wavered,

letting everyone know he'd made an alteration from his presentation menu. Night turned into day. "Before we get into that,
let me give you some history, kind of put events into perspective."

As the class followed Solomon through the transition, mountainous country appeared around them. Broken, hilly land
spilled out in all directions, and herds of elephants, black
wildebeest, giraffes, and antelope roamed the wide lands filled
with brush and short, scrubby trees. A pride of lions lay in tall
grass to the left, waiting patiently for the antelope herd that
would pass their way. Vultures heeled over in the sky.

Some of the students laughed and joked, and whipped up
safari outfits to wear in veeyar. A stern look from Dr. Dobbs
quieted the joking, but the safari gear remained.

Andy briefly thought of joining in the joke, but he didn't.
This was too close to home for him. He waited for Solomon
to spring his trap.

"This is the Transvaal," Solomon said. "Today it's a game
reserve and home to the Kruger National Park. But it's also
home to the gold-mining center in the Witwatersrand, now
called Gauteng."

The surroundings became more mountainous. They stood in
a modern mining community. Excavation machines and huge
dump trucks rattled around the hard-packed earth. Andy felt the
heat soak into him and his skin become grit-covered. Solomon
almost had to shout to be heard over the clank of machinery.

"More than half the world's gold is produced in South Africa. Pretoria is another major producer of gold." Solomon led
them to the smelting operation, and they watched as small
stacks of gold ingots were carried to cavernous warehouses
under the watchful eyes of uniformed security officers. "That's
one reason for the Western powers to involve themselves in
the civil war that broke out in South Africa in 2009."

"The peacekeeping effort was there to protect the people,"
Debbi Toth said. She was a trim brunette with a pug nose and
killer fashion sense she got from her mother, who was a model.
But her father, Andy knew, had served with the Marines in
South Africa. "You make it sound as if they were there trying
to get their hands on the gold."

Solomon folded his arms across his chest. "Dr. Dobbs, I'd
like to finish this presentation without interruption."

The professor hesitated. "I understand your personal feelings, Miss Toth, but Mr. Weist isn't offering any new conjectures here. He's allowed to speculate on the background of the conflict."

Debbi clearly wasn't happy with the decision. She walked to the back of the class where Andy was. "I'd like to pull the plug on him," she whispered.

"Only if it was for life support," Andy joked.

She smiled at him, and a smile from Debbi Toth went a long way toward making Andy's day better.

Andy continued watching. He knew Debbi's reaction to Solomon's presentation was probably the only thing keeping most of the rest of the class interested. Of course, those who really knew Solomon and the things he was capable of were waiting to see him pull his rabbit from the hat. It was even more interesting to speculate whether Solomon would get the rabbit out before Dr. Dobbs took the hat away.

"Gold was only one of the reasons the Western powers involved themselves with the South African civil war," Solomon went on. "Of course, they protected themselves under the political umbrella of the United Nations." Solomon started forward again.

Andy followed reluctantly, watching as the surroundings changed once more, becoming a gentle slope that led down to a winding river. Huts lined the river, located between shady trees and brush. Men and boys used spears and nets from small canoes to catch fish.

"This is near Kimberly," Solomon said, "on the Orange River, one of the two largest rivers in South Africa. In 1867, Dutch farmers called Boers, which is Dutch for farmer, discovered diamonds here. South Africa is still a major player in the diamond market. The discovery of the Kimberly diamond pipe eventually led to the Boer War against the British, who fought to keep control of the gold and diamonds South Africa was producing. This was the age of colonization, remember? And some people believe the world hasn't outgrown that age."

As Solomon went forward again, the riverside community transformed into an urban setting. Tall buildings stabbed into the sky, and paved streets carved civilization into orderly squares. Traffic congested the downtown area.

"South Africa has been divided for a long time," Solomon

said. "First it was split along race lines, separating blacks from whites. Even back then it was also split along class lines, and wealth and breeding played a part in that. But race was the most important division. Apartheid became official policy, requiring black citizens to carry passes or papers verifying their identities if they left their homelands."

Andy stared out at the checkpoints set up around the city in disbelief. Uniformed and armed white military personnel managed lines of black men and women trying to get into the city. Some of them were turned away even though they obviously needed the kind of help only available in the city.

Andy's best friend was David Gray. David had helped him get into the Explorers. Andy couldn't remember a time when they hadn't been friends, or think of any reason why they wouldn't be. Skin color wasn't an issue. But he knew some people still felt that way about race.

"Even in 2009," Solomon said, "South Africa was still divided. Only, this time the divisions had nothing to do with race. They were those familiar everywhere: between the haves and the have-nots. Or, as they became more popularly known, the Nationalists and the Patriots." He smiled. "And if you look in the dictionary, you'll find those two terms are synonymous. But the media needed a way to tell them apart."

Following Solomon's lead, Andy stepped into a large room filled with men in suits yelling out prices for stocks. Huge tote boards covered screens at the center of the room and constant price indexes. Andy had seen similar surroundings on Wall Street when he scanned the HoloNews for current events for other classes.

"Trading," Solomon said, "became a big issue with the South African Nationalist government after the millennium. They wanted to trade with the emerging Chinese market rather than the Western nations. Taking that much gold and that many diamonds out of the free market and Western industry would have destabilized several major economies."

"I don't think that's exactly the case," Megan said. "My mother covered those issues during the war as a reporter. Losing those resources concerned a lot of people, but the world would have survived it."

"Not happily," Solomon said. "And might I remind you, this is *my* presentation."

Megan reluctantly nodded.

"So those are the main reasons I see for American, British, and European involvement in the conflict." Solomon moved forward, and the scene changed again to night.

The tanks still sat quietly beneath the trees at the little village north of Mandelatown. People tended their campfires, talking and eating. The moonlight gleamed, clear and unimpeded now.

"Which brings us back to here," Solomon said. "It's 2014, near the end of the war. With the U.S. and European powers supporting the Nationalist rebels who wanted to continue their relationship with the Western world, the South African government was slowly being beaten into submission. The Western powers had bigger and better and—most important—more guns to put into the field."

"Not to mention the Patriots were hammering the Nationalists every chance they got," Debbi said. "They made sure there was less and less for them to have-not."

Solomon shook his head in annoyance and kept talking. "Then on August 12, 2014," he continued, "a plague descended on the area that became known infamously as Site Forty-three."

Andy swallowed hard. His father had died on the morning of August 13, only a few hours after the scene playing out before them. He made himself breathe. *Why did Solomon pick this war, and why a time so close to Dad's death? Is that his rabbit this time? A dig at me?*

"In seventy-two hours," Solomon said, "that plague spread down into Mandelatown and killed people by the thousands. The plague didn't show any favoritism. It killed Nationalists and Patriots alike."

"The plague was stopped thanks to American intervention," Megan said. "If America hadn't been involved in the war, there's no telling how many people would have been killed."

"Yeah," Solomon said. "But there was also some speculation that the United States was behind the biological weapon's release."

"As I recall," Dr. Dobbs said with audible restraint, "the biological weapon you're referring to proved to be a leftover Soviet weapon from the arms race. It was believed to have been delivered by a Middle Eastern terrorist group hoping to cause mass fatalities among the American and European forces."

"That's the official story," Solomon agreed. His smile never left his face.

Andy's stomach tightened, knowing Solomon hadn't dropped his bomb yet. Thinking quickly, remembering everything he could about the time and the events, Andy tried to guess where Solomon was heading, but couldn't come up with anything.

"No one ever proved the existence of the Middle Eastern terrorists," Solomon said. "Although the Western powers and the Nationalists agreed on that story."

"Obviously you disagree with that assessment, Mr. Weist," Dr. Dobbs said. "Otherwise we wouldn't be standing here in the middle of nowhere with you. Get to the point."

"My point is that the winner gets to rewrite history." Solomon snapped his fingers for effect.

The next transition wasn't a smooth one. Andy felt his stomach flip-flop, then realized the entire class—thanks to the magic of veeyar—had crowded in behind the pilot of an Apache helicopter gunship skimming across the treetops. The veeyar made it possible for them all to share the backseat and observe the action.

Andy looked through the helo's Plexiglas nose, watching as the land slid by beneath them like a great, dark ocean. Suddenly a fireball dawned in the darkness and threw flaming debris in an inverted cone. Andy knew from his Net Force Explorers training that the charge was shaped deliberately to hurl the deadly contents into the air so they could be blown by the wind toward Mandelatown. *And my father.*

"Homebase, this is Falcon Twelve," the Apache pilot said over his radio. "I spotted an explosion north of my position at ground zero. Do you want me to take a closer look?"

"Acknowledged, Falcon Twelve. Homebase is a no-go on the sat-com relay. We have no visual confirmation. You have the ball."

"Roger, Homebase. Falcon Twelve has the ball." The pilot pulled on the control stick and altered the helo's flight direction, then raced for the detonation area.

Andy relaxed a little. What Solomon showed now was stock footage of the incident. The scene had been played and replayed on HoloNews dozens, if not hundreds, of times. There were no surprises here.

Lieutenant Joe Dawkins, the Apache pilot, had been the first confirmed American casualty of the biological weapon. He'd infected twenty other men upon his return to base, then had died a day later, long before the med teams could identify what had happened.

Solomon let the footage run through, showing the pilot's view of the target area. Then he ended the sim, bringing them all back to class.

"Old news, Mr. Weist," Dr. Dobbs said. "Frankly, I'd expected more from all the research time you say you've put into this."

"There is more," Solomon offered. He snapped his fingers again. When the sim took over the veeyar again, they were back in the jungle at Site 43. "As some of you may also know," he looked directly at Andy, "the Nationalist army at Site Forty-three flatfilmed the delivery of the biological weapon. What I give you now is a re-creation of that event."

Andy watched apprehensively. A screen dropped into view at the lower right of his vision.

"The screen is the actual footage shot by the Nationalist tank crew," Solomon said. "I based the sim on what was filmed."

Silent shadows roved through the bush, closing in on the tanks. Andy recognized the shadows as American Special Forces troops from their gear and weapons and the sleek way they moved. He'd seen Marines at Quantico who moved the same way.

The Nationalist tank crews went into action, opening up with machine guns and their main cannon. The bullets chopped branches down, and the big cannon rounds ripped whole trees from the ground.

The Special Forces group returned fire, taking out the tank crews.

"Mr. Weist!" Dr. Dobbs interrupted. "I told you no more cheap theatrics would be allowed, and I meant it!"

"Here!" Solomon said, pointing, and his tone of voice, the sheer excitement in it, froze even Dr. Dobbs in his tracks. Tracer rounds tracked through him, never touching his veeyar image due to the sort utility programmed into the sim.

Following Solomon's pointing finger, Andy saw the big, unmarked deuce-and-a-half truck plowing through the bush. Its powerful motor whined at the abuse it was taking. Small trees went down before the truck's bumper like child's toys. This had been in the footage, too, so Andy wasn't really surprised.

"Remember what I said about the winners getting to rewrite history?" Solomon asked. "Officially, maybe the South African Nationalists didn't lose the war, but they didn't get to go through with the trades with China like they wanted, either. The biggest winners were the Western powers."

Andy watched as men in camouflage with no identifying insignia debarked from the distant truck. They carried a wooden crate from its rear, charging across the river into the village. Some of the villagers hid in their huts, and many others fled into the bush.

"Prepare the weapon!" one of the soldiers ordered.

"Yes, sir." Men pried at the wooden crate with crowbars and opened it.

The commanding officer was draped in shadows and wearing some kind of helmet and protective suit. His face couldn't be seen. He ordered the rest of the team back to the truck once the box was in place. They vanished into the distance, leaving the officer alone with his task.

"Watch carefully," Solomon said.

The sim played out in slow motion.

Almost breathlessly, knowing that Solomon was about to produce his rabbit and that Dr. Dobbs hadn't taken the hat away yet, Andy watched.

The bright green glow of the control panel for the opened weapon almost revealed the commanding officer's identity, but his face somehow remained in the shadows even as light played across his chest and the faceplate of his helmet. Once the weapon was set, the officer ran for the distant truck. But a Nationalist soldier hidden somewhere in the bush opened fire, pinning the man down by the riverbed for a few precious moments.

"They're using Russian technology," Solomon said. "*Old* Russian tech. Otherwise, the world won't buy their story. But those men weren't Russians, or even Middle Eastern terrorists."

The commanding officer raced across the river, dodging bullets. His boots sloshed through the water. Then the plague bomb blew, filling the sim with bright, harsh light and sudden thunder that vibrated through Andy. He blinked his eyes against the glare, watching as a wall of vapor pushed out from the bomb.

The concussive wave knocked the commanding officer from his feet.

"It wasn't Middle East terrorists who delivered the bomb," Solomon said.

The commanding officer pushed himself to his feet and tried to run. But it was too late. The deadly cloud issuing from the biological bomb had surrounded him.

The officer frantically checked his suit to see if it was compromised.

"It was us," Solomon said. "An American Special Forces team on a black op."

Clearly leaving the matter to fate, the officer waved to his men as the deadly cloud roiled around him, ordering them to proceed to some unknown destination without him. In the distance the truck roared away downwind. He turned back to watch the village, soon to be a charnel house when the effects of the plague kicked in. The moon broke through the intermittent clouds. And in that moment the man's face was finally revealed. Solomon froze the image in the sim, and the screen in the lower right-hand corner froze as well.

Andy knew the man's features immediately. Pain roared through him.

"This was the commanding officer of the special ops team," Solomon said. "Colonel Robert Moore, who the next day earned the Medal of Honor for sacrificing himself to save a battalion of U.S. Army Rangers surrounded and pinned down by Nationalist troops outside Mandelatown." He turned to face the class, the image of Andy's dad hanging over his shoulder. "Now you tell me: Was Colonel Moore a hero or a villain?"

4

"What did Andy do?" Matt Hunter asked, trying to imagine how Andy had felt. He sat across the booth from Megan O'Malley at Cecil's Spaghetti. The lunch buffet crowd was mostly Bradford students. The restaurant was homey and smelled like baked bread, garlic, and spaghetti sauce. Matt liked the place a lot.

Megan crunched a carrot stick. "What do you think Andy did? He freaked." She underscored her words with the carrot stick remnant. "This was his dad, Matt, the man who didn't come home from the war, someone he lost when he was just a kid. All Andy has of his father is this big hero image. Solomon ripped that to shreds, then had the nerve to ask Dr. Dobbs if the presentation was worth an A."

Matt shook his head, feeling even worse as he twirled his fork in his plate of spaghetti. "I'm surprised they didn't have to pull Andy off Solomon."

"Trust me," Megan said, "it's only because Andy couldn't figure out how to get out of that come-along hold I put him in."

"So where's Andy now?" Madeline Green, better known as Maj, asked as she walked over and caught the last of the conversation. She sat at the table when Megan scooted over. Like the others, Maj was a member of the Net Force Explorers. Her brown hair trailed over the thin straps of the peach sundress she wore. "Weren't you supposed to have lunch with him?"

Matt nodded. "Yeah. I looked for him at school, but when I didn't find him, I thought maybe he'd already come here."

"After something like that," Maj said, "you'd think he'd want to talk."

"Not Andy," Matt said. "He's one of those guys who plays hurt and never tells, remember? He'd make smart-aleck remarks in intensive care. So where did Solomon get this new flatfilm footage?"

"He won't say," Megan replied.

"Dr. Dobbs didn't ask him?" Matt was sure the professor wouldn't let the report go by unchallenged.

"Solomon said it's all in the hard copy he'll hand over later, when the whole class turns in their documentation."

"Why later? What's wrong with now?"

Megan shook her head. "Solomon told Dr. Dobbs he had some things to finish first."

"Dr. Dobbs let him get by with that?" Matt asked.

"Nope. Dr. Dobbs told Solomon that the presentation was an incomplete until proper reference materials were produced." Megan ate as she talked, managing both tasks elegantly.

"As an academic scholarship student, and as proud of his grades as he is," Matt said, "you'd think Solomon would have knuckled under."

"He didn't. Instead, the creep told Dr. Dobbs the reference materials would be made public soon enough."

"Cryptic," Matt commented.

"Solomon loves cryptic," Maj said.

"But Solomon's not going to tank on a grade," Matt went on. "Especially not in Dr. Dobbs's class."

"I know." Megan frowned. "That's why we have to treat this seriously."

"You mean we should believe that Andy's dad set that biological weapon off?" Matt shook his head. "No way. My mom flew missions in South Africa, remember? She never met Colonel Moore, but she knew he was a respected officer. The kind who gives—*gave*—everything for his country."

"Hey," Megan said, "I didn't say we needed to believe Solomon's story. I said we needed to take it seriously. If Solomon says he's got documentation, then he'll have documentation. He's that way. But it wouldn't hurt to look at it closely."

Matt released a tense breath. "Sorry. I knew that. I remember the first time the war came up in a history class. I did a project on my mom's time there, showed pictures that Dad gave me of her and the fighter jet she piloted. Some of the other kids did the same thing. But Andy—he never talked about it even when the teacher covered his father's last mission."

They were quiet for a time, and Matt felt responsible for bringing up the subject.

"So what we need to do is figure out where Solomon got his information," Maj said. "And keep an eye on Andy. He's probably going to either go after Solomon or try to keep all this stuff inside and crater."

As usual, Matt reflected, Maj calmly got to the heart of the problem. "That sounds like a plan. But we're dealing with the irresistible force meeting the immovable object when we're talking about Andy and Solomon. Neither one of them is likely to tell anybody what's going on."

"Right," Megan said. "We'll hand off watching Andy. He only has two classes with Solomon right now. I'll keep an eye on him in strategic analysis, and David can keep an eye on him in English lit. If anybody can keep Andy's head on straight, it's David."

"Without the come-along hold?" Matt asked.

Megan grinned at him. "I'll give him a demonstration. Just in case."

"That leaves us with Solomon," Maj stated. "Did the HoloNet footage look real?"

Megan nodded. "Very. I've got it downloaded on datascrip. When I get back to class, I'll E-mail copies to your home computers. Maybe you'll see something I didn't."

Matt finished his spaghetti and pushed the plate away. "I've never been able to figure out why Solomon and Andy go at each other. Both of them are bright guys. Solomon's a stellar student as far as knowledge and performance go, but he's a big pain. And Andy's the class clown but doesn't hit the books as hard as Solomon does. You'd think they'd get along—opposites attract and all that."

"Solomon gets the grades because he doesn't have Andy's knack for winning over crowds," Maj said. "Andy's popular and figures he doesn't need the grades. But the major difference is in their fathers."

Matt listened. What Maj said made sense. She was probably the best among the Net Force Explorers at understanding people and relationships.

"Andy's dad is a hero," Maj said. "And Solomon's dad—" She stopped.

"Isn't," Megan finished. It was no secret that Solomon's dad had abandoned his family as soon as the gates at Leavenworth Prison had rolled open.

"I think Solomon does identify with Andy in some weird way." Maj sipped her drink. "And I think he believes bringing Andy down is going to make him feel better about himself."

"If Andy doesn't clean his clock." Matt glanced at his watch, then started cleaning the mess from the table. "And speaking of clocks, we'd better hustle if we're going to get back to school on time."

Matt enjoyed the walk back to the academy from the autobus stop. He always felt better when he was in motion. The best feeling of all was flying, but he wasn't going to get the chance to do that today. He listened to the girls chatting beside him for a bit, but their conversation seemed centered around martial arts styles, so he tuned them out.

On autopilot he slipped through the cars parked in the student lot. Then he heard tires squealing against the pavement.

Matt glanced up. The academy had strict rules. Peeling out in the parking lot guaranteed somebody wouldn't be driving to school for a long time if they were caught.

An older car, a big, flat-black corporate transit model, charged through the last line of vehicles in the parking lot. The front end wobbled a bit as the driver compensated for the increase in speed and the temporary looseness of the steering. The car stayed on track, rushing toward a lone figure standing between the rows of parked vehicles.

Matt recognized Chris Potter, one of the Bradford students, from classes he'd had with him. Tall and gangly, his blond hair cut in a mohawk that had been died chartreuse on the ends, Chris froze in the car's path, obviously too stunned to react. He was a self-confirmed dexter, living for veyar and having no interest or talent for sports or much else in the physical world. Besides, even if Chris did move, Matt knew it wouldn't be in time.

His stomach churning, sure he'd never reach Chris, Matt vaulted onto the hood of the Dodge Durango SUV in front of him and slid across. His feet hit the pavement on the other side and he ran toward Chris as the big car bore down on him.

5

The big car was almost on top of Chris Potter when Matt saw Megan break from the line of cars to the right. Without hesitation she threw herself at Chris, knocking both of them from the vehicle's path.

Matt lost sight of them as the car bore down on him. The roar of the racing engine filled his ears. He thought he heard Maj scream out in warning.

Twisting, Matt threw himself to the left, toward the closer line of cars. He landed on a hood and slid, then collided with the windshield.

Matt hooked his fingers into the groove between the hood and the glass and held himself tight against the windshield. The black car slammed into the parked vehicle, driving it back more than a foot and riding up onto it for an instant. Then it pulled free.

Metal shrieked as the car passed by. The impact left a long tear in the car's side. *That's going to make it easy to identify,* Matt thought. Glancing after the retreating vehicle, he tried to get the license number, but the plate had been removed.

"Matt!" Maj called.

"I'm okay," Matt said, breathing hard as he climbed off the parked car and landed on his feet amid the clutter of broken glass, shattered ceramic polymer, and crumpled metal that had torn free of the car's front end.

Maj dashed across to help Megan pull Chris to his feet.

Rubber shrilled again with grim persistence.

Matt watched in disbelief as the black car came around in a tire-eating semicircle and reversed directions. He spotted two shadows behind the windshield, letting him know there was a driver and a passenger. He ran toward Megan, Maj, and Chris.

"Move!" Matt ordered. "It's coming back!" He crouched down and ran with his friends between the rows of parked cars, reached into his back pants pocket, and pulled out his wallet. Flipping it open, he punched on the power to the foilpack keycard, then selected the phone option from the menu. Immediately the flexible circuitry inside the tough polymer case reconfigured itself into the cellular phone module. He tapped in 911 while Megan and Maj yanked Chris along.

"What's going on?" Chris demanded.

"Keep moving!" Megan ordered.

The phone connection snapped through at the same time the car slammed into the parked vehicles Matt had followed his friends and Chris through. He felt the vehicle next to him shiver. He leaped forward just as it slid over to smash into the car beside it.

"Washington, D.C., Police Department," a computerized woman's voice answered. "Please state the nature of your emergency."

Matt ran, trying to talk to the dispatcher as he did so. Megan pulled at Chris while Maj pushed from behind. The black car reached the far end of the line of parked cars. Matt watched, half-expecting it to swing around for another try.

Instead, the driver steered for the gate and roared out into the traffic on the street. As it merged lanes, it slammed into another vehicle and knocked it out of control into the lane of oncoming traffic. Horns blared and tires screeched, followed by the hollow booms of too many cars plowing into each other.

Finally able to concentrate on what he was saying to the dispatcher, Matt ran down the events, described the black car with the missing plates and the dents, and added information about the wrecks in front of the academy. By then school security officers had run out into the parking lot. Some students, too, headed toward the wrecked cars to see if they could help.

Matt closed the foilpack and put his wallet away. He looked over at Chris. "Are you hurt?"

"Banged up my knee some." Chris pulled at his pants leg. Blood stained the denim.

Megan inspected the tear, pulling the material away from the wound. She gave a sigh of relief. "He's going to need this cleaned up, Matt. Maybe a couple stitches, too. But it looks like it's all surface damage. It can wait till after the police talk to him."

"Police?" Chris shook his head. "No police, man. We're definitely not going there with this." He started to back away.

Matt dropped a restraining hand on Chris's shoulder. "Whoever was in that car was trying to run you down. The police are going to want to know why."

"*Why?*" Chris repeated. "Man, you think *I* know why?"

"Look, Chris," Matt said, trying to lighten up the situation, "the police are going to talk to you. That means they're going to check your records with Juvenile Crimes. They're going to know, just like I do, that you've got a history of hacking into computers and trashing them. But this time you're the victim, not the perp. You know that makes a difference."

Chris Potter was a legend around Bradford. Net Force had showed up on campus more than once to shut him down. Mark Gridley, the son of Net Force head Jay Gridley, had told Matt about some of the hacks Chris and his friends had made.

The last time Chris had gotten arrested, he'd turned himself in. The corporate sector sometimes handled seriously troublesome hackers outside the legal system. A French computer software designer had scrambled an execution and sweeper team to take out Chris and his family. Net Force had only just managed to save Chris and his folks.

Chris shook his head. His eyes flared. "Matt, I swear to you that I haven't done anything illegal in seven months. Not since those guys came to my house. I learned my lesson. My mom's still taking physical therapy after what they did to her."

Matt clapped Chris on the shoulder. "I believe you," Matt said, "but I think, under the circumstances, it's going to be hard to get anyone else to." He looked back at the wrecked cars. "That car was definitely after you."

"It tried to get you, too," Chris pointed out. He wiped at his running nose.

"The driver was trying to get *somebody*," Maj said. "You can't ignore that. You were the first person they tried to run down, Chris. And they made another pass at you when the first one missed."

Matt nodded, spotting the first Washington, D.C., patrol cruiser swinging into the Bradford Academy parking lot. "Yeah, I know. And a lot of people are going to want to know why."

Once he'd given his preliminary statement to the uniforms securing the area with the help of the Bradford Academy security staff, Matt took out his foilpack again. He flipped it open and started to punch in the phone number for Captain James Winters, the Net Force Explorers' liaison to Net Force proper.

"Hold up," the barrel-chested patrol sergeant who climbed out of the second arriving vehicle bellowed. "Son, you can't make any phone calls until you clear them through me." The sergeant was tall and had graying temples and a gray mustache.

"It's okay, Sergeant," Matt said, turning the wallet over to show his Net Force Explorers ID. "I'm calling Captain Winters at Net Force."

The brass tag above the sergeant's left breast pocket identified him as Sergeant Lance Cooper. "Maybe I'll need to make that decision."

Matt bridled at the restriction, but he didn't fight authority. "Yes, sir, Sergeant Cooper. Then I expect you'll explain to Captain Winters why I didn't call him. As liaison for the Net Force Explorers, he likes to know whenever any of his people have any problems."

Winters *was* very protective of the Net Force Explorers. Not only did he act as liaison, but he'd also originated the program concept and put it into operation.

"Your Captain Winters doesn't cut any ice with me," Cooper said.

"Then maybe I will, Sergeant," a deep voice rumbled.

Cooper stepped back, dropping some of the aggression. "Yes, sir."

Matt recognized Martin Gray at once. David's father was a detective on the Washington, D.C., police force. Tall and fit, showing the build David would one day grow into, Detective Gray was at least three or four jacket sizes bigger than the patrol sergeant. He had short hair and ebony skin, and his pants had the sharp creases David's mom Janice ironed into them so her husband would look his best.

"Good," Detective Gray said. He flicked his eyes to Matt. "Call Winters. And tell me if there's anything he thinks I should know about this."

Matt nodded. Detective Gray then took Chris away from the uniformed officer who'd been in charge of him and guided him to the back of the unmarked car where another man in plainclothes waited. Matt finished keying in the number and listened to the phone ring as he watched.

"You've reached the desk of Captain James Winters," Winters's gruff voiced answered. "I'm away or on another line. Leave your name and number after the beep and I'll get back to you."

Caught off-guard, Matt almost missed the beep before he started his message. He'd never gotten that kind of response on Winters's line before. Usually either Winters picked up or his secretary did. Matt left his name and number, and a brief report on what had happened.

"What's going on?"

Matt turned and found David Gray at his side.

David was tall and lean, dressed in jeans and a plaid shirt. He kept his head shaved for the swim season.

Matt told the story quickly, gazing out at the parking lot as the first of the media vehicles arrived. *Must be a slow news day,* he thought. But then again, with a student body whose parents were often high-profile Beltway insiders, Bradford Academy represented a potential for huge stories.

"Doesn't make any sense," David said when Matt finished.

"What? That someone would try to hurt Chris?" Matt blew out a breath. "Don't you remember when that French corporate security team firebombed his house with his family in it?"

David nodded. "Sure, but they did that in the middle of the night, remember? They had a witness potential of zero. The only reason they were caught was that Chris hacked into their computers and found out they'd been turned loose on him. So Net Force was able to scramble a team in time. But that was a fluke. So my question stands. Why did they try this here at Bradford in broad daylight when it would have been easy to find out where Chris lived and take him out quietly?"

"Unless perhaps they *wanted* witnesses?" Matt said.

"Why would they want witnesses?" David asked.

Both boys were silent as they thought about it.

The security personnel and uniformed police officers worked quickly in an effort to keep the media people from interviewing students. It was wasted energy, though, because several of the students simply went to the reporters.

"To make a point," David finally said.

"To who?"

David grinned. "Ah, now there's the real question, isn't it?" He paused. "They didn't want to make a point to Chris, unless they figured they could just run over him a little."

"As opposed to running over him a lot?" Matt's mind flew through the possibilities David's line of thinking had stirred up. He didn't like where he was headed.

"Maybe. Was anyone else with Chris?"

"No."

"But you, Maj, and Megan weren't the only students in this area?"

"It was after lunch," Matt said. "There were a lot of people here." *And a lot more here now,* he thought, looking out over the gathering crowd. Cameramen had set up on the roofs of the autovans and the feeds went directly to HoloNet and the other local channels they represented.

"Maybe the point was to be made to one of them," David suggested. "And maybe it was to be made to one of Chris's hacker buddies."

"Chris says he's clean," Matt said.

"Wouldn't you?"

Matt nodded. Through the windshield he saw Chris protesting vehemently with waving arms to Detective Gray, who remained calm and showed no emotion at all. "Your dad usually works homicides, right? I don't think anybody was killed here, even out in all those collisions."

"Yeah," David said. "It's possible that he's here because this *is* a violent crime against somebody. But you're right. Him being here is kind of curious."

"Want to know something even more curious?" Matt asked. "I called and got Captain Winters's automated message system."

"I didn't know he had one."

"Neither did I," Matt replied. "And he still hasn't gotten back to me."

"Kind of gets your attention, doesn't it?" David asked.

Matt nodded, then led the way back to where Megan and Maj had finished being interviewed by uniformed officers. Megan was restless, while Maj quietly studied the crowd.

"You know," Maj said, "it's possible that whoever drove that car is back in the crowd by now."

That got Matt's attention. "What makes you say that?" He started looking at the crowd with new eyes.

"The villain always returns to the scene of the crime," Megan quipped. "My dad's used it before in his mystery novels."

"It has a basis in fact," Maj said. "Arsonists and terrorists often return to the scene of whatever they've done to see how it affects people."

"It's true." David pointed at a cameraman in a dark gray Washington, D.C., PD jacket. "When something like this happens, one of Dad's first procedures is to order holograms shot of the crowd. If nothing else pans out later, they go through the film and see who was there right after whatever happened. He's cleared some cases that way."

"There's not going to be a repeat of this." Megan looked at them. "Is there?"

Matt nodded toward Detective Gray and Chris. "I guess that depends." He scanned the crowd again, feeling slightly paranoid. Then his gaze locked on a slim man dressed casually and wearing aviator sunglasses. Despite the casual dress, the man's black boots shined like he'd just stepped off parade drill.

The man's name floated at the back of Matt's mind, just out of reach. He turned to David, quietly getting his attention. "Hey, isn't that a Net Force agent?"

"Where?" David asked.

Matt glanced back to where he'd seen the man only to find that he'd disappeared. Matt couldn't believe it. "He was there," he told the others. "And he was Net Force. I've met him."

"Okay," David said. "But they don't generally run solo. If you spotted one of them that means you missed at least one other, maybe more."

Matt knew that was true. But what was going on? He'd called Captain Winters and hadn't gotten his call returned, but Net Force agents were showing up? That made no sense.

Detective Gray stepped out of the unmarked car and waved at Matt.

"Looks like they want me. Keep an eye out for Net Force agents," Matt told the other three. "I'm curious about what they're doing here."

They agreed to look. "But you know you're only going to find out what they're doing here if Captain Winters okays it," Megan told him.

On his way to Detective Gray's car, Matt thought about the last couple of hours—Solomon's attack on Andy and Andy's father, and Chris Potter's narrow escape from the unknown car were both *way* out of the ordinary. The odds of both of them happening on the same day were staggering. What was going on at Bradford?

6

Hey, Mom, what do you think the odds are that Dad headed up the mission that set off that plague bomb in South Africa?

Even as the question ran through his mind, Andy scowled at his pale reflection in the autobus window. There was no way to ask her that question in a calm way. Not without dropping a bomb himself.

And there was no way he was going to drop that bomb on his mother.

He sat curled up in his seat, his knees drawn up against the seat in front of him. The seat beside him was empty, which was a rare thing. Usually somebody sat with him on the ride home so they could hear the latest jokes he'd learned or the funny stories he only halfway made up to tell. Real life was almost always funny enough if viewed from the right perspective.

Today, though, everybody seemed to sense the Stay-Away-From-Me vibrations he was putting out. Or maybe it was that stupid scowl on his face.

When the autobus rolled to a stop at his corner in Alexandria, Virginia, he grabbed his backpack from the overhead compartment and bailed without a word to anybody. He was running by the time he hit the curb, dashing across the sidewalk and listening to his shoes slap the pavement.

He didn't stop running till he reached the small three-bedroom house he shared with his mom. He looked at the elephant ear plants in the garden that he'd helped put in. He studied the scarlet crawl of impatiens threading between them, and the ceramic animals scattered through the greenery that he and his mom had bought each other for every birthday that he could remember.

They were all part of the yard that he'd taken over mowing after he'd turned ten. They were part of a yard his dad had *never* mowed, he realized. His mom had done it before it became Andy's responsibility. It was funny that he'd never really thought about that before. Dads on both sides of the Moore home and across the street had mowed their yards, turning it over to their sons when they got old enough, then taking the job back when the sons moved away.

Andy breathed shallowly, unable to take a deep breath with all the effort it took to keep the emotion locked up inside him. Mr. Crewes next door had taught him the simple lawnmower repair and maintenance skills that had kept the Moores' machine virtually breakdown free. *That was something Dad should have taught me,* Andy thought bitterly. *Just one of dozens of things he should have been there for.*

But he hadn't been, and Andy had gotten along fine in spite of it.

He tried to shelve that line of thinking because it was getting him nowhere, but it wouldn't totally go away. He stood in front of the door scanner and spoke a couple of phrases into the mike. His identity established, the door opened and he went inside.

This house was home, the only home he could really remember. His mom had bought it when he was five years old, moving them out of the military housing where they'd stayed until she got on her feet financially after his dad's death.

He raided the refrigerator out of habit, slapping a BLT with mustard together and grabbing a juice pack. Then he went back to the annex in the backyard and tended the three hedgehogs, the Golden Retriever, two potbelly pigs, a boa constrictor, two sugar gliders, and the Persian cat his mom had brought home for special attention away from all the constant noise at the clinic.

Andy fed them and watered them, checking his mother's notes for behaviors and visible changes in their conditions, making notes of his own. It made him feel good to know how big a difference he could make. He didn't know how many animals he and his mom had worried over, lost sleep over, and cheered over in the past dozen years. But he did know that together they'd saved lots of animals.

"*So,*" Solomon's mocking voice taunted in his head again. "*How does it feel not to have a hero dad anymore?*"

Being alone with his thoughts wasn't a good thing, Andy decided. He gave the dog a final pat, kicked up the climate control, locked up, and headed to the house and his room. Posters of holos and Net games covered all available space. Shelves filled with model cars, planes, rockets, and gaming figures, all part of his endless search for the perfect hobby, lined one wall. He hadn't found it yet, but each exploration had given him new ammunition for gags and jokes.

He dropped into the computer-link chair by the small study desk at the foot of his bed and slotted in his school datascrip. Leaning his head back, he felt the buzz of contact in his implants, then he shifted into his personal veeyar. His veeyars changed a lot, too, depending on his current enthusiasm.

The current one was a Spanish pirate ship, a sixteenth-century galleon, racing across a turquoise sea filled with marine creatures from legend and myth. The ship's white sails strained in the wind under the clear blue sky, and he felt the gentle roll of the deck beneath his feet. The crew only noticed him when he wanted them to. He could be alone without feeling too alone.

He went back to the stern castle where the wheel was and stood beside the plotting desk. "Bring up menu," he said.

Immediately icons surfaced in the map of the ocean he was currently sailing. Andy tried the Net first, but Mark, strangely for him, wasn't on-line. So Andy called Mark Gridley's home number.

A window opened up in the map, revealing Mark sitting in front of the vidphone at his desk in Georgetown. His olive complexion, straight black hair, and precise features showed his Thai-American heritage. His almond-shaped brown eyes glittered warmly. At thirteen, Mark was the youngest of the Net Force Explorers.

"Hey, Andy," Mark greeted.

"Hey, yourself," Andy said. "Catch you at a bad time?"

"Nah," Mark said. "I'm getting ready to run some moves against some of the new software Mom's created for Net Force use in a little while. Debugging the encryption stuff mostly, making sure it's as hacker-proof as it can be before they bring it on-line."

Mark's dad was Jay Gridley, head of Net Force. His mother was the top computer tech for the agency. It was no surprise that their only son was a computer prodigy.

"Got a minute?" Andy asked.

"For you, sure." Mark gave him a sympathetic look. "I heard about this morning. That must have been rough."

Andy nodded, grateful for the breeze that blew over him in his veeyar. "I'm getting around it. I guess that's why I'm calling." Despite the veeyar's sensory input, he felt his heart pounding back in the real world. "I'm going to ask you a favor."

"What?" Mark asked.

"I know the accusations Solomon made about my dad can't be true."

"He wouldn't have gotten the Medal of Honor for that," Mark agreed.

No, he got that for dying. Actually, Mom got it. Andy didn't say what was on his mind, though. "I want to prove that Solomon's wrong. To do that I need a copy of my dad's files."

"I thought your mom had them."

Andy paced the deck of the pirate ship. "She has what she was given."

"What do they say?"

"The same thing I've always heard," Andy replied. "That Dad was killed during the rescue of a Rangers battalion pinned down by Nationalist guns outside Mandelatown. But there's nothing about the plague bomb. Or whether my dad was involved with it."

Mark suddenly understood, and he didn't look happy about it.

Andy didn't like it that he'd made Mark feel that way. "Look, I hate to put you on the spot like this, but I need help. This is what I'm up against." He reached for the icons, then brought up Solomon's presentation file from the strategic analysis class. He watched in silence, seeing his dad's face revealed again when the biological weapon blew.

"Did Solomon say where he got this?" Mark asked when it finished.

"No. The flatfilm's supposed to have come from the Nationalist tank crews."

"Did it?"

Andy shrugged and went back to pacing. The wood felt and sounded real underfoot. "Nobody ever saw this version if it did. That's only one of the questions I want answered."

"You could do a comparison check on the flatfilm with the official version," Mark said. "The speed of the flatfilm, frames per second, lens size, get an idea of the developmental process."

"Already done," Andy replied. That had been lunch. "It specs out as a probable match."

"Then you have to figure out what nonstandard avenues are open to Solomon."

Andy gazed out at the turquoise sea and watched the Loch Ness Monster surface briefly, then plunge back under the water. "Solomon's a hacker. One of the best at Bradford. You want to try to guess where he got his information?"

"Not from U.S. military files," Mark said. "Net Force manages the security on those. There's no way he could have gotten in."

"I thought about that, and I agree. So if we rule out our military files, who does that leave us with?"

"The South Africans."

"Okay, let's say it was them. Why would they sit on something like this? Something that could blow American and European intervention during the war out of the water?"

"I don't know."

"Remember, after the plague bomb was used, how the Nationalists tried to blame the United States?"

"Sure. The charge didn't stick."

"It would have if they'd had this footage."

"So I guess your question becomes why didn't they have it."

"Yeah. If they'd had it, they would have used it then. It's either fake, which the data doesn't bear out, or somebody took it from them before they could use it. But how did Solomon find out about it? And how did he track it down?"

"It could be hard to find out," Mark said. "But it's doable."

"Over time, maybe. Solomon's going to have his stuff hidden away. Even if he left it on his veeyar, I'd have to be really lucky or really good to hack into his system. I don't feel that lucky or that good."

Mark hesitated. "Do you want me to give it a try?"

Andy knew his friend didn't like the idea much. Mark had a lot of friends among the hackers because he was an excellent designer, but he definitely rolled on the straight and narrow most of the time. "Actually, I was thinking more along the lines of the Defense Department files."

Mark shook his head. "I couldn't get in there if I wanted to. Net Force set up and maintains the security over those Net sectors. Nobody without clearance gets in there."

"I thought maybe you had clearance with all the testing you do," Andy said.

"No. And even if I did, Andy, I couldn't use it for something like this." Mark frowned sympathetically. "I'm sorry. I hope you're not mad."

"No." Andy sighed. "You're right." *I'm frustrated, yeah, but not mad at you.* "And I guess I shouldn't be so impatient. The answers are out there. I just have to find them. Thanks for listening and not getting bent out of shape with me for asking."

"Maybe I can take a run at Solomon's computer," Mark offered. "Sure, he's smart, but I've beaten a lot of systems."

"Not yet," Andy said. "Solomon would know who was behind it even if I didn't do it myself. He'd know how much he's gotten to me. I don't want that to happen yet." He thanked Mark, said goodbye, then blanked Mark out of the veeyar.

Andy abandoned the stern castle and went back down to the main deck. He stood at the railing and watched the curved horizon, idly wondering what shore the sea would finally wash up against. He'd never gotten close enough to know.

Just like he'd never gotten close to his dad. *What if the military put Dad up to it? What if they somehow convinced him the plague bomb's deployment was necessary to end the war?*

The South African War had ended within days after the biological weapon had been used. The Nationalists hadn't had any choices about continuing the fight with the plague running rampant through their country. They'd given in to the economic demands of the Western nations, but they'd remained in power. *What if that was the deal the Western powers made with them?* Andy couldn't help wondering. *Keep your cushy government jobs in return for not telling everyone that the plague bomb had been used by an American special ops team operating under Dad?*

He didn't like thinking that way, but he couldn't help it. And what was worse was thinking that while maybe he could handle it if Solomon's story was true, what about his mother?

The ship's first mate, a rumpled stump of a man with a fierce, fiery beard, walked up beside Andy. "Begging yer pardon, Cap'n Andy, but there's someone to see you."

"Connect," Andy called out.

Immediately a window opened beside him, overlaying the view of the ocean and sky so they could still be seen. Matt gazed at him through the window and grinned. "Permission to come aboard, Cap'n."

"Come ahead," Andy answered, knowing why Matt was dropping by and really wishing he didn't have to deal with this now.

7

In reality Matt just moved into the veeyar from his own scenario, but Andy's system made it look as if he grabbed the
edges of the screen framing him and pulled through. Matt
stepped down onto the deck, looking around. "I don't think
I've been to your veeyar since you came up with this."

"It's new." Andy kept his answers short. Less talk meant less
opportunity to ask questions.

Matt faced into the breeze and took a deep breath. "I like it.
So where are you headed?"

Andy shook his head. "I'm not headed anywhere. I'm just
going." Matt Hunter was a guy who always knew where he
was going. Andy had never felt like there was a place he really
needed to be.

"I thought maybe we'd try out Hooper's zombie game
again," Matt suggested.

"And that's why you're here?"

"Maybe not entirely."

"I can handle Solomon and his story," Andy said.

"I just didn't want you to handle it alone if you didn't want
to. What Solomon did was wrong, Andy. Even if it was true—"

Andy turned on Matt and took a step in his direction. "You
think it's true?" His hands balled into fists, and all the unvented

anger he'd stored since morning threatened to spill out.

Matt eyed him levelly. "Not even for a second. Your dad was a good man, Andy. What Solomon's saying is garbage."

Trembling from the sudden swirl of mixed emotions that filled him, Andy let out a long breath. "I know. But I can't let him sit back and say those things."

"Then what are you going to do?"

Andy shrugged. "I'm still working that out."

"You sound like you have doubts," Matt observed.

"About my dad?" Andy nodded. "It's funny. Until this morning, I didn't doubt anything. I didn't doubt my dad was a hero, and I didn't doubt that he just decided that whatever he was fighting for over in South Africa was more important to him than Mom and me."

"Being kind of hard on him, aren't you?"

"I don't know, Matt. I mean, how do you suppose you'd feel if your mom hadn't come back from that war?"

"I don't know how I'd feel. She came back."

Andy flashed his friend a half grin. "Yeah, well, I was dealing with that okay for a while. Then this happened. You haven't seen Solomon's footage."

"Yeah, I have. Megan gave me a copy. I scanned it before I called you."

"What did you think?"

"It's pretty tough to take."

"It doesn't look fake," Andy said. "I compared it to other footage that was filmed over there at that time, including the official footage released of that incident. It specs out right."

"That doesn't mean that it *is* right."

"I know. Did Megan tell you Solomon wouldn't tell Dr. Dobbs where he got the footage?"

Matt nodded.

"Solomon's planned this," Andy said. "He's not going to rest until he sees it through. I have to ask myself what that could mean to Mom."

"What are you talking about?"

"Suppose Dad was ordered to put that weapon there, Matt? It *did* end the war."

"Andy, listen. This is America you're talking about. We're the good guys."

Andy nodded morosely. "I guess I just want to be sure. I don't want any more surprises."

"What do you mean—any more?"

"It's just surprising," Andy said, "that after all these years it matters so much to me. It shouldn't. I never knew him, and I never will."

"I wish I knew what to tell you, buddy."

Andy smiled. "I'm not somebody you can just tell things to, Matt. You should know that as well as anybody. I'm stubborn. I have to find things out my own way. That's why I get into all the trouble I do." He paused. "Look, I've got to get to some homework I've been putting off. Really. I appreciate you stopping by, but this is on me. I've got to deal with this myself."

"Sure," Matt said. "I just wanted you to know that you didn't have to go through this alone."

"I appreciate that." Andy said goodbye and watched Matt step back through the opening to his own veeyar. After the opening closed, Andy retreated back to the stern castle and pulled the menu out of the map again. He pressed a utility icon and brought up his strategic analysis presentation. After seeing Megan's in action that morning, he'd thought of some ways he could tweak his own.

He opened the file where he kept his homework, then pulled himself through the opening. He dropped a few feet on the other side, landing on a grassy hill overlooking the Irthing River in Great Britain. He was now clad in the leather armor of a Roman foot soldier. He carried a spear and wore an eighteen-inch gladius—the short sword carried by Roman soldiers—at his hip.

He walked down the slope and watched the men building the wall. At this point in the presentation the builders of Hadrian's Wall had reached Carlisle, near the western coast of Great Britain, not far from where the Irthing River drained into the Solway Firth. The wall was ten feet thick, made of stone, and had forts at regular intervals along its length. It was meant to protect Roman-occupied Great Britain from the northern barbarian tribes. By the time it was finished, it would run all the way across the island from east to west.

When Andy had first started his research, he'd thought slaves had built the wall. Instead, he'd discovered that the soldiers had built it themselves. The Roman Army at that time was made up of volunteers from all over the Empire. Many of those men were masons, architects, and carpenters. They were accustomed to building—the Roman Army built most of the roads that crisscrossed the empire, as well as forts, fortifications, and government buildings in all the distant lands the Romans had settled or conquered. The wall had provided work that beat sitting around waiting for orders.

With the research Andy had done, he'd been able to sit and talk with the legionnaires. He'd learned a lot about them, about what they were doing and what they hoped to do. Most of them, he'd discovered, were regular guys hoping to become landowners. After twenty-five years of serving Rome, a soldier could retire from the Army and would receive an estate somewhere on the borders of the Empire. About half of the soldiers even lived to collect it.

For a while Andy had enjoyed building the wall with them, but he couldn't hope to sell Dr. Dobbs on that experience for his presentation.

Now Andy watched the soldiers as they worked, joined by the citizens of the nearby city who benefited from the protection the wall offered. Gates through the wall were spread far apart, protected by forts that straddled the wall.

Usually Andy had been able to lose himself in talking to the men, working on the wall, or training with the gladius. Today, none of that distracted him. Irritated, he logged off the computer, leaving his report as it was.

His mind was totally locked on to the problem Solomon had given him.

"Hey, what's going on here?"

Andy looked up from the living room floor and saw his mom standing there. She was blond like him and wore her hair short. She stayed trim by working hard and long at the clinic and by watching what she ate. Her work clothes consisted of jeans and a work shirt under a white smock. She was a couple of inches shorter than Andy was these days.

Andy glanced around at all the family photo albums, holo cubes, flatfilm, and holo footage he'd gathered from all over the house. He had a photo album open in front of him that showed his mom and dad's wedding.

"Personal project," he told her.

She glanced at the pictures. "I thought you didn't like looking at these."

"I never said that," he protested, feeling a flush of guilt. His mom sometimes brought them out on rare weekends and spent hours going over them, even though he was sure she'd memorized them.

"You didn't have to say that," she told him. "I can tell by the way you quietly leave the room every time I start looking at those."

Andy didn't bother to deny it. He hadn't liked the way looking at the pictures and holos obviously made his mom feel, and he hadn't liked the way they made him feel. She had memories; he had no clue. He saw pictures of his dad holding him when he'd been small, but couldn't remember it.

"So why the interest tonight?" she asked.

"I don't know," he said finally. "I just feel like I need to try to get to know my dad."

Tears glittered in his mom's eyes, and Andy felt bad about that. He hadn't lied to her. Exactly.

"Can I help?" she asked hopefully.

"Sure," Andy said.

His mom settled in beside him. "Where do you want to start?"

"At the beginning," Andy said, passing her the wedding album.

She grinned at him, a single tear sliding down her cheek. "Actually, Andy, it didn't begin there." She got up and went to her room, then came back with a college yearbook. She sat down again and opened the yearbook. A single yellow carnation flattened and preserved between wax paper and wrapped in plastic slid out. She caught the flower and held it tenderly. "It began here. With two young people who had their whole lives ahead of them." She turned to a page that had a picture of a guy who looked way too young to be his dad and way too much like his dad to be anybody else.

"What kind of guy was he?" Andy asked. "Was he a good guy?"

"The best, Andy," she replied. "And don't you ever let anyone tell you any different."

What does she mean by that? Andy knew it could have just been an innocent comment, but Solomon's footage twisted all his thinking. *Does she know about the plaque bomb? Has she been keeping that from me all these years?*

The possibility was real, he knew, and sent chills down his spine.

In his veeyar at home Matt floated in a crossed-leg position with a starry sky spread out all around him, thinking. Watching Andy suffer, thanks to Solomon's project, hadn't been good.

Matt wished there were something he could do for Andy, but couldn't come up with anything useful. So he turned his thoughts to the mystery of Chris Potter's attack. He reached out for the marble slab floating in front of him and touched the inch-high Net connection, giving it Mark Gridley's location.

A window popped open, revealing Mark dressed in a silver suit of armor that appeared to be all angles. The helmet was a huge crystalline polyhedron that seemed to change shape constantly. Mark called it his crashsuit.

"Hi," Matt said. "Busy?"

"Kind of," Mark said. "I'm running diagnostics on some software Mom's developing. Want to go on a run with me?"

Matt only thought about it for a moment. Going up against Net Force security programming was usually an exercise in futility even when it was in the testing state, but it was exciting nonetheless. He knew Mark had sometimes found weaknesses, and had even been with him a couple times to share in the victory.

"Sure." Matt pushed himself from behind the marble slab and through the window, joining Mark in the pure black of true cyberspace. By the time he arrived, he had on a suit like Mark's. In this scenario, he moved by venting jets in the gloves, boots, and back of the crashsuit.

The target hung before them, looking like a diamond-studded Möbius strip that doubled back on itself endlessly. It winked and sparkled and gave off the occasional blue flash.

"Man," Mark said over the helmet radio, "you have to love non-Euclidian geometry."

"What is it?" Matt asked.

"Mom wouldn't tell me," Mark answered. "I don't know if it's a standard security program or a Trojan horse they're hoping to use against subversive Net elements. For all I know, it could be a Wonderland Black Hole."

A Wonderland Black Hole, Matt knew, was a piece of impressive tech. It sucked a potential hacker into a system, then created an interactive near-AI world that kept him or her occupied without letting on that it was a complete fabrication. Some were called Looking Glasses, modeled on the real sites the hackers tried to break into. And some were called White Rabbits and were filled with disconnected errata that made no sense. Of course, logging off was always possible, but hackers tended to stay engaged by the challenges in Black Holes until it was too late.

"Ready?" Mark asked.

Matt checked the suit controls. The left glove contained all the mobility controls, and his right glove held the attack programs Mark had packaged for the run. "Yeah."

"I've got the lead." Mark accelerated, boosting from his boots and starting a glide path toward the crystalline shape. "Let's see what's out there!"

8

Matt followed Mark as they dived into the crystalline shape. The program spat out lime-green rays that touched their suits.

"Simple IFF tag," Mark said.

"Got it." Matt tagged the identify-friend-or-foe server routine in his glove and watched as his suit suddenly took on the aspects of the crystalline shape. Ahead of him, Mark's did the same. The green rays washed over them but sent out no alerts.

"So far so good," Mark said, "but that was the easy one." He accelerated again, closing on the crystalline shape. "I talked to Andy earlier."

"Me, too, for all the good it did."

"I think I may have gotten somewhere."

Matt listened as Mark told him about the discussion, paying just enough attention to the whorls and loops inside the program to survive. Disguised as a general information statement bouncing back from the earlier query, he still had to stay within the channels of the datastream feeding through the program. One touch along the program and his thin cover would be blown.

Matt watched as the interior of the program erupted in a sudden flurry of missiles from the walls. They were tiny, no longer than his finger, but they represented the secondary wave of security programming. Getting hit by any of them would throw him out of the program.

Mark barrel-rolled smoothly ahead of him, flaring out programming sequences that looked like laser beams. The homing missiles vanished like popped soap bubbles, convinced by Mark's programs the boys belonged here. The route they used got tighter, and the channel they moved through suddenly bottlenecked.

"First of the firewalls ahead," Mark announced. A cone of violet light sprayed the narrow opening.

Matt watched as the opening irised closed. At the speed they were going, if they hit, the crashsuits would shatter and they'd be evicted. "Have you talked to Chris Potter?"

"No." Mark increased the violet light's wattage, then added two small missiles, actually programming sequences designed to make the firewall accept them as an ordinary part of the data flow. "These are a series of the most-used server codes in the government NetWare. They should do the trick, but we might buy it here if they don't."

Matt braced himself. It wasn't possible to really get hurt in the Net, but getting shaken up was a common occurrence.

The firewall suddenly irised open again and allowed them passage. It closed immediately after they shot through.

Ahead of Matt, the tunnel vanished, replaced at once by a tangle of cyber representations that looked like a cityscape spread out before them. All around that cityscape, however, comets whirled in interlocking orbits. And several of the buildings had tentacles.

"If you get the chance," Matt said, "stay close to Chris and his buddies."

"I'm not exactly a friend of theirs."

"Yeah," Matt agreed, "but you guys do hang out together a little. Just keep your eyes and ears and browser open. That attack today at school left me feeling that whoever did it isn't through."

"I heard the police found the car."

"Yeah," Matt said as he adjusted his speed, falling in behind Mark. "Nobody in it and wiped clean of prints. It was stolen less than an hour before it showed up at Bradford."

"You're assuming the target may be bigger than Chris."

"He says he's clean," Matt said. "And I believe him. Even

if I didn't, we'd need to broaden our coverage."

Mark threaded through the comets with split-second timing. "Have you talked to Captain Winters?"

Matt struggled to follow Mark. It would have been easier to plot his own course and take his chances. Except that he didn't know for sure what he was doing. The security program they were deep into now was nothing he recognized.

"Briefly, this afternoon," Matt replied. "Captain Winters didn't seem interested."

"Probably has a bunch of other cases he's working on," Mark suggested. He barrel-rolled away from a comet.

Matt saw it too late. He moved his controls desperately, trying to break the collision course he was on, but couldn't. The comet smashed into him. He recoiled from the crash, watching gleaming shards of his crashsuit spin away.

"I'll let you know if anything comes up," Mark promised, his voice fading as the log-off procedure initiated by the security system ejected Matt from the Net.

The security program kicked him all the way out. When Matt opened his eyes again, he sat in the computer-link chair in his bedroom. *Oh, man, that was embarrassing,* he thought.

"You look like something the cat dragged in."

Andy dropped into the computer-link chair beside Megan the next morning in strategic analysis class and said, "Now, there's that bit of self-confidence I've been looking for all morning."

"Sorry. Late night?" Megan asked as the first bell rang and more students started to file into the classroom.

"Yeah." Andy and his mom had gotten lost in the albums and stories last night. They'd been up till three. He glanced at the empty seat Solomon usually occupied. If Solomon wasn't there, what was he doing? Andy's stomach rolled sourly.

"He's here," Megan said.

"I didn't ask." Andy slid his classroom datascrip into the computer-link chair.

"You didn't have to. I saw the look on your face." Megan slid her own datascrip into place and checked the chair's systems. "This is really bugging you. Maybe you should protest to Dr. Dobbs, see if he won't assign Solomon another topic."

Andy shook his head. "And if I protest Solomon's research, what am I to base it on? Personal conflict?"

"The story's not true," Megan said. "Somehow he's twisted things around."

"Are you so sure about that?" Andy demanded, more harshly than he'd intended.

"Yes. You've seen the military report on your father. They don't give traitors Medals of Honor."

"Megan," Andy said, struggling to keep his voice at a normal tone, "I tried to get into my father's military files. They're locked up tight, buried beneath layers of security programming—and not typical stuff. Some of that programming was put there by Net Force. I have to ask myself why they've got that locked away."

"National security," Megan replied. "They don't want tactics, weapons, and intelligence services released where terrorist groups can get hold of it. Information is a weapon. You know that. Or maybe they want to protect the personnel involved in that operation. Commanding officers and men in the field could become targets for revenge by groups like the South African Nationalists that split from the main party after the treaty agreements were made. You know that, too, Andy."

Andy made himself breathe out. He felt as if he was about to explode and didn't know how he was going to make it through class today. "I know. I just don't like wondering."

"He was your dad," Megan said. "How can you wonder?"

"Because I didn't know him." When a few students' heads turned in his direction, Andy knew he'd spoken louder than he'd intended.

Megan was quiet for a moment as other students continued to file into the room. "Maybe you should talk to Captain Winters about this."

"I thought about it," Andy said. "I decided not to."

"Why?"

"Because if Winters finds out about this and starts poking around, and he discovers out my dad really did set off the plague bomb, he's about the last person I'd want to know that."

"I'm sorry, Andy. I wish there was something I could do to help you believe."

"Believe what?"

"Believe in your dad for starters," Megan answered. "Everything else is really secondary to that."

"That's going to be hard to do," Andy said, "without being able to sit down and talk to him."

Solomon swept into the room just after Dr. Dobbs and just ahead of the last bell. He grinned maliciously at Andy and dropped into his computer-link chair.

"Mr. Weist," Dr. Dobbs asked after he'd punched the attendance verification program to take role, "have you brought that bibliography concerning your presentation?"

"No, sir," Solomon replied. "But you'll be getting it before the class deadline."

"As you say, Mr. Weist, but I want to remind you that should you not turn that in, you'll be getting an incomplete on the assignment."

Solomon nodded. "It won't be incomplete."

Dr. Dobbs leveled his gaze on Solomon, usually something that made most students wish they were half a world away. "Your presentation lacked a motive for the United States military yesterday, a reason why they would employ the biological weapon as you say they did."

Solomon grinned and shook his head. "I didn't know I was going to have to spell it out."

"If you want your grade to reflect a job well done," Dr. Dobbs said evenly, "you will."

"Unleashing the plague was designed to wipe out Nationalist resistance," Solomon said. "One way or another. If most of the South African population had died, it wouldn't have mattered to the U.S. government, because they still would have had what they set out for—access to the gold and the diamonds. That didn't happen. Instead, they bargained with the South African Nationalists, threatening to withhold the plague's cure."

"You have documentation on this?" Dr. Dobbs asked.

"Stating the U.S. government's position?" Solomon said. "No. That's conjecture on my part."

"So noted then."

"But it's good conjecture," Solomon argued. "What other reason would they have for using the plague bomb?"

"Exactly," Dr. Dobbs said. "Maybe there are a few things you haven't investigated yourself."

The statement sent a chill through Andy. Dr. Dobbs had been involved in both the military and diplomatic corps before turning to teaching. There was even a rumor that he occasionally helped handpick candidates for Net Force. *Is there something Dr. Dobbs knows or found out?*

The suggestion that he hadn't quite nailed his report turned Solomon's face white. "That footage is enough to get me an A in this class, Dr. Dobbs. I researched that and discovered it when no one else has."

"And that situation obviously begs another question, Mr. Weist," Dr. Dobbs said. "If the South African Nationalists had this information, why didn't they use it back in 2014?"

A slow grin spread across Solomon's face as he leaned back in his chair. "Ah, I never said they had this information, Dr. Dobbs. I only said that it came from flatfilm shot by their tank crews near Site Forty-three."

"So you did."

"You'll find out where I got the footage in my bibliography," Solomon said. "Not one moment before."

"And not one moment after the deadline next week, Mr. Weist."

Andy sat back in his chair, barely hanging on to his calm. He was filled with hurt confusion and worry about his mom. He was also concerned about where Solomon had gotten his information. If the South African Nationalists hadn't used it, they must not have had it. And since there was no way to get it from the United States Department of Defense with Net Force watchdogging everything, where had it come from?

And where was he going to find information about it? He couldn't let Solomon take his dad down. Maybe his dad had never been there for him, but Andy knew his dad had never been far from his mom's heart. He didn't know what it would do to her if the footage were true, and she got wind of what was in it.

"Mr. Moore, I'd like a moment of your time."

Andy glanced back at Dr. Dobbs and stepped out of the line of students headed for the door. Even though the computer-link chairs provided for students would have allowed them to simply go on-line into whatever classroom the next teacher was in, the administration recognized the value of getting a few minutes of physical movement between sessions.

Solomon caught Andy's eye, but Andy turned away too quickly for him to say or do anything.

Dr. Dobbs assembled his notes for the next class. They were neatly printed on 3x5 cards, bound by a rubber band. He returned Andy's gaze. "I must permit Mr. Weist some leeway in his presentation to follow the dictates of the structure I intended for this class."

"I understand," Andy said.

"I realize that it hurts you. That's why I wanted us to speak."

"Not just me. My dad, too. And if Solomon takes this very far, it'll hurt my mom. I'm not going to stand for that."

"My suggestion would be to let Mr. Weist continue to grind his ax for a time. Eventually he'll hang himself."

"What makes you so sure?" Andy asked. *What do you know that I don't?*

"I've spent years working for my country," Dr. Dobbs said. "First physically defending it in the military. Then defending its practices in the diplomatic corps. Now I've devoted myself to teaching the young who will continue building this country after I'm gone. I'm giving my life to this country. And I'll never believe that we engineered the atrocities Mr. Weist's accusation contains. You know the kind of man your father was. Trust that."

"That's the problem, Dr. Dobbs," Andy told him bitterly. "I don't know my father at all."

For once Dr. Dobbs, who seemed to have an opinion on everything, didn't have anything to say.

9

"Hey, mind some company? Or do you want to be alone?"

Seated at the table in Bradford Academy's noisy cafeteria, Andy glanced at Mark standing across from him. There were plenty of empty seats. The cafeteria posted the menu on the Net, which gave everyone plenty of time to make other arrangements on mystery meat days.

"No," Andy replied, even though he didn't want company.

"I saw you and thought I'd come over and ask." Mark stepped over the bench seat on the table and sat down, sliding his tray onto the top.

"Ask what?"

"How you managed to get your chin that far down on your chest?" Mark poked a disposable straw through the side of his juice gel-pak and sipped.

"Practice," Andy said. "Good genes. A past life as a giraffe."

"I thought I'd take a minute and brief you on the latest Net Force Explorers meeting." Quickly Mark did that, relaying that Matt wanted the Net Force Explorers to pay attention to the hacker community in case any more attacks happened. "It's not like you to miss a meeting."

"I'll square it with Matt."

"He's not upset. Just concerned."

"He doesn't have to be concerned about me. I'm handling things."

"Are you?"

"Yeah." Andy gulped milk from his gel-pak. He twisted one of the broccoli sprigs on his plate. "Maybe. The truth is, I don't know. I forgot about the meeting this morning because I was ducking Solomon in the halls. This is all my fault."

"That's not true," Mark said.

"Solomon wouldn't have looked at my dad's record so closely if he didn't dislike me so much. And he wouldn't have found this stuff if—"

"If your dad didn't do it?" Mark shook his head. "That didn't happen. Your dad was a hero."

"Maybe," Andy said. "But he was also the guy who didn't come back to Mom. For me, that takes away a lot of hero points." He and Mark ate in silence for a few minutes, and Andy knew it was more than just the meal that was unappetizing.

"Where have you checked for information about your dad?" Mark asked.

"Everywhere. I pulled HoloNet records, hard copy, text files, everything I could think of. I sifted back through all the information the military gave Mom. The official story's there, but no details. I can't seem to find out what really happened on August 12, 2014. The info's all wrapped up in red tape."

"There is another option you haven't used." Mark kept his voice quiet, which wasn't hard to do over the general noise made by the cafeteria crowd.

"What?"

"Interpretive programming."

Andy shook his head. "You're talking about near-AI sounding boards? The kind of stuff that's supposed to be interactive with CEOs and artists?" He was familiar with near-AI software that worked as an audience, devil's advocate, and second opinion. The software gave feedback as well as constructive criticism, and even helped guide decision-making based on an individual's past work record.

"No," Mark replied. "I'm talking about the software that National Treasures, Incorporated, puts out. They create sims, but not just any sims. People like Benjamin Franklin, George

Washington, and other famous people who existed way before computers."

"That's no big deal," Andy said. "I can talk to a history sim of Benjamin Franklin anytime. Even go on that little kite-flying mission of his and find out who suggested he do that. And I'm betting that whoever suggested it wasn't playing nice."

"No bet." Mark grinned. "But that's not the kind of sim I'm talking about. Those sims can't act out of character, commit anachronisms, or do or think about something they didn't do or know about back then."

"So?" Andy struggled with finding a nice way to tell Mark he really didn't need or want the additional help. *This is something I've got to do for myself.*

"With National Treasures' software, you can create a sim and bring it into your own time frame, your own house. Or school. With the near-AI interactive programming National Treasures puts out, you can build a sim of Benjamin Franklin and ask him how he feels about the moon landing in 1969. And he'll have an answer. Their sims are like having that person around, but as educated about the present world or situation as you are. Or as you program them to be."

"Sounds fascinating," Andy said dryly. "But I don't see how it applies to me."

"Build a sim of your dad," Mark suggested. "You've already built your database."

Andy's stomach turned queasy as he considered the idea. "No."

"Andy, I don't mean to push, but with a sim like that, you could ask all the questions you wanted to about your dad. And it'd be like him answering them."

"Except it wouldn't be my dad," Andy replied. "And he's the only one who really knows what happened that night."

"Andy, if you do the sim right, it'll be like having your dad there. No, it won't be able to tell you what your dad did that night since you're not programming that information in, but you can interact with it. Maybe get to know your dad better. Maybe you can convince yourself about what kind of person your dad was."

The thought continued to make Andy sick. *Bad idea. I've been mad at Dad nearly all of my life.* "Look, I don't want to get to know my dad. I just want to try to get Solomon's mess straightened up so it doesn't hurt my mom. She's already hurt enough."

"But if you make a sim of your dad, it'll help you do that."

Andy gazed at the students around them. All of them were involved with each other, talking and goofing off. He couldn't believe he was having this conversation in the middle of them. "It won't have the information I need."

"But it may lead you to other information, other ways of thinking about the problem," Mark said.

"Mark, I just don't like the whole idea. It creeps me out for one thing, and for another if I know it doesn't have the answers I need, what's the use?"

"It's a really good program," Mark said. "I thought it was something you should think about."

"Oh, I'll do more than think about it," Andy said, clearing his tray and standing up. "I'll probably have nightmares about it."

"Sorry."

Andy knew Mark's feelings were hurt, and he felt miserable about that. "Hey, no sweat. You were just trying to help, right? I can't hang you for being a friend, can I?"

"I hope not." Mark didn't sound certain.

"There you go. I'll catch you later. And if you see Matt before I do, let him know I wanted to apologize." Andy took his tray to the counter line and tried not to think about anything Mark had just told him.

Matt got off the autobus at the mall that afternoon after school. Seeing Leif at the meeting that morning had reminded him how close it was to Leif's birthday. And he thought he'd found the perfect present.

He strolled through the mall crowd, looking in the windows of the software stores, wishing he had more time to go in and browse. He could shop on the Net from his room, but it wasn't the same.

On the Net the clerks who worked on-line concentrated totally on selling their merchandise, and their attention was divided in several different directions, just like any chat-line host. If the system was jammed, getting quick answers to questions was sometimes impossible. And getting a dry run through a demo might be informational, but it lacked conversation.

Matt liked interacting with the other people in a store, swapping information and ideas. Most of the time he learned as much from the other people as he did from the dealers.

He stopped for a gel-pak soft drink at a booth next to the sports card store. After swiping his Universal Credit Card through the scanner to pay for the drink, he walked to the sports card store and peered through the window.

One of the interests he shared with Leif was baseball. Although he sometimes suspected Leif's interest in the sport bordered more on fanatical than fan.

Luck and persistence had led Matt to the sports card store a couple weeks ago when a new shipment of old cards had cycled through. He'd turned up a Monte Irvin baseball card from 1951.

Monte Irvin had an interesting history, Matt had discovered. Irvin had started out playing for the Newark Eagles for the Negro National League and had a shot to become the first black player in the major league just before he had been drafted for World War II. Jackie Robinson became the first instead, but Irvin had returned from the war and played for the New York Giants beginning in 1948. In 1951 he'd had his best year in the majors, batting a .312 and hitting twenty-four home runs.

Matt studied the week's HOT BETS through the window as he sipped from the gel-pak. He noticed two men's translucent reflections in the glass as they stepped in behind him. His mind was already registering danger because they were getting too close to him.

Matt started to turn, but one of the men dropped a heavy hand on his shoulder. The man pulled Matt closer, keeping him slightly off balance. Then a cold cylindrical shape pushed against his side.

"You feel that, boyo?" the man asked hoarsely.

Before Matt had a chance to move, the second man stepped in close on the other side. "Yeah," Matt answered. "I feel it."

"Good. Then you got a bloody clue what it is." The man ground his point home by shoving on the hidden pistol. "Now, you be a good boyo. Take a few minutes and talk to us and ain't nothing going to happen to you."

Matt didn't believe him, but there was nothing he could do at the moment. He nodded, and set about finding a way to escape.

10

"You step lively here, boyo, and we're going to get along fine," the man with the gun instructed.

Matt nodded, afraid but controlling it. His training in the Net Force Explorers covered situations like this, as did some of the martial arts training he'd had, but it was different playacting a scenario and actually being held at gunpoint.

"You follow my friend," the man ordered. "I'll be at your back. I don't have to tell you what a bloody mistake it would be for you to try something asinine, do I?"

"No." Matt stared at the reflection of the man, memorizing him as well as he could.

The man looked rough, a square-hewn face framed by a scraggly dirty blond beard. Wraparound midnight blue sunglasses hid his eyes. He looked as if he was in his early twenties. He wore a duster and black jeans.

Matt looked at the man's feet, noting the worn motorcycle boots. From criminology classes he'd taken, he knew that most criminals who changed clothes immediately after committing a crime failed to change their footwear. It was one of those details that the Net Force Explorers had laughed about after the class, but the detail had stuck.

The translucent image trapped in the plate glass of the sports card store wasn't as generous with the other man, but Matt picked out some details. The man looked to be in his early forties and balding. He was thin and narrow, shorter than Matt.

"Let's go," the man said.

Matt followed the older man, staying back about six feet. He looked around the mall desperately, not believing no one had noticed he was being taken away at gunpoint.

"Now, don't be filling your head with nonsense," the younger man told him. "This gun I'm carrying has a silencer. I can put a couple bullets in you quick-like, then turn and be gone before anybody knows I did a bleedin' thing."

Matt nodded and followed the leader through a door into the corridor leading to the public rest rooms. The gray-walled corridor was empty except for a mom and two kids in a double walker. Matt's mouth had gone dry.

The metal double doors at the end of the corridor held a plaque that read: NOT AN EXIT. AUTHORIZED MALL PERSONNEL ONLY. The older man pulled something out of his pocket and pushed it against the lock. A sudden pneumatic hiss filled the corridor, followed immediately by the *chunk!* of metal hitting metal. When the man stepped back from the door, Matt saw the neat round hole that had been bored through the locking mechanism. Tiny bits of metal gleamed on the flooring.

The older man opened the door and stepped through into another corridor. The gray walls continued, but there was an office on either side, and the tunnel dead-ended less than twenty feet away.

End of the line, Matt thought desperately.

The older man turned around and brought out a blued 9mm pistol. Without hesitation he pointed it at Matt's face. "No sudden moves, no stupid moves. Otherwise, *bang*, you're dead."

Matt nodded, noticing that one of the offices belonged to the security people out in the mall. It offered a little hope.

"Back against the wall, boyo." The older man turned Matt around roughly, then shoved him back against the wall. "Arms out to your sides."

Matt lifted his arms, facing both men.

"Cool one, ain't you?" the younger man asked.

"No," Matt replied honestly. "I'm scared." He wanted there to be no mistake about that. That way they wouldn't feel they had to scare him.

The young man smiled. "We've been hired by some people who want their property back."

"Who?"

The young man shook his head. "Now, that's a stupid question, isn't it? If they'd wanted you to know who, they'd have up and come done this themselves."

"How am I supposed to know what to return?" Matt concentrated on getting as much information from them as he could. If he survived the encounter, he wanted to have something to give Captain Winters. The men who'd seized him gave every indication of being professionals.

"Wiseacre," the younger man said, drawing a hand back.

"Now, hold up, mate," the older man said to his partner. "Maybe our clients aren't the only people he's taken stuff from. This could be a legitimate question."

The younger man lowered his arm.

Matt relaxed a little, but his breath remained tight in his chest. He was buying time, that was all, and he felt it wasn't going to be enough time no matter what.

"Unfortunately for you, boyo," the older man said, "we ain't at liberty to be giving out information. Maybe you'll just have to give back everything you've took of late."

"How late? The last week or two?" Matt was desperate to gain some clue. Even a time frame might help.

The older man smiled. "Been at this for a while, eh? All right then. This particular package we're looking for has gone missing almost a week."

"What is it?" Matt asked. "I need to know what you're looking for."

The younger man exploded then, putting his hands flat out against Matt's chest and shoving him back. Matt bounced off the wall behind him, knocking the wind from his lungs and hitting his head hard enough to cause momentary black spots in his vision.

"Don't be playing no games with us," the younger man warned. He stayed in Matt's face, letting him see his own terrified images reflected in the hard blue lenses. "We're on a deadline here, and you ain't going to chip no time off it."

"You've got the wrong guy," Matt said. "I don't know what you're talking about."

The older man stepped in front of the younger man and faced

Matt. "We got the right boyo. Matt Hunter, son of Gordon Hunter and Lieutenant Colonel Marissa Hunter, formerly a fighter pilot and now serving at the Pentagon in an advisory position for the U.S. Navy Special Operations Command."

Matt swallowed hard and forced himself to think clearly. "You guys came after Chris Potter on Monday. Now you're after me. How can you be so sure you've got the right guy?" It was a guess, but an educated one.

"Chris Potter wasn't the one," the older man said. "But you, you're the one. Ol' Chris, he's got a rep for hacking into computers, but you, boyo, you're a bloody Net Force Explorer. You're the one we're told we want. And now we've got you."

"I don't know what you're talking about," Matt said. "I haven't hacked anybody. If you know anything about the Explorers, you know Net Force wouldn't put up with a member getting involved in something like that."

"We know about Net Force," the younger man said harshly. "And we know about you. A smart kid like you, you wouldn't mind trying to make a few brownie points tapping into something that ain't your business. Problem is that you done took a piece of the wrong thing this time."

Matt considered that. *So it was something Net Force would be interested in? Something they don't think Net Force is already looking into?*

"You give it back to them what you took it from, boyo, you'll be out of this clean as a whistle." The older man eyed him directly.

Matt thought furiously, trying to find something he could work with.

"He's stalling," the younger man grated. "I say I muss him up some, see if he comes clean then."

"No, I said." The older man stepped in front of Matt again, presenting his back to the Explorer. "Let's give him another chance."

Taking advantage of the men's proximity to each other, Matt lunged out suddenly. He bent slightly as he came off the wall, then rammed his palms against the older man's back and knocked him into the younger man. Both men hit the wall on the other side of the hallway. By then, Matt was in full flight.

Heart pounding, raising his knees high and driving his feet against the concrete hallway floor, Matt exploded through the door. He dived on the other side, going low in case they opened fire. He wasn't disappointed.

Bullets ripped through the metal doors and buried themselves in the ceiling, chopping holes in the acoustic tiles and knocking them from their aluminum casements. Still sliding across the floor, Matt checked to make sure the hallway was empty and pushed himself to his feet. He hit the door letting out into the mall at full speed. He caught the corner with one hand, barely staying on his feet.

All the nearby mall attendees looked at him with concern. Some of them moved away immediately. Matt turned right, sprinting back the way he'd come, searching for a mall security uniform.

When he found a security guard down by the pretzel shop, Matt grabbed the man. The guard tried to calm him, but words kept pouring out of Matt. Once the guard understood the situation, he called other guards.

Matt watched them converge on the hallway area while he tried to get his wind back. His heart beat rapidly, but he kept it together. He opened his wallet and configured his foilpack into a phone, then punched in Captain Winters's number.

Andy stood on the stern castle of his pirate ship and flipped through all the files he'd retrieved on his dad and the South African War. In veeyar the files were represented as documents rolled around wooden spindles. There were hundreds of them, neatly racked in a carved storage bin he hadn't even known the ship possessed.

"Cap'n Andy."

Andy looked up at the first mate. "Yeah."

"Got a call comin' in. Swabbie says his name is Dale Fisher."

Dale Fisher had been one of the men in his dad's Special Forces group down in Mandelatown.

"Thanks." Andy touched the phone icon. A window opened up on the plotting table, revealing a leathery face tanned a deep mahogany that made the china-blue eyes stand out even more. His sandy hair was cut in a flattop.

"Are you Andy Moore?" Fisher asked.

"Yes, sir." With the tone of voice the man used, there was no other way to answer.

The china-blue eyes flicked down to the table in front of

Fisher. "Says here you're Colonel Moore's boy."

"Yes, sir."

Fisher gazed at Andy. "I'm sorry about your daddy, boy." His accent was Deep South. Fisher lived in Charleston, South Carolina, and worked in the private security field.

"Thank you." Andy felt uncomfortable. He'd looked up the numbers of the names of the men he'd uncovered in his search for the truth, and culled the ones he'd found. He'd even practiced what he was going to say, but now that he was actually talking to one of the men, everything he'd thought of had vanished.

"I thought about looking you and your mom up at some time," Fisher went on. "The colonel was a good man, and I'd wanted to know if there was anything I could do. But things at the end of the war—" He shrugged. "Time got away from me."

"Yes, sir. I read that you were wounded."

Fisher nodded. "Took a shrapnel burst. Almost cost me my leg before the docs got hold of it, kissed it, and made it better. Now I get around pretty good, but for the first few months things weren't fun." He gazed at Andy. "Your daddy saved my life that day in Mandelatown. Packed me up on his back and put me in a med-evac helo. He hadn't done it, I'd have been KIA. They don't make 'em like your daddy much these days."

Listening to the emotion in the words, Andy felt pride sweep over him. Then he felt an immediate surge of guilt over having to find out if his dad would have been involved with anything like the plague bomb. "No, sir. I suppose not."

"Too bad you didn't get to know your daddy, Andy," Fisher said. "You'd have liked him a lot."

Andy nodded, his throat aching. He tried to speak but was afraid his words would only squeak out.

"Is your mom doing okay?" Fisher asked.

"Yes, sir."

"What about you?" The concern on Fisher's face was evident.

"I'm doing fine, sir. Thank you. I called to ask you a favor."

"How can I help you?"

Andy breathed out, trying not to show his tension. Despite the fact that Fisher was out of the military, Andy knew the man was still bound by the military edicts. "I need some information. I need to know about Mandelatown."

Fisher hesitated. Andy noticed it at once. It jarred the down-home demeanor the man exuded. "What do you need to know?" the man asked.

"Everything you can remember."

Fisher scratched his chin and the audio pick-up even got the scratchy noise. "That was a long time ago."

Getting a little firm, knowing he couldn't get the answers he was looking for unless he pressed, Andy said, "I don't think it's something you'd forget."

Fisher nodded. "No, you're right about that." His eyes got a faraway look in them. "Most of that stuff you can read about in electronic format in the media archives. And there's a lot about it in the HoloNet you can download from their site."

"I've got all that," Andy said.

"I'm willing to bet they can remember more than I can." Fisher grinned, but the expression lacked real enjoyment.

Andy took a deep breath and decided to go straight to the heart of the matter. "I need to know about my father's involvement with the plague bomb."

Fisher's eyelids drooped to half-mast, but the easygoing smile stayed on his face. "Where'd you get an idea like that?"

Andy didn't want to go into the story about Solomon's research. Telling his friends in the Net Force Explorers was one thing, even knowing most of the students at Bradford had heard was another. But he wasn't going to repeat the story. "I just wanted to call and ask. And I figured that since you knew my dad, maybe you'd talk to me about it."

Fisher shook his head. "Nothing to talk about."

Andy lifted his chin and dropped it, accepting the answer. "Yes, sir. Well I'm sorry to have interrupted your day. I appreciate your time."

"Wait," Fisher said.

Andy stared at him.

"Look, Andy," Fisher said, "some of the things that happened in the war, we've been ordered not to talk about. A lot of your dad's activities—and ours—over there are still black-listed, strictly on a need-to-know basis," Fisher replied.

"I need to know," Andy replied. "It's come to my attention

that my dad might have been involved in setting off that plague bomb."

"No way," Fisher stated gruffly. "Whoever told you that is a liar."

"My dad wasn't involved with the plague bomb?" Andy asked. "He was nowhere near Site Forty-three when it went off?"

Fisher's jaw clenched and his eyes slitted. "No."

Andy knew the man was lying then. He wasn't sure if Fisher was lying to comply with the military restrictions or to protect himself. Andy suddenly realized Solomon's discovery of the flatfilm of Site 43 was going to affect a lot of people who were still alive and probably hoping it never came out. After all, it had been hidden away for almost eleven years.

"Well, thanks for your time," Andy said, feeling uncomfortable.

Fisher gave him a short nod but let out a deep breath. "This thing you're digging into, Andy, you might want to give it some thought before you start calling a lot of people."

"I have given it a lot of thought," Andy said. "I just don't see a way around it."

"Old ghosts and old dogs," Fisher pointed out, "are often better left alone."

"Yes, sir. I'll keep that in mind."

"Tenacious." Fisher softened a little. "That's something you got from your father. Don't watch it, though, it could get you in trouble."

Is that a warning? Andy suddenly didn't know.

"You take care," Fisher said, and blanked the connection.

Andy pushed back from the plotting table and gazed out at the sea. For once, there was no relief found in it.

‖

"Dad, I'm okay." Matt felt bad about the worry that showed on his father's face.

Gordon Hunter gazed at his son again, then gave a short nod. They stood in the kitchen at the family home, the chosen place for all family discussions because, even with their busy schedules, they all ended up in there eventually.

Matt sipped some milk. His stomach still hadn't settled, but now the upset was more from the anxiety his father was showing than from what had happened at the mall.

"The security guards never found the men who did this?" his father asked.

"No. The police think the men got out through the ventilation system."

"This has me really concerned," his father said. "Does it have something to do with your involvement with the Net Force Explorers?"

Matt shook his head. "No. They didn't want me. They wanted to scare me so I'd tell other people about them."

"That doesn't make much sense."

"It does," Matt pointed out, "if they're not sure who they really want."

The phone rang then, and his father went to answer it. It was

Matt's mom, who wanted to be filled in. Taking advantage of the opportunity, Matt retreated to his room. Captain Winters hadn't been able to talk much when he'd called him from the mall. Now was a good time to get back in touch.

In his room Matt dropped into the computer-link chair, leaned his head back, and buzzed into veeyar. A moment later, sitting cross-legged at his black marble tabletop, he called Captain Winters.

A window opened in the star-filled sky around Matt, giving him a view of Winters and the captain's office. "Matt," Winters said, "I'm looking over the preliminary police reports concerning your incident. It doesn't look promising. They're holding out hope that perhaps one of the security cameras picked up footage of your abduction."

It was the first time Matt had heard it called abduction. Somehow that made it more disturbing.

"However," Winters said, "that doesn't look good, either. Most of the security cameras aren't set to take in the outer hallway, and the outside cameras didn't get anything because they're set over the exits and entrances."

"The men might have known where the cameras were," Matt suggested. "They seemed professional."

"I noted that." Winters sat hunkered over his big desk, scanning reports. "You didn't hear any names?"

"No."

"And they didn't say what they wanted?"

"*It,*" Matt answered. "Whatever *it* may be. But I also think they knew I didn't have it."

"What makes you think that?"

Matt had thought about that all the way home from the mall with his dad. "They didn't search me. Not once. And they didn't ask me if I had *it* on me."

"Which they should have done," Winters agreed.

"Yes. And my escape was way too easy—almost handed to me," Matt said. "They even shot high when I was getting away. I don't know what they'd have done if I hadn't tried to get away."

"That could be one of the reasons they went after you, Matt," Winters said. "They figured you'd know how to react in that situation."

Matt nodded.

"Do you know what it was about?" the captain asked.

"Not really. But it has to do with Chris Potter's attack on Monday. I think that was supposed to be a message to someone. They admitted the link to Chris, and that's something two guys as professional as they seemed to be wouldn't have done."

"Unless they'd wanted you to know that."

"Yes, sir. They're putting the pressure on, and even if I keep quiet about it, the news is going to get around school. A lot of Bradford students go to the mall after class. I know some of them saw me when I was talking to the security guards and the police."

"So the message will spread." Winters didn't sound happy.

Matt let the man have a moment, then asked, "Captain Winters, is there something going on at Bradford that I should know about?"

Winters looked at him keenly. "Matt, if there was something you should know, I'd be the first person to tell you."

Matt nodded, feeling a little awkward about asking.

"However, I will say this. I want you and the other Net Force Explorers at Bradford to keep your eyes open, both while you're at school and away from it."

"There is something going on."

"Maybe," Winters said. "We don't have enough information yet. As soon as we do, you and the other Explorers will be briefed. That's all I can tell you now."

"So the man I saw Monday afternoon *was* a Net Force agent?"

Winters nodded. "And that goes no farther than the Net Force Explorers. Are we clear on that?"

"Crystal."

"I'm glad you're safe, Matt," Winters stated. "Just work at staying that way."

"I will. What are we supposed to be looking for at school?"

"Anything out of the ordinary. If something does come up, get to me immediately."

Matt nodded.

"I've got another call waiting," Winters said. "Good night, Matt."

"Good night, sir."

Winters exited the veeyar, leaving Matt floating in the blackness of space. But he wasn't alone. There were a lot of questions dancing around inside his head. *What is Net Force doing at Bradford? What are they waiting for?* IT?

Before he could pursue that thought, an incoming call beeped at him. He hit the phone icon. A man in a suit with a Washington, D.C. detective's badge in hand appeared.

"Matt Hunter?"

Matt nodded.

"I'm Detective Duran. I'm following up on the report you filed earlier about the attempted kidnapping. I've got some questions for you, but I need a parent or guardian to give consent before I can ask them."

"I'll get Dad." Matt logged off veeyar long enough to find his dad. He wasn't looking forward to more questions covering the same answers he'd already given.

Trying to contact other men his dad had served with, Andy ran into trouble almost immediately, and it only got worse. Duncan Richmond, the first man he'd gotten hold of after talking with Fisher, had chatted with him briefly, then totally locked up when Andy had asked about Site 43. Riley Taggert had lasted all of a minute and twelve seconds before he said he had another call coming in that he had to take.

After that, Andy had tried twenty-three other numbers in straight succession, getting only answering services or no answer at all. He left messages, but he didn't expect any return calls.

He had no doubt at all that Fisher had passed the word around. Andy paced the pirate ship's deck in an effort to work out the anger he felt, but it didn't do any good. The clock was ticking on whatever Solomon had planned.

He considered calling Captain Winters and trying to get some help there, but even as he thought of it, he knew he wouldn't. In the end, despite every misgiving he felt, he knew there was only one answer. He jogged back to the stern castle and up the steps, feeling the ship roll on the waves.

He touched his Net icon and asked for Mark Gridley. The connection went through at once.

Mark was dressed in his crashsuit, sliding through some kind of multicolored tunnel that twisted constantly. He negotiated the turns with ease.

"Hey, Andy." Mark pointed his arm out ahead of him and

fired a dozen violet bursts that Andy knew represented lines of code. Andy had gone on some of Mark's runs but lacked the patience to do something over and over, testing every little strand of programming.

"Hi." Andy took a deep breath. "Look, I've done everything I can on my own. I've researched files, nagged my mom, and talked to everyone who'd talk to me about my dad. But I still don't have any answers."

"You want to try the National Treasures' software?"

Andy nodded, unable to say it out loud. His stomach knotted up. *How am I supposed to talk to my dad?* He knew if the program was as good as Mark said it was, that was precisely what he was going to have to do. *And if it's that good, isn't it going to have an opinion—or form one—about me? What if I don't measure up?* That thought bothered him deeply.

"Be right there." Mark ended the program he was running, saved it, and popped into Andy's veeyar. "Are you ready to upload?"

"Yeah," Andy croaked.

Mark punched some unfamiliar icons. Immediately Andy felt the quiet buzz of his veeyar system booting up with Mark's.

"If you want," Mark offered, "I can show you how to set up and get you started."

"Sure," Andy said. There was no way he wanted to be alone when he initiated the program.

"He was shorter than that," Matt said, gazing at the representation the police artist was making of the two men in the mall. The images were amazingly lifelike, resembling statues in a wax museum. They even had physical presence when he'd touched them out of curiosity.

Matt stood in one of the Washington, D.C., police department's veeyars used for interrogation and witness interviews. It was a gray cube of a room, nearly filled to capacity by the short conference table and half-dozen chairs. Blank gray walls surrounded him on three sides. The fourth held the door they'd entered the veeyar through.

The artist looked old enough to be his mom. Her white-blond hair was cropped short and kept spiky, and her long silver earrings brushed at her shoulders. She wore black, a sweater and a skirt. Even her eyes were black. But she was quick with her work. Her fingertips controlled unseen palettes of color and clay—at least, that's how Matt thought of the way she continually built the image and colored it.

She stood in front of the representation of the older of his two captors. Her long-nailed hand touched the image, and it lowered a couple inches.

"There?" she asked.

"Yeah," he said.

"What about his face?"

Matt went through the description again, amazed at how close the woman had already come from his description. "The ears were a little bigger and stuck out more. His eyes were closer together. The right one wasn't quite centered."

The artist touched the image again and bursts of color popped when contact was made. The man's ears got bigger and stuck out, and his eyes got closer together. Another plink and one of them was no longer quite centered. "More like this?"

Matt walked around the man. She'd even gotten his clothing right, although according to her that wasn't really important. "That's him."

The artist made a couple more adjustments to the image, then stepped back. She smiled. "You've got a very good eye for detail."

Matt shook his head. "I've seen people build proxies from scratch, but those are generally borrowed from another source or just loose caricatures. I've never seen anything like this."

She looked at him. "I'm good at what I do and I enjoy my work. Let's sharpen up the second man now." She turned and brought the younger man into the veeyar. She spent only a few more minutes on his appearance, then animated the images, asking Matt how his captors had moved, how they'd held their heads, their arms, whether they'd glanced around often or stayed focused.

Watching the two men walk around the veeyar at the artist's bidding like cybernetic puppets was eerie. They *were* the two men who'd grabbed him in the mall.

"That's amazing," he told her.

"Only partially," the artist told him. "Your memory of these two men is really good. Your ability to describe what you've seen is way above normal. It's also good that you can handle this. A lot of potential witnesses tend to spazz out when they see the image sims I create for them."

Matt nodded, staring at the two men. "I can see how that could happen."

"But this is our best chance of identifying those men." She gazed at him with those black eyes. "And I've got a real good feeling about this. Good luck with it. I'm logging off now, but I'll get Detective Duran for you." She vanished in a swirl of rainbows.

Matt grinned at the exit. Somehow the flashy departure was exactly what he'd expected of her. He approached the proxies and examined them more closely. They could have passed for twins of the men. Movement caught his eye. *Are they breathing?*

"Hey."

Matt jumped and stepped back from the sims of the two men, turning quickly.

"Sorry." Detective Duran stood behind him, crisp and clean in a brown suit.

"It's okay. I'm just a little tense."

"That's understandable." Duran walked around the sims, taking them in. "She said you had an eye for detail. She was right."

"Thanks." Matt shifted uneasily.

"Now let's see how good the two of you are." Duran stood in front of the two men again. "Computer, access and run the two identification modules in this veeyar. Search for matches beginning in violent crimes against persons, covering domestic and international databases. As a secondary corollary, expand search to known and suspected terrorists."

"Accessing," the cool automated voice replied.

"It shouldn't take long," Duran said.

Matt nodded. From the time he'd first talked to the detective, he'd been impressed with Duran's professional courtesy. For his part, Duran had been impressed with Matt's Net Force Explorer standing.

"Reporting two matches," the computer stated less than a minute later.

"Bring them up," Duran instructed.

Instantly two windows appeared in the veeyar. They stacked one on top of the other beside the older man. Both images were of him, but they had separate names. The top name, Harry

Cavendish, had a New Jersey address. The second name, Liam McDouglas, reportedly lived in Belfast, Ireland. Cavendish was a licensed bodyguard, and McDouglas was a suspected terrorist with ties to the Irish Republican Army.

Matt was familiar with the IRA from his studies. The IRA was responsible for a number of attacks against Great Britain in the real world and on the Net, and had a long history of violence. Even though Northern Ireland had merged with Ireland, the fighting between religious factions continued.

Cavendish hadn't been an angel, either, according to the computer's voice-over of the men's backgrounds. Since arriving in the United States seven years ago, Cavendish had almost lost his license three times for using deadly force.

"Well, well," Duran said. "Now this gets interesting."

"He's a thug for hire," Matt said, interpreting the reports. It was no big leap of logic.

"Yeah," Duran agreed. "Things must have gotten too hot for him in Ireland, so he decided to set up shop here. He's going to regret that. You're willing to press charges against him when we find him?"

Matt nodded.

A moment later the computer announced it had a match for the younger man. According to the files he was Neal Tomlinson, an Irish citizen, and he'd gotten shot and killed in Paris three years ago.

"That's what he wants us to think, anyway," Duran said wryly. "Computer, reset parameters for search. Check databases regarding handgun licensing. Start in New Jersey, then branch out from East Coast to West Coast."

Less than a minute later, another match came back. Matt looked at the new image, realizing it was close to the holo the police artist had made. The younger man's name was Danny Luck and he was a licensed private investigator in New York.

Duran uploaded the information in the veeyar to his personal unit in the police station. "Chances are even these addresses are blinds," he told Matt. "But we'll follow up and see what we get. If we find them, we'll call you and let you know. And we'll need you to confirm the IDs in person when we catch them."

Matt nodded, his mind whirling. *What are professional thugs doing at Bradford?*

"Have you got any idea what these guys are looking for?" Duran asked.

"My best guess is that they're looking for a hacker or computer specialist," Matt replied. "They went after Chris Potter, and then they came after me. I'd say they were definitely looking for someone who moves through the on-line subculture on a regular basis."

"I would, too." Duran studied the open files. "But I guess the real question is who hired them."

Matt silently agreed. "I couldn't tell you."

"Net Force has been known to share information in the past with local law departments," the detective said. "In fact, if jurisdiction can be handed back to the local agencies once Net Force has gotten information that will help the local guys, they usually do. Unless it involves one of their own. Then they tend to get proprietary."

Matt knew that was true. Captain Winters played things very close to the vest when it was a Net Force operation.

"If you find out anything I can use, I'd encourage you to see that it gets into my hands. Detective Gray mentioned I should ask."

"If I can," Matt agreed.

Duran nodded and Matt logged off. At home he sat in the computer-link chair and pushed ideas around. Bradford Academy had some high-profile students, kids whose parents were involved in high-level political, economic, military, and even religious arenas. Any one of those might have spawned the interest of someone who could hire men like McDouglas and Tomlinson.

But Matt's parents—not a chance. So who was hiring thugs, and why? Once he had the why, Matt was certain it would lead him to the who.

12

"Are you okay?"

Andy glanced at Mark and tried to sound normal. "Yeah. I'm good."

They stood in an interactive veeyar that the National Treasures' software had programmed to respond to the database and Andy's own commands. At present it was a featureless cube with a console in the center.

Occasionally images flickered across the walls, floor, and ceiling. Andy recognized a lot of the images. They came from the files he'd put together regarding his dad. It was a compilation of flatfilm, holos, and military records he had access to— dental records, medical records, psychological profiles, and testing that had been done throughout Colonel Robert Moore's entire military career. There was further documentation from men who'd served with, under, and over him, and his mom's personal pictures, flatfilms, and holos.

It was the most complete job Andy could do with the resources available to him. Mark thought it would be enough, pointing out that historical personalities like Franklin, Washington, and Jefferson had only had posed paintings, their writings, and writings by other people to base them on. National Treasures, Inc., had still created fully interactive sims of them.

Mark turned from the console that hung in the air before him. "That's everything you have at the moment. We can bring the sim on-line now or you can continue feeding in more information as you discover it. Are you ready to bring him on-line?"

Him? Andy felt his pulse suddenly speed up, and his mouth dried. It was disconcerting to hear Mark talk about the sim like it was real. "Let's do it."

Mark touched an icon on his console and the board winked out of existence. He gazed at the veeyar's center.

A shimmer took shape, forming slowly. The veeyar pulsed slightly. The upload from Mark's computer had been tremendous, the biggest program Andy had ever loaded onto his system. Thanks to Mark's mom, Andy was getting a chance to test a beta version of the newest program, one not yet on the market. Andy knew he could never have afforded this if he'd had to pay for it.

A vague man-shape came into view, as white as a ghost and translucent as glass.

Andy's breath locked in the back of his throat as the process continued. It was the image of his father standing there, more defined with each passing moment.

"Computer," Mark called out, "freeze program execution."

Andy looked at him. "What's wrong?"

Mark pointed. "Your hands are shaking, Andy. If this is too much—"

"It's not," Andy gritted. "I have to catch up to Solomon and figure out what he knows if I'm going to do anything about it."

Mark didn't say anything.

"Computer," Andy called out, "continue execution and build of subprogram Moore, Colonel Robert A."

Smoothly the program reintegrated itself and continued processing. Slowly color filled the sim. The close-cropped hair turned black, eyebrows arched sharply over bright blue eyes that were half closed. The face was hard-planed, and a small scar showed just to the right of the chin. A deep tan from constant outdoor exposure covered his face, forearms, and hands. He wore unmarked camouflage BDUs, the uniform looking neatly cared for and fitting him exactly. He wore no rank insignia. A Kevlar helmet hung over one shoulder, balanced by an M-16A4 on the other. He carried a field pack and looked ready for action.

In the next instant the stasis that held the sim vanished. The figure glanced around the room, taking in everything in a long glance. Then its eyes focused on Andy.

Andy froze, feeling like an elephant had stepped on his chest. He'd seen a lot of flatfilm and holo footage of his father over the years, and had studied it intensively during the last few days. But never once in his memory had his father looked at him so directly.

The sim gave a small smile, like he was shy. "Hello, Andrew," he said quietly.

The words ripped through Andy's control. "Oh, man," he gasped. "Computer, end program."

In an eyeblink the sim vanished.

"It *knew* me," Andy said in disbelief.

"I programmed him to recognize you."

Andy shook his head. "That sim is no *he*. It's an amalgam of programming and images. That's all. It's not alive."

Mark waited a moment, then said gently, "He's not alive, and he knows that, too. But he also knows he's not an it, Andy. You can't think of him that way. He's a near-AI character. Referring to him in those terms is going to cause problems with the programming."

Andy opened up a window and stepped out of the veeyar onto his pirate ship. He felt immediately better when the salt breeze wrapped around him.

"I know this is hard," Mark said, following him. "But it may be the only way to answer the questions you have."

"I know." Andy held onto the railing tightly, like he was going to hang onto the real world somehow. *That* thing *is not my dad. No way.* He shuddered, struggling with stomach-twisting nausea.

Mark stood quietly beside him. "I can stay for a while. That way you don't have to be alone while you learn how to interact with him."

Andy shook his head. Part of it was stubbornness, not wanting to need anyone. But the other part of it was because he didn't want Mark to see him in a potential moment of weakness. More than anything at the moment, he was mad at Solomon. *Maybe I ought to use the National Treasures software and create a sim of Solomon's dad, then stick it*—him—*into Solomon's personal veeyar. See how* he *likes dealing with this.*

But it wouldn't be the same and Andy knew it. Despite the bad feelings that might have existed between them, Solomon had known his father. That situation wouldn't have been anything like what Andy faced.

"No," Andy said in a tight voice. "This is something I have to do by myself."

"Okay." Mark didn't push.

"Look," Andy said after a moment, "I know you've got things to do. Why don't you cut on out of here and let me deal with this?"

"That's how you want it?"

Andy turned to Mark and gave him a shrug. "That's how it's gotta be. Thanks for helping me."

"No prob." Mark nodded. "You'll let me know if you need anything?"

"You're the first person on the list."

Mark stepped out of the veeyar, leaving Andy alone.

When the window closed after Mark's exit, Andy took a deep breath and opened a window to the sim veeyar. Dark shrouded the cube. Andy stepped inside. "Computer," Andy called, "reengage sim."

Almost immediately the featureless room lit up, and the sim reappeared in front of Andy. It—*he*—waited patiently.

"You know who I am?" Andy asked.

The sim nodded. "You're my son. Andrew."

"Call me Andy."

"Andy."

"Do you know why you're here?" Andy paced nervously, trying to get a grip on the whole situation. *How could anyone deal with their dead parent or friend dropping back into their lives after so long?*

"You have a problem you think I can help you resolve. And I can help you, Andy, if you'll let me."

"Right." Andy tried to figure out where to go from there, but his mind spun helplessly. In school he was the one everybody could always depend on to come up with a joke, a quick volley in an exchange of insults or digs. But now his mind was blank.

"What am I supposed to call you?" he asked.

The sim regarded him frankly, then shrugged. "I guess Dad's

out of the question. Otherwise you'd have used it."

Andy studied the sim-dad's face. *Did a hurt look just flash through his eyes?* A chill twisted his stomach. He could only nod. Calling the sim Dad *was* out of the question. But the way it—he—sounded so much like a dad left Andy even more confused.

"That leaves us with Colonel Moore, but I'm not exactly comfortable with that. How about Robert? Or Bob?"

Andy had trouble clearing his throat. "Bob's fine with me."

"Good, then Bob it is." Bob extended his hand.

Andy took the proffered hand, feeling the tactile realness of it. Bob's grip possessed warmth and strength. He held Andy's hand for just the right amount of time, then let go.

"What do you need from me?" Bob asked.

"Can you remember the South African War?" Andy knew Mark had programmed that information into the sim.

"Of course. I fought and died there." Bob seemed to take the information in stride.

Would my real dad have sounded so cold? Andy stared at the sim and felt a momentary pang of regret. He should have known it—*he*—would remember what had happened to him. "Do you remember the plague bomb that was set off near Mandelatown?"

"Of course."

Andy's words caught in his throat for a moment. "Did my dad set that bomb off?"

Bob looked away for a moment, then stiffened. Abruptly his image blurred, like a television signal that traveled through heavy interference. Bob jerked and broke apart, then came back together again. He opened his mouth, and his voice sounded tinny and mechanical. "Warning. Parameters for possible interpolation have been exceeded. Withdraw, rephrase, or redefine question or risk damage to subprogram build: Bob."

Mark arrived late to the meeting after leaving Andy's veeyar. Getting through the checkpoints to the current veeyar was easy since he had the passwords. The veeyar resembled Victor Frankenstein's laboratory, complete with pieced-together monster lying on a raised table in the center of the room. Yellow forked lightning flickered across the dark sky above the domed glass-paneled ceiling, almost but not quite touching the rod extending up from the castle.

Mark wasn't sure who'd come up with the Frankenstein motif for the veeyar, but it always kind of creeped him out. He wasn't afraid of monsters, especially animated corpses. Though the time one of the unofficial members of the unofficial club programmed the lightning to strike the rod and cause the monster to come to life and lumber around the room had been disconcerting.

Actually, it was nothing less than a miracle that more pranks weren't pulled in the veeyar. All of the members were heavy into software and computer systems. They ranged from designers to pirates to hackers, from professionals to amateurs, from law-abiding users to outright outlaws who hadn't been caught yet. The membership had changed a lot even over the time he'd been part of the select community. Some people simply lost interest, some got into arguments with other members, and some were convicted of crimes.

And Mark was certain at least two of them were Net Force agents.

Over thirty people were in the lab now. Like all good veeyars, no matter how many people were present, the castle was just the right size. All of the people wore proxies.

Mark wore a proxy as well, disguising himself behind the image of Thor, the Norse god of storms. He looked like a Viking, wearing a hair vest and pants tucked into knee-high cracked leather boots, a horned helmet, a fierce red beard, and he carried a war hammer.

"—almost got kidnapped at the mall," a girl with wings said. She sat on one of the laboratory tables, test tubes and copper tubing arranged behind her. Instead of hair, she had feathers that trailed down her back.

"Who?" a man made of marshmallows asked. He leaned against one of the coffins Victor Frankenstein had emptied while gathering parts.

"Matt Hunter," the bird-girl said. "He's a student at Bradford Academy."

Mark's heart rate sped up. He walked over to join the group. "What happened?" He hadn't been in touch with Matt since school.

Quickly the bird-girl told Mark about Matt's near abduction

at the mall. "Why are you so interested in him? Do you know him?"

Mark smiled, though he knew the expression didn't look too friendly on his Viking face. "That question is out of bounds." Everyone who attended the meetings was supposed to remain unknown to everyone else. Of course, that wasn't the way it worked. Mark had already identified three people who attended Bradford. Chris Potter, the multifaceted iceman lounging against one of the back walls, was one of them.

The bird-girl smiled. "You must know him if you're so interested."

"I might be interested," Mark said, "because I don't want to get nabbed, too."

"That's right." A fairy no bigger than Mark's hand dived down from the ceiling where she'd been standing on one of the rafters. She hovered in place just above the group. Her wings threw off glowing gold dust. "I heard someone tried to run down another Bradford student on Monday."

"Why?" the marshmallow man asked.

The fairy shrugged. "I haven't heard. But the guy was a known hacker."

In back, the multifaceted iceman shifted nervously.

"Somebody told me Hunter was one of the Net Force Explorers." The speaker looked like Captain Venn from the science-fiction holo show *Ultimate Frontier.*

"Sounds like some kind of conspiracy, if you ask me," the bird-girl said.

Paranoia settled in over the group at once. The biggest fear all hackers had, in Mark's opinion, was of getting noticed for the things that they did. Oddly, for most of them, their second biggest fear lay in not getting noticed for the things they did. That allowed agencies like Net Force to catch them.

"Targeting Bradford Academy?" Chris spoke up in the back. "Do you think they could be doing that?"

The bird-girl looked at him. "Does that bother you, Ice? Usually you're *soooo* cool."

Chris shifted and his multifaceted body reflected the light from the lanterns illuminating the room. "I just think that—"

Darkness descended over the veeyar, startling everyone there. Some of the more senior and more cautious attendees logged off on reflex. The veeyar had defenses, maybe nowhere near those of Net Force or even most corporations, but it wasn't unprotected.

Mark knew at once, even before the shapes started to take form in the center of the room, they'd been invaded.

13

The new arrivals cut through the veeyar's defenses as easily as fingernails through silk. Three shapes shimmered and took form in the center of the room. When the haze cleared, Mark saw the invaders weren't human, and that the term *invaders* clearly fit. The three were chuggorths, aliens made popular by a recent Japanese anime series on holo.

Oh, man, this is definitely a close encounter, Mark thought as he prepared to log off.

The "aliens" fanned out at once, raising slender rod devices that were evidently weapons. Gangrenous egg-shaped heads sat on top of narrow shoulders, and their arms were spaghetti ribbons. Purple tunics covered them all the way to their four cloven feet.

"We want *it* returned," one of the aliens said in a shrill automated voice. "One of you has taken something that doesn't belong to you. It must be returned or all will suffer. There will be no more warnings." A sizzling violet ray streamed from the rod the alien held and set the patchwork creature on the table on fire.

The action told Mark that the invaders had not only slipped into the veeyar, they'd hacked into it so that they also controlled the environment. "Get out!" he yelled at all the people still frozen by the sudden intrusion. "Get out now!"

People logged off immediately, their proxies vanishing at once.

The veeyar environment shifted, giving way to the outside interference. The laboratory melted away, leaving the bleak nightscape of a huge downtown area behind. Black skies gathered overhead, totally oppressive.

The violet beams slashed through the night, looking even more terrifying. Less than a dozen people remained in the altered veeyar. Two of them vanished even as Mark sprinted down the dark street and took shelter in an alley.

Breathing fast, Mark reached into his hard drive, pulling out programs he wanted. The first utility he used helped mask his signature within the Net.

The second was a trace-back utility. In the real world the trace-back was an awesome piece of programming strategy. Lines and lines of code he'd written created an almost foolproof bloodhound capable of tracking program origination anywhere in the Net. In the veeyar the trace-back took shape as a glowing green glob about the size of a baseball that filled Mark's palm.

Peering around the corner of the alley, Mark saw an alien approaching his position. A violet beam blasted the corner of the alley only inches from Mark's face. Brick and mortar exploded outward as Mark pulled back to safety. *Man oh man oh man!* Maybe they had him on some kind of radar.

Mark pushed out of the alley, knowing if they hit him with one of the beams he was definitely going to be thrown out of the veeyar and he wouldn't get to use the trace-back utility.

He rolled, using some of the same skills he had back in the real world, not bothering to try to reprogram his proxy for superhuman speed or flight or the ability to crawl along the wall. He didn't have time to do that before the alien was on top of him.

Instead, he instructed his trace-back to lock onto the nearest person that wasn't Mark. Then he casually dropped the baseball-shaped glob and watched it streak after the alien.

A heat beam tore a hole in the street, covering Mark in debris. *Come on, come on! Lock on already!* He watched the trace-back ball splatter the alien, throwing out tentacles of green slime. The alien couldn't see it. The trace-back was visible only to Mark because of its programming.

The creature aimed the rod at Mark again, catching him flat-footed in the street with no place to run. The violet beam ripped toward him.

Without hesitation Mark logged off the Net, crashing back into his physical body. He gazed around his bedroom, breathing rapidly from all the adrenaline hitting his system, jerking his head away from the implant-connect on the computer-link chair for an instant to make sure he was totally clear of the Net. Then he dropped his head back into the trough and shot back into the Net.

He returned easily to the Net sector where the veeyar was. In the Net a whirling obsidian pyramid floating high above the rest of the Net community below represented the veeyar. He didn't enter.

Enabling the trace-back, Mark studied the whirling pyramid and watched as the utility activated. Programming interlaced with the aliens' programming as tightly as DNA and RNA spat up a single green thread like a spider tracking a web. It spun swiftly across the Netscape.

Excited, Mark clothed himself in his crashsuit testing gear, then accelerated after the green thread. He stayed low within the Net, aware that some of the corporations he came close to might register him on their outer perimeter line of security sensors. He got pinged twice from other sites, but both times managed to mollify the automated sys/ops watching over those systems.

Mark became a rocket hurtling across cyberspace, accelerating still more as he followed the thin green thread of the trace-back. He tracked it through the huge com-complex that served Washington, D.C., then out into space itself. The cool blue of sky gave way to the deep ebony of space. A glittering multi-faceted diamond spinning above him was a major com-relay satellite in geosynchronous orbit.

Slamming through the com-relay satellite's circuitry was a log ride through ice-slick chutes surrounded by glaring lights, memory modules that resembled cobalt blue towers, and constant datastreams consisting of a dozen different colored shapes that spread out in a spider's web of activity. Mark hung on tenaciously.

Come on, come on, he urged, trying to work up greater speed. The man could log off at any time and be gone. The green thread raced to the European Exchange in Great Britain.

The Great Britain location surprised Mark. He'd expected the point of origin for the computer link to be in the United States. Mark landed in London, then raced through the com-relay circuitry, getting tangled quickly. He fought through the systems, sliding through like a greased eel, twisting between bits of binary code that would have tried to categorize him and file him away. He stayed hidden in his programming, following the bouncing green thread.

Once through the Great Britain exchange, the trace-back headed spaceward again. He wove through the com-relay stations over Europe and Asia. He'd been that way before, doing other trace-backs for his mom and for Captain Winters. And he'd practiced against hackers in contests as well as real attempts to locate and identify cyber-outlaws working a string of wildings on the Net.

He went to ground again in Germany, bouncing through their com-relay towers in Berlin. *Gotta be getting close,* Mark told himself.

He slipped through the landlines out of Germany, prowling the newly laid lines leading into Romania and other points in Eastern Europe. He guessed he was headed for the Middle East. It was the only thing that made sense.

The trace-back doubled back through Eastern Europe, then headed north, deep into Russia.

A warning peeped inside Mark's skull. *Trace-back utility has been disengaged,* his computer told him emotionlessly.

No! Mark concentrated on the green thread, striving desperately to go even faster to stay up with the com-data. But it wasn't possible. Even traveling at com-rate speed, he knew he couldn't keep up with the signal fragmentation that happened when his target discommed at the other end.

He crashed through the Russian systems, setting off at least three alarms. Out of the Russian systems, he flew spaceward again. Just as he started to leave the cool blue of the sky for the deepening dark of space, the green thread from the trace-back utility zipped by him, fading and leaving nothing for him to follow.

Mark never even made it through the com-sat relays over the Pacific bloc. Another warning peeped inside his head, letting him know he was dangerously close to getting tagged with an IFF program—not good.

Disgusted, totally frustrated, Mark stopped his pursuit. *Another couple of minutes,* he told himself. *Maybe even only one, and I'd have had them.*

Three Russian IFF utilities, zipping through the Net like ICBMs launched from the com-sat relays above him, vectored in on him. They were twisting red representations that flared fiery embers behind them in ever-widening cones—no finesse at all.

Completely lost as to where he was supposed to proceed next, Mark logged off, evading the IFF utilities with nanoseconds to spare.

"Warning!" the computer stated again. "Question has exceeded safe parameters. Subprogram Bob has become unstable."

Andy peered anxiously at the sim of his dad. The staticky waves still ran through the holo, blanking it out in places, then moving on to other places while the other areas struggled to rematerialize. He was almost mesmerized by the look in Bob's eyes. *Was it—he—in any kind of pain?*

"Computer," Andy said hoarsely, "end interrogation." *Was that what he was doing wrong? Interrogating instead of interacting?*

The staticky charges disappeared, and Bob reappeared. He ran his hands down his body. A look of wonder filled his face.

"Now, that's going to take some getting used to," Bob said.

Andy heard the quaver in Bob's voice and felt guilty. But he felt confused, too. The real Colonel Robert Moore had decided to stay in South Africa and die instead of returning home to his wife and son. *I don't owe him anything,* Andy thought, hardening his heart and his resolve. *Especially not to a sim of the real thing.*

"I'm sorry," Bob apologized. "I tried to answer the question, but I can't. I don't have enough information."

His tone sounded sincere, and that made Andy feel a little worse. Still, all he had to do was think of his mom and how she would feel if Solomon's information got back to her.

"Why don't you have enough information?" Andy demanded.

Bob's chin came up and his eyes narrowed. "Why don't you?"

The steel in the sim's voice surprised Andy and ignited the anger that lay boiling deep inside him. "You don't ask the questions here, I do."

Bob shook his head. "You can run this program or you can end this program, but I'm fully interactive, son."

"Don't call me that!" Andy snapped.

Bob laced his hands behind his back. "You can redefine the nature of our relationship. At this point I recognize you as my son Andy, and I know I wouldn't let any son of mine address me like that without good reason. You don't have one. I can still remain interactive without that personal relationship—"

"Computer," Andy commanded. "Redefine the nature of relationship between subprogram Bob and me."

"I'm sorry you feel that way, son," Bob said gently. His regret appeared genuine.

Andy almost weakened, wishing there was some other way to handle the situation. But there wasn't. He couldn't tolerate the familiarity the sim showed toward him.

"Query: How do you want nature of relationship reconfigured?" the computer asked. "Present primary function, interactive. Choose from following menu. Opposing views for debate skills. Adversarial for combat skills. Fully interrogative, no personal relation, for investigative."

"Maintain present interactive mode," Andy answered. "Are there any adjustments that can be made to redefine the relationship?"

"Present settings show father-son relationship," the computer answered. "Established at onset of program launch. Do you wish to redefine that?"

"Andy," Bob said in a quiet voice, his eyes focused on him, "I wish you'd reconsider this."

Andy shook his head, his throat tight. "I can't. This isn't going to work."

"You haven't given it a chance," Bob replied.

"You and I never got a chance," Andy said. "You saw to that when you chose to stay and die in South Africa instead of coming home." He was surprised to feel tears hot on his cheeks. Their presence made him even angrier.

"Then give it a chance now."

"Why?"

"Because," Bob said, "there is a chance now."

"Did Mark program this into you?"

"No," the sim answered patiently. "This is the core feature of the program, to reveal the nature of the personality being reincarnated. The sims are designed to be fully interactive, including on an emotional level."

Andy shook his head. *Is this the way my dad would have sounded?* No way was this his father. Bob was just trying to relate to him in the only way he knew how.

"I can't handle the emotional level," Andy said.

"Then you're going to miss out on some of this experience that could have been uniquely yours," Bob told him.

"What?" Andy grated. "Not having a father? Sorry. Been there. Done that. That's old news, Bob, and I'm just fine in spite of it."

"You're sure?"

Andy ignored the question. "Computer, redefine nature of present relationship between subprogram Bob and myself. Have him recognize me as a commanding officer."

"Affirmative," the computer responded. "Complying."

Bob stood a little straighter as a whirling amber mist surrounded him. "Goodbye, son."

Andy didn't say anything, having to fight to keep back an angry retort.

The mist vanished. Bob stood ramrod straight, then his right arm came up in a crisp salute. "General, Colonel Robert Moore reporting, sir."

Andy drew on his own experience, gathered from classes he'd taken with the Explorers, from being around Captain Winters and the other Net Force agents, and from stories he'd been told by other students whose parents were in the military. "At ease, Colonel."

"Thank you, sir."

"I'm going to debrief you," Andy stated. "You'll be asked questions about your service record, particularly your involvement in the South African War."

"I understand, sir."

Andy studied the sim, noting several changes. This Bob was more reticent, tighter in his body language. No less confident, but definitely not as open. "Did you set off the plague bomb near Mandelatown in 2014?"

The staticky interruption started again, blurring Bob at once.

"Computer, end question," Andy snapped in exasperation. "Why does the program keep becoming unstable?"

"The question exceeds the parameters of the subprogram Bob's definite answers," the computer answered. "It can only know what you put into it. Suggestion: If you know the answer to this question, simply enter it and Bob will answer appropriately."

"I don't know the answer," Andy said, frustrated.

The computer cycled a moment. "Conclusion: Without proper preparation, subprogram Bob cannot know the answer."

Andy considered the response. *Interactive, Mark said. In its near-AI capability, it can interpret data and form logical conclusions. But it can't know what it doesn't know.*

He took a deep breath and looked at Bob standing at attention before him. "Colonel, would you knowingly ever use a biological weapon?" Andy asked.

"No, sir." Bob showed no hesitation before answering.

Andy felt good about the reply. Despite his own feelings about his father, he had known his dad would never use such a weapon. "Would there ever be an occasion you would use one?"

"I can't imagine one, sir."

"You'd never consider using one in South Africa?"

"Sir," Bob said, showing a little irritation, "this line of questioning, if you don't mind me saying so, sounds preposterous. Pure speculation. The South African Nationalists have no such weapons in their possession."

But, Andy thought, *that statement has to be incorrect. Unless there really was a team of Middle Eastern terrorists who'd gotten involved in the war.* He thought furiously, wondering if he could take the sim into Dr. Dobbs's strategic analysis class. Except he knew Solomon would tear it apart. Even asking Bob if he'd used the plague bomb rendered the subprogram unstable.

Playing devil's advocate to the hilt, remembering what he'd learned about the time the atomic bomb was used in Japan to accelerate the end of World War II, Andy looked at Bob again.

"What if you were commanded to use the plague bomb, Colonel? Would you use it then?"

Bob hesitated. "Then, sir, if it was necessary, I would."

The answer hammered Andy, stripping away all of his confidence and reawakening all the fears Solomon had started within him.

14

Matt listened to Mark's story about the alien invasion of the hacker veeyar, growing increasingly agitated. They'd met in Matt's veeyar, floating on either side of the black marble table.

"You talked to your dad about this?" Matt asked when Mark had finished.

"Yeah," Mark said. "He said he'd investigate. But I've got more news. While I was talking to Dad, I had nearly a dozen other messages left in my E-mail. Since Monday, three other hackers from Bradford have gotten attacked on their way home. From the descriptions I got, it sounds like it was done by the two guys you met in the mall today."

"When?"

"Another one Monday evening. One on Tuesday. And one on Wednesday."

"And these people are just now talking about it?"

"Hey," Mark said, "these are hackers, remember? They have that little credo: Don't talk to anybody, don't admit to anything, keep a low profile. The only reason I found out as much as I did this afternoon was because they heard what happened in the veeyar."

Matt blew out a frustrated breath. "What really bothers me is Captain Winters's refusal to do something about this."

"You can't say that," Mark said. "Captain Winters can have you shadowed by some of the Net Force agents and you'll never know they're there until he wants you to. Don't forget about the guy you thought you spotted on Monday."

"I haven't," Matt said. He glanced at the spacescape around them and watched a comet hurtling past. "But Bradford is *our* school. And if we're in training to become potential Net Force agents sometime in the future, you'd think we'd be allowed to help out on any investigation Winters might be conducting around Bradford."

"It's still possible that none of these things are connected."

"Do you think that?" Matt asked.

Mark grinned ruefully. "Not even for a second. Whoever's harassing the hackers, they know too much about the Bradford Academy students. They knew you. They knew Chris and these other people. And they knew about the hacker veeyar where some of the Bradford hackers hang out."

"They don't seem to know who has whatever it is they're looking for," Matt said. His mind seized on that. Somewhere in there, a clue existed that would take them to the people stalking the Bradford hackers. "But this afternoon they sent a team after me and raided the hacker veeyar. They're stepping up their pursuit. Why?"

"There's only one reason," Mark said. "They're facing a time crunch."

Matt nodded, agreeing. "That means we are, too." He sighed. "If Captain Winters is running an operation at Bradford and we're being left out, I don't appreciate that. We deserve to be involved. After getting to meet those two guys at the mall and knowing the hacker veeyar got hit, I'd like to be a little more aggressive than what we've been."

"Well, I've got an idea." Mark sat up straighter. "I can try to install some secondary interfacing utilities in Bradford's security systems. Maybe we can keep an eye on things around the campus."

"Okay." Matt felt uneasy about the prospect of getting caught. Mucking around in the school's Net-based security systems was a flagrant violation of the academy's rules. "But it'll just be you and me who knows about this."

"You don't have to be involved in this," Mark said. "I can do it by myself and let you know how it went."

"No way." Matt shook his head. "We'll take the heat together if it comes to that."

"Okay. I'm going to get home and knock out some homework, then put together the utilities and programs we're going to need. We can run uploads through the homework interfaces Bradford has, so that won't be a problem." Mark waved goodbye and left.

Matt sat quietly for a while, trying to figure out how all the pieces they'd seen fit together. But it was like having a lot of the inside pieces on a jigsaw puzzle without having any border pieces. He couldn't even begin to see what it was starting to add up to.

Clad in black combat BDUs, Andy raced after Bob, running through the dark jungle around them. They were in South Africa now. It was August 13, 2014. Bob's unit was en route to rescue the battalion of U.S. Army Rangers pinned down outside Mandelatown. The colonel maintained an easy lope despite the heavy field pack he carried.

Andy tightly gripped his optically sighted M-16A4 in his hands. Even though he knew the gun was only a sim rendering, he didn't much care for it. He'd carried lasers, bazookas, machine guns, swords, knives, and bows in hundreds of veeyar games, and battled other people, zombies, wizards, armies, dragons, and robots. But never before had a sim-rendered weapon seemed so much like a *weapon*.

The black matte finish of the barrel and the other machined parts didn't stand out from the nylon and ceramic stock at all. The assault rifle was as invisible in the night as he was in his high-tech DuPont/Rockwell D-1B Battlesuit.

Bob went to ground behind underbrush surrounding two trees that had grown together. He tilted his fully computerized and networked helmet with head-up display back, the chin straps hanging loose on either side of his sweat-streaked face. Black camouflage cosmetic broke the hard planes of his features and turned them dark.

"We're getting close." Bob pulled his helmet back on and consulted the digitally enhanced information mode of his all-purpose battle visor. A sat-com relay fed him information directly from the U.S. strategic operations command set up on an aircraft carrier out at sea. "Shouldn't be more than another klick out from their position."

Andy checked his own display.

A map of the surrounding terrain pulsed into view. It showed the rocky and broken land pouring down from the hillside where they currently were. Less than twenty yards in front of them, barely visible in the night, a gorge spilled down to a shallow streambed. The gorge was seventy yards deep, and the slope on either side was steep enough that traversing it couldn't be done in a hurry.

Nationalist forces on the other side of the gorge blocked the tactical retreat of the Rangers. More Nationalist reinforcements, including tanks, were on their way toward the American troops and would overtake their position in less than half an hour. The wooden bridge across the gorge was the only way out.

Andy tapped the nav-datapad, drawing back on the com-sat top-down view till he could see the bright yellow blips that were the Nationalist troops and the bright blue ones that represented the Rangers.

Bob gave orders to his men, assigning the positions they'd hold on the other side of the gorge. Their response was immediate and professional. Andy had to credit his dad with the ability to command. The special ops team was excellent, and they appeared willing to follow the colonel anywhere.

Andy looked at Bob as the man flagged his point team across the bridge. "You know you're going to die when you go over there," Andy said.

"Yes, sir." Due to the program modifications Bob still saw Andy as a commanding officer.

"Then why go?"

Bob shifted in his crouch, turning to face Andy directly. "Why go now? Or why go then?"

"There's a difference?" Andy asked.

"Yes, sir." Bob pointed his chin at the bridge. "That's the only way out for those Rangers, sir. And my team is the only thing that can buy them enough time to get clear before they're pounded by the Nationalist armored cavalry. The armored cav, sir, they're not going to take prisoners."

"I know that." Andy glanced at the wooden bridge as it swayed a little in the wind.

"I'm going now because it's something I did in the past,"

Bob said. "By allowing you to witness this, maybe you'll get a clearer answer to the questions you have. In reality, none of this makes any difference. We can sit here and watch those Rangers get chopped to pieces between the two Nationalist forces. The software is capable of extrapolating that, though not of informing you exactly who would have died and who wouldn't have."

Andy swallowed hard. *I'll stop the program before I have to watch that.*

"As to why I went then," Bob said, "I believed it was my duty. The military is important to me."

"Is that what my da—" Andy halted. "Is that what the real Colonel Moore thought?"

"I don't know. That's my extrapolation based on the events and the man as my programming understands him."

It was no real answer, Andy knew. He tried another tack. "Aren't you afraid?"

"Yes, sir. What good is a soldier who doesn't know how to be afraid? A soldier who doesn't fear is as bad as a soldier who can't control his or her fear. Neither one is going to serve the military, their group, or their mission very well. One will be dead and the other will be unable to act."

Andy hesitated. "What about your wife? Do you think she's going to like being a widow?"

Bob took time to consider his answer. "Sir, with all due respect, I think that's a question best left between Sandra and me."

Andy took a deep breath of the fetid jungle air and felt guilty. He *was* stepping into an area that really wasn't any of his business, but he couldn't help himself. The interactive software presented so many possibilities. He wanted every answer he could get. "Answer the question, Colonel."

For a moment, Andy thought Bob wasn't going to answer. Then Bob's mouth firmed into a thin, hard line.

"Yes, sir. Sandra and I talked about the possibility of me getting killed in the line of duty. It was one of the reasons I suggested she not marry me."

The statement angered Andy. *That isn't true!* He stood up and walked away from Bob. "Computer, freeze veeyar." Immediately the scene turned into a two-dimensional state, leaving Andy stranded outside of it.

Even Bob remained behind. "Computer, check out Bob's last answer. That can't be true."

"According to the database formed for this veeyar," the computer responded, "subprogram Bob's answer is referenced from letters to your mother prior to her marriage. Those letters further refer to conversations that took place between them over a period of months. This appears to have been a major consideration for Moore, Colonel Robert A. Moore, Sandra (maiden name) Creel didn't exhibit the same concerns."

A headache formed at the base of Andy's skull. He paced, but in the blank veeyar he had no sense of going anywhere. He and Mark had scanned his mom's letters from his dad into the database, but Andy hadn't read them. He'd tried to, but they'd been overwhelmingly personal and painful, he just couldn't.

He turned back to the frozen scene, wishing Bob had made an error so he could erase the whole program and realize what a mistake even trying it had been. But Bob appeared to be correct about so many things.

"Run program," Andy ordered.

The flatflim image suddenly exploded out for him, enveloping him again and surrounding him with the jungle. He heard night creatures in the distance, far from the invasive special ops team, and smelled the thick air tainted with dry heat. A slight breeze stirred against his skin.

"But Sandra wouldn't hear of not marrying me," Bob continued. "She said she knew the risks and could accept them if I could. For myself, I couldn't imagine a life without her. Maybe I was selfish. Even though the military separated us at times, we were there for each other when my missions were over." He looked down the bridge across the gorge. "I really didn't think this time would be any different."

"But it was," Andy said.

"Yes, sir." Bob looked at Andy. "Are we going or are we staying, sir?"

15

Andy knew there was no choice about crossing the bridge. If his dad had faced what lay over the gorge, he would, too. "We're going."

Bob swiftly relayed his orders. Separating into groups, the special ops team broke cover and streaked across the bridge. Andy followed Bob, staying close.

Only minutes later they encountered the first of the Nationalists. Bob and his team took them down without mishap. Andy watched, finding himself unable to leave the veeyar. Men died quietly, fearfully, and he knew none of the on-line games he watched would ever seem the same to him.

This was his dad's world, the world of the warrior, and it wasn't nearly as glamorous as holo shows made it out to be. Andy felt a lot of guilt piling up on him even though he stayed on the periphery of the action. Shadows moved, bled, and died. Knowing they were sims didn't lessen the impact.

"Are you okay, sir?" Bob asked after they'd secured their position.

"Yeah," Andy croaked. "I'm fine." He scanned their surroundings. None of the bodies were in view. He wished he could talk to Bob more one-on-one, but the commanding officer role was limiting when he wanted to speak his mind.

"Tanks will be within firing range by the time we get the Rangers out there," Bob stated.

Andy glanced at his display, noting the yellow cubes on the screen that marked off the advance of the Nationalist tanks. They approached the gorge in a loose semicircle. Small yellow dots represented the infantry between the armored cav. In front of them, marked in neon blue, the Rangers were in full retreat. They'd used the last of their ammo to blow through the Nationalists ring.

Bob looked at him. "You don't have to be here for this, sir. You could end the program or just leave and let it run."

"No," Andy replied. "I'm staying." Airborne buzzing drew his attention.

"Helo," Bob said, opening a channel on his comm-set. He ordered two teams equipped with LAW rockets to stand ready. "Spotter aircraft for the Nationalists. The Rangers have already called it in."

Andy watched helplessly, wishing he could break out of the veeyar. But he couldn't.

Bob called the maneuvers to his teams and guided the Ranger retreat to the bridge. The Nationalist helo sped toward them. "The pilot knows they're headed for the bridge."

Andy gazed at the slender wasp-shape cutting the air above them. He knew enough about helos from veeyar mil-games to recognize the weapons it carried. "It's got rockets."

"Yes, sir." Bob commanded the rocket teams into action over the comm-set.

Both LAWs launched their 94mm warheads and struck the helo. The attack chopper disintegrated, wreathed in flames and roiling smoke. Flaming debris tumbled into the gorge.

The next few minutes turned into a blur for Andy. The Nationalist tanks rolled into range and locked down. They opened up with their main guns at once. He recognized the scene from HoloNet broadcasts.

When the armored cav finished pounding the area, the Nationalist infantry swept in. Jeeps and fast-attack vehicles sped toward the American special ops forces. Machine-gun fire strafed the hillside and tracers lit up the night.

Miraculously, heavily outnumbered, the special ops forces held their positions. Under Bob's orders, the warriors broke the advancing Nationalist lines in several places with rocket attacks and squad-attack weapons. They also filled the battlefield with smoke that fouled normal vision as well as infrared.

When the front line broke and retreated so the armored cav could hammer the ridge again, Bob pulled his teams from the area. They traveled in staggered groups that fell back and covered each other all the way back up the ridge.

Andy turned to Bob. "You could go now."

Bob shook his head. "Not till the last one of my boys gets across the bridge."

"Your boys?" Jealousy, anger, and fear bubbled over inside Andy in a fierce Molotov cocktail. "You've got a son back home who's never going to get to know you if you die over here."

"Then I'm going to do my best not to die over here," Bob stated calmly. "Now, sir, if you'll allow me, I've got an exfiltration to command." His voice held bared steel.

Andy subsided.

The special ops retreat continued even after the tank shelling began again. Bob waited till the last of his men had gathered in the gorge, then fell back with them. Tank rounds smacked into the ridgeline, blasting rock and trees high into the air and filling the night with swirling dust.

Andy watched as Bob commanded the group to mine the bridge. The plan was to blow it after they got across, preventing infantry pursuit. But a cold, dead feeling filled Andy because he knew what was coming next.

The four-man special ops team worked quickly to lace the bridge supports with explosives. But it wasn't quick enough to beat the Nationalist group that had come up the ridge from the western slope, protected from the shelling of their own tanks.

"Look out!" one of the special ops men yelled in warning. He lifted his rifle and started blasting.

Bob raised his own weapon, adding to the firepower. "Finish the bridge!" He took shelter behind one of the bridge support poles. Bullets ripped long wooden splinters from the pole.

Andy stood behind another pole and watched. His stomach lurched sickeningly and his throat constricted so much he could barely breathe. The special ops team finished wiring the bridge as the Nationalists came up over the ridge in a rush.

Bob fired into them, running the M-16A4 dry and reloading.

He ordered his men across the bridge, stayed for a moment to cover their backs, then ran after them.

Bullets chopped into the bridge and tracer rounds flamed across the night. Cover fire from the opposite side of the gorge broke some of the advancing Nationalist line. But they were too close. Rounds hit one of the special ops warriors and knocked him down.

Bob stopped and lifted the man bodily, throwing him over his shoulder and trying to sprint to the other side. He didn't make it halfway before Nationalist bullets cut his legs out from under him.

Numb, feeling the hurt waiting somewhere outside himself, Andy said, "Computer, freeze program."

All the motion came to a stop as silence filled the veeyar. The three-dimensional world shrank to flatfilm.

Andy stared at Bob lying on the bridge, wine-dark blood rushing out across the wooden surface. He walked toward the man and looked down at him. "Why did you stay?"

The two-dee image shimmered, and Bob stretched into holo again, still lying down. "I couldn't leave, sir," Bob answered. "Why didn't you leave?"

"It's not the same," Andy protested. "I knew I wasn't going to die."

Bob grinned painfully. "I don't believe I thought I was going to either, sir."

Hot tears stung Andy's eyes. "Didn't you even think of your son?" he demanded.

Bob looked at him with slight surprise. "Every minute, sir. Andy was never far from my thoughts. I worked hard to come back to him alive. I wanted to see him. More than anything. We've never had any time together. He's so young. I can only hope he understands."

I don't! This isn't fair! Andy made himself look away from Bob. "Computer, run program." He stood on the bridge.

The Nationalist forces swarmed onto the bridge, firing at the special ops squad. They didn't get far. The explosives packed onto the bridge blew, ripping the structure to toothpicks. The roiling mass of flames surrounded Andy in a sudden super-heated gust. He let the concussion blow him out of the veeyar and back into his bedroom, aching with the loss.

•   •   •

Andy waited in the hallway outside the Strategic Analysis class the next morning. He felt hollow and empty—he'd had no real sleep. The little he'd gotten had been filled with recurring nightmares of South Africa. But that didn't take the edge off the anger that pounded at his temples.

As usual, Solomon Weist was nearly late to class. His gaze locked onto Andy at once.

Andy pushed off the wall and threaded through the few students separating him from Solomon.

"Something tells me you want to speak to me," Solomon said coyly and smirked.

"I want to know where you got that footage of my dad." Andy blocked the way.

"You mean 'the *hero*'?" Solomon tried to step around.

Andy took another quick step and blocked him. Solomon outweighed him by sixty or seventy pounds and was built like an ape, but Andy didn't care. "This is between you and me. Whatever you're pulling, it's not going to work. That footage isn't true."

"Right," Solomon replied sarcastically, "and you knew your dad well enough to say that."

"The military knew him." Andy glared at Solomon.

"They have a vested interest in heroes," Solomon returned. "Having heroes is good for them. Having dead heroes is even better."

"Tell me where you got the footage." Andy clenched his fists.

Solomon puffed out his chest. "Do you really think you can take me, shrimp? Do you think you're enough like your dad that you can stand up to me?" He put out both hands and pushed Andy.

Andy fell back a step, then swept Solomon's arms away with his. Angry himself now, Solomon swung a big hand at Andy's head. Only Andy wasn't there when the blow passed. He ducked and punched Solomon in the stomach.

Solomon cried out in surprise and pain, but he flailed with his hands again. One of the blows landed on Andy's jaw and knocked him back a couple steps and down to one knee.

Recovering, Andy pushed up and launched himself at Solomon. He couldn't control the anger and frustration anymore. He blocked another of Solomon's blows with a forearm, then hit Solomon in the nose with a short jab. Cartilage snapped and blood spurted. Even though he was hurt, Solomon came for Andy, yelling angrily. He wrapped both arms around Andy in a bear hug, pinning Andy's arms and slamming him up against the wall near the classroom doorway.

Andy's breath left his lungs in a rush. He headbutted Solomon in the face twice, then broke free of Solomon's loosening grip. Andy fisted Solomon's shirt, slipped a leg behind Solomon's, and bore his bigger opponent to the ground.

On top of Solomon, Andy drew his fist back as Solomon tried to cover his face with both arms.

"Andy!"

Despite his anger, Andy recognized Megan's voice. Before he could turn, she seized his wrist. Applying pressure in a martial arts grip, she held his fist back and levered him off Solomon.

Cursing fluently, Solomon shoved up from the floor and stood woozily. Then he started for Andy.

Megan's friend Maj stepped in front of Solomon, her hands raised before her. "No," she told him.

Blood streamed down Solomon's face. "He started it!" he roared at the girls.

"Let me go, Megan," Andy said, pushing against her grip.

Megan shook her head. "No, Andy. You've gone too far."

"He's gone too far," Andy shot back. "He started all of this." He jerked his arm but it hurt so he quit.

"Look," Megan said, maintaining her grip, "you're already in trouble. Don't make it any worse."

Andy tried to wriggle free but couldn't. Megan knew what she was doing.

"Release him, please, Miss O'Malley." Dr. Dobbs stepped through the crowd and fixed Andy with his gaze.

Even though he didn't want to, Andy put aside his anger at Solomon, still held firmly in Maj's grip. Andy breathed heavily, panting. It felt like someone had removed most of the air from the hallway.

"Mr. Moore, Mr. Weist," Dr. Dobbs commanded, "you'll both accompany me to the principal's office." There was no arguing with the tone the professor used. Maj let Solomon go and backed off.

Solomon held his fingers pinched across the bridge of his

nose in what was obviously a practiced procedure. Despite his pain, he grinned maliciously at Andy. "You're going to regret this. I've got an interview after school with a reporter who's going to go international with this story. You think it's so bad that maybe people here at Bradford know about your dad, wait till the whole world knows."

Andy turned away from his tormentor. All the satisfaction he'd gotten from hitting Solomon drained from him. If what Solomon said was true, there was no way he could protect his mom from learning about the footage.

Matt and Mark walked through the virtual representation of Bradford Academy. They were dressed in veeyar crashsuits. Matt stared through the school's hallways and felt really uncomfortable. Mark had gotten them into the veeyar despite the security safeguards.

"It's up here," Mark said, pointing at the principal's office. He let them through the door, bypassing the security system there, then went back to the security systems in a room by themselves. The security firewall was represented by a series of staggered orange laser beams that went from floor to ceiling.

"Can we get through that?" Matt asked. Seeing the firewall, he felt less confident. Still, Mark had gotten by the other security systems with what looked like almost no effort. And Matt knew that Mark's skills were top-of-the-line.

"No prob." Mark suddenly flattened, becoming a two-dee image. He grinned at Matt, then reached out and touched him. "Nifty little program, isn't it?"

Matt felt a tingle that ran from his head to his feet. When he glanced down at his hand, then the rest of his body, he discovered he was two-dee as well.

"Now we can just walk through." Mark took the lead, sliding easily between the lasers.

Matt followed his friend into the computer room.

Mark took a seat in front of the system. "Wow."

"What?" Matt asked.

"There's something new here." Mark leaned over the table. The computer system used at Bradford was elaborate. It looked like a dozen high-rise apartment buildings done in miniature. Each one of the rooms inside the buildings was a compartmentalized function. They resembled towering versions of the mazes the lab rats ran in during biology class. Lights flashed in each of the compartments, cycling through a pattern that Matt couldn't quite catch.

"What's new?" Matt asked.

Mark pointed one of his two-dee fingers, a blade that almost touched the computer. "Somebody's got this computer wired up already."

Matt looked more closely and spotted what Mark was talking about with difficulty even after it was pointed out. Some of the rooms in the representation were double-layered, thin sheets of the translucent programming added to create a new interior inside certain rooms. To the casual observer the additions wouldn't have been immediately noticeable.

"Someone layered their programming right in over the top of the existing programming," Mark said. "Looks like a room within a room here. Do you see it?"

"Yeah," Matt replied. "But who?"

Mark shook his head. "As well as this is built, I'm not even going to try to find out. This is Net Force quality stuff. If I do anything wrong, whoever put this here is going to know we're here in a heartbeat. The best thing I can do is attempt to weave in the programming we're going to use to allow us into the school's system. And hope whoever built this doesn't find us."

"Get it done," Matt said. "We're running out of time."

Mark reached out without hesitation and touched the representation in three places. Immediately rooms formed within rooms there. His new layers weren't quite as thin and unnoticeable as the ones he'd shown Matt. Mark quietly surveyed the microcosm of the Net that was Bradford's computer system.

"Those are some of my best snooper programs," Mark said. "They'll allow us to get in and take a look around from the school or our home veeyars whenever we want to."

Matt nodded. "You said those other programs were Net Force quality."

"Yeah. Just looking at them and the way they interface with the Bradford system, I'd say so."

"Maybe they are," Matt said. "Is there any way of checking it out?"

"Not without possibly giving ourselves away or alerting them that we're in here, too."

Matt sighed. *It would be good to know if Winters really is operating on this.* "Okay, for now let's just leave everything in place and see what we can scam off the snoopers."

"That would be the safest thing to do," Mark agreed.

"Catch you later," Matt said. "You did good."

"Thanks." Mark disappeared when he logged off.

Still trying to wrap his mind around the extra programming, Matt logged off the Net as well. Time to get cracking. He had a full day ahead of him. He knew he'd have a hard time focusing on school activities after the excitement he'd just been through.

Who else was out there spying on the school? Net Force? Or the people who'd lost *it*—whatever *it* was?

16

"Solomon? Yeah. He was just leaving the principal's office last I saw of him, after getting his hide chewed."

"When was that?" Andy asked impatiently. The echoes of the last bell ending the school day echoed through Bradford Academy. Students jammed the hallway, their voices so loud it was almost impossible to hear the guy he was talking to.

"Ten minutes ago. There he is—"

Andy followed the pointing finger, scanning across a sea of people. It took him just a moment, but he spotted Solomon down the hall by the library.

"Thanks." A smile touched Andy's lips when he saw the large white adhesive bandage across Solomon's nose. The principal hadn't been too enthusiastic about the fight, and Dr. Dobbs had let his own disapproval be known. At the same time, though, Andy had the feeling that the professor had gone to bat for him behind closed doors. After all, he was still in school—pending review—when most students would have been out for at least three days' suspension. He had a feeling that Solomon wasn't so lucky.

Andy set off through the hall, tossing out jokes and comebacks as other students recognized him. He stayed back far enough from Solomon that he was certain none of the talk was overheard.

Solomon walked to the autobus stop in front of the school.

Andy veered off, spotting an approaching gypsy cab behind the autobus. He flagged the driver to the curb, then hopped in the cab. It was deep burgundy, a big Dodge, an older model that still carried an air of luxury and elegance.

"Where to?" The driver gazed in the rearview mirror at Andy. He wore a pale green turban and a long, curling beard.

Andy pointed at the autobus as it pulled into the flow of traffic. "Follow that bus."

"Haven't heard that line since the talkies changed over to holos," the cabbie said, but he pulled out and followed the bus just the same. The driver skillfully wove through the traffic.

The autobus followed its route, stopped at a booth on Nineteenth Street N.W. The cabdriver pulled over four car lengths behind the autobus. Solomon got out of the autobus and looked around for a moment.

"Wait here," Andy told the cabdriver as the autobus drove away. He watched Solomon turn and walk toward a restaurant called Sam & Harry's. Andy had eaten there a couple times with his mom on special occasions. Sam & Harry's was an upscale restaurant where a lot of business deals were made and political matters were discussed away from the Capitol buildings.

Solomon entered the restaurant. Andy swiped his card through the reader, added a tip, and left the cab. He felt nervous. There was no way Solomon would drop into a restaurant like Sam & Harry's for an after-school snack.

He wasn't kidding. He's meeting somebody here, Andy thought. Anger and worry made his hands shake.

"Table for two," Andy told the hostess.

She was young and pretty, and looked at him doubtfully.

"I'm meeting my mom here," Andy said, then passed his swipe card over for inspection.

The hostess scanned it quickly, then gave it back, and grabbed a menu. She led him to one of the small round tables in the front. Andy asked for a table in the back, telling the hostess it was what his mom had asked for.

Sam & Harry's was open and friendly, a bright space for elegant meals, but had private dining areas in the back consisting of high-walled booths that offered the diners privacy.

The hostess led Andy to a table in the back dining room. When she left him there, he looked around and spotted Solomon sitting at a table halfway down the room and on the right. Andy moved, sliding out of direct view behind one of the walls at his own booth, but by leaning forward he could see Solomon easily. He also saw the man Solomon was with.

The man looked tall, even seated. Gray touched his temples, and he had a square face that invited trust. He wore a dark suit that fit him perfectly. He appeared to be very happy to see Solomon.

Andy knew he recognized the man's face. He'd seen it somewhere before, but he couldn't remember where. Hating to bring anyone else into the situation, but needing to know what he was facing, he took out his foilpack and reconfigured it into a phone. He punched in Matt Hunter's number, hoping Matt was home. His foilpack phone also had a video component that would allow him to show Matt the man.

He listened to the phone ring, growing more nervous as he watched Solomon talking animatedly. Andy couldn't hear anything because of the way the booths were constructed, and he didn't dare move any closer.

The afternoon crowd consisted of nearly three dozen people, all scattered around the dining room. Andy pegged them as businessmen and politicians, all of them jockeying to make a deal. None of them paid any attention to him or Solomon or the man Solomon was with.

The phone continued to ring in Andy's ear.

Solomon sat across from Keith Donner, the *Washington Post* reporter he'd contacted about the South African footage, and felt great.

Donner was one of the top men in the media field, a guy who'd been responsible for breaking a ton of stories on what went down in Washington, D.C. Also, as a young reporter, Donner had covered the South African War. He'd first made a name for himself by reporting from the front lines where the action was heaviest. He'd been wounded twice.

Solomon enjoyed being the center of attention. Especially this kind of attention. He couldn't imagine life being any more perfect.

Donner smiled. "So what happened to your nose?"

Solomon reached up and touched the thick adhesive bandage across his nose. Okay, so maybe life *could* have been a little more perfect. "An accident."

"At Bradford?" Donner asked.

"Yeah."

"Was somebody trying to keep you from making the meeting with me?" Donner asked. "Because if you don't feel safe, I'm sure we can make other arrangements."

Solomon grinned and visions of a palatial hotel and room service danced in his head. But he didn't want to draw any more attention to himself. Yet. "Yeah, somebody was trying to keep me from telling the story. But nobody knows about the meeting I have with you. I wanted that to be a surprise."

A waitress appeared at the table and left Donner a coffee and Solomon a fruit drink with a small umbrella in it. Solomon sipped his drink happily, trying not to think of the ache in his nose. According to the school nurse, Andy had broken it, but luckily it didn't require setting.

"Who tried to stop you?" Donner asked.

"Andy Moore," Solomon answered.

"Colonel Moore's son?"

Solomon nodded.

"Why would he try to stop you?"

"I told him I was going to the media with the story about his dad."

Donner stirred sugar into his coffee.

Solomon admired the way the man acted so calm. He knew the story he was giving to the reporter was the kind that made careers.

"Have you been able to get a copy of the footage yet?" Donner blew on his coffee and took a sip.

"No," Solomon answered. He hadn't told Donner that he had the footage already. He never told anybody much till he'd negotiated all he could for himself. Besides, by acting like someone else had the footage, he made his role in the story seem even more clandestine. It fit his sense of importance. Plus, he didn't have to worry about the reporters coming after him until he was ready. He thought maybe someone had already searched his house, but he wasn't keeping the datascrip that contained everything at home. He still had his hiding places at school.

Donner nodded. "You know, Solomon, we're going to need a copy of this story before I can break it properly. I need to show that Colonel Moore was the one who set off the plague bomb in South Africa. You're going to have to give me solid proof."

"I'll get it," Solomon promised.

"Soon?" Donner pressed.

"Soon," Solomon agreed. *Soon enough. And I'm going to enjoy seeing Andy's face around Bradford after this story gets out.* It would be worse than any white adhesive bandage.

"Look at this."

Inside his home veeyar Matt glanced up at Mark, who was staring at a screen hanging in the air before him. Both of them were accessing the archived security tapes Mark's programming allowed them to get into.

The screen in front of Mark showed footage from the security vids that were shot around the school 24/7—round the clock, seven days a week. The present scene showed two of the after-school janitors mopping the floor and talking to each other.

"Janitors?" Matt asked doubtfully. He and Mark had been fast-forwarding through the archived vid hoping to see something fishy.

Sitting in midair the way Matt was, Mark nodded. "Yeah, but don't let the uniforms fool you. I've been watching these two. They're not exactly what you think they are."

Matt stared at the holo more intently. "What makes you say that?"

"Watch them. This is the part I found that shows it best."

Matt did. At first he didn't see what Mark was talking about. Then he saw how the two men moved. Even though they were just mopping the main hallway, they kept each other in sight. The mops hit the buckets regular as clockwork, and the work was evenly divided. Then Mr. Thomas, the science teacher, who sometimes worked late in the lab preparing lessons for the next day, came out of the door between them.

Both janitors went into motion at once, flanking the man in an obviously practiced maneuver that was so discreet Thomas never even noticed it. The mops were held across both janitors' chests and Matt knew they could be used as weapons in an eyeblink. Thomas just waved at them. The janitors went back to mopping without a word.

"Those," Mark said, "are Net Force agents. Or somebody like them."

Matt nodded, not doubting it. They had all the moves and they stayed paired up in a buddy system. Matt let out his breath. "Okay, something is definitely going on. Did you check out their IDs?"

"First thing." Mark opened windows in the veeyar. The personnel records of the two janitors scrolled through the windows.

"Let me guess," Matt said, "there's nothing outstanding about either man."

"Got it in one," Mark replied.

"How long have they been here?"

"According to their files, they're part-time help, brought in as needed, but they've been involved with the school for three years."

Matt considered that. "It stands to reason that since so many students at Bradford have parents involved in sensitive government operations, Winters would keep a semi-standing army to look out for things here."

Mark nodded.

"I've got something, too." Matt pointed at the holo he'd been watching. It also showed a man in a janitor's uniform. He was of medium height and build, with dark skin and short-cropped hair. "According to his file, this is Gordon Mbuta. He's one of the night cleaning crew."

"There's a name you don't hear often," Mark commented. "Where's he from?"

"Alexandria. American by birth."

"Okay," Mark said, "I'm puzzled. We have janitors *and* a night cleaning crew?"

Matt nodded. "Yeah. The janitors take care of the light work, the surface stuff. The night crew does the deep cleaning, buffs the floor, cleans the vents, stuff like that."

"What interested you in Mbuta?"

"Watch." Matt rolled the holo forward. "This is from Tuesday night."

In the holo Mbuta pulled an industrial floor buffer into a hallway. After plugging it in, the man grabbed the buffer's handle and switched it on. Without warning, the floor buffer jumped and the buffer pads grabbed the floor. Mbuta was slung around for a moment, then started battling the mechanical beast until he got it under better control. He cursed fluently with a heavy accent.

"He's better with the profanity than he is with that machine. He sounds British," Mark said.

"Not quite. It's derivative," Matt replied. "I think maybe it's South African."

"Maybe he got the accent from his parents."

Matt nodded. "I've looked into his files, and everything checks out. But I still think he's worth checking into. His file says he's worked here four years. You think he'd learn how to operate a floor buffer better in that amount of time."

"Okay. I'll search through the system and see if there's anything else I can turn up."

Now that the first, critical stage was done, Matt reactivated his phone interface. He normally left it on while he was in veeyar, just in case, but there were times he didn't want to be interrupted. This had been one of those times. But the worst was over now, so he set the system to route through emergency calls only.

The phone rang immediately.

Matt touched the icon and a window opened but remained blank.

"Hello," Matt said.

"Hey, it's Andy. Where've you been? I've been calling and calling!"

Matt started to answer, but Andy cut him off.

"Never mind—I've got a favor I need."

"Sure. What's up?"

Andy sighed. "Solomon's at a restaurant with a guy I need identified. I know the face, but I can't put a name to it. I thought maybe you'd know him, and if you didn't you could run him through the Net and see what you came up with."

"Okay," Matt said, "but you're going to have to open the vid on the foilpack."

"Yeah. Here you go."

The window in the veeyar filled with color, revealing the interior of a restaurant. The view shifted slightly, then Solomon and the man came into view.

Matt recognized the man at once. "Andy, I know him."

"Who is he?"

"Keith Donner. He's an investigative reporter for the *Washington Post*. What's Solomon doing with him?"

"Telling all, I guess," Andy said disgustedly. "He threatened to this morning."

As Matt watched, two men suddenly stood up from a back table. They wore suits with long jackets. When Matt saw their faces, he recognized them as McDouglas and Tomlinson, the Irish terrorists who'd seized him in the mall.

"Andy," Matt said, "those guys are—" He didn't have time to finish.

In the next instant McDouglas and Tomlinson pulled their jackets aside and yanked mini-Uzis from holsters. They aimed at Donner, never giving the man a chance. The bullets caught the reporter as he tried to stand, then drove him back against the booth. Solomon was a sitting duck.

Further back in the restaurant three men erupted from their seats and pulled weapons as well. Matt knew corporate executives and Congressmen frequently traveled with bodyguards in the city, either their own or ones assigned to them by the Justice Department. One of the men grabbed a fourth and hustled him toward a back exit. The other two opened fire.

McDouglas and Tomlinson moved quickly, staggering back as bullets slammed into them. Even injured, they returned fire, spraying the restaurant impartially.

Then one of the bullets must have struck the foilpack. The window in Matt's veeyar went dark and silent. "Andy!" Matt shouted.

There was no answer.

Matt ordered the computer to trace the call and got the restaurant's address. "I'm going," he told Mark. "I need you to call Winters and the cops and get them over there with reinforcements, then stay here in case we need anything on-line."

Mark nodded tightly. "Take care of yourself."

"I will." But even as he logged off the Net and returned to the school library, Matt knew that whatever violence was taking place at the restaurant would be long over by the time he got there.

And Andy appeared to be in the middle of it.

17

Andy dived beneath the table as gunfire filled the restaurant. When the explosive detonations slowed, the first of the screams from frightened people started.

He stayed on the floor, the tiles cool against his cheek. He couldn't call for help because a bullet from one of the bodyguards had smashed his foilpack, sending it flying from the table.

The two men who'd killed Donner didn't turn their weapons on Solomon as Andy had expected. They pointedly kept their fire away from him, exchanging shots with the bodyguards. Solomon wrapped his hands around his head and cowered in one corner of the booth. Donner's body lay sprawled across the booth's opposite side.

The bodyguards staggered back as bullets hit them. Andy knew their jackets or vests must have had some kind of Kevlar weave under them because they'd have been dead otherwise. As it was, he was sure one of them was injured—a nasty-looking wound in one thigh. That bodyguard was down, but the other one reloaded and spun around from cover. He kept his weapon aimed low and cut the legs from under both of the killers, knocking them to the floor. Before they could get up, the bodyguard rushed forward and fired point-blank into their faces.

Sudden silence filled the restaurant as the bodyguard swept the room with his hard gaze. Then he retreated back to his partner. He wadded up one napkin and tied it tightly against the wound with another—a rudimentary pressure bandage. Then he helped the wounded man to his feet. With the other man's arm across his shoulders, he exited as well, a trail of blood marking the passage of the two men.

Shaken, almost not believing the carnage that had taken place before his eyes, Andy crawled out from under the table. He pushed up and went to confront Solomon. "You okay?"

Solomon looked around the room fearfully, his chest rising and falling in shivering, rasping pants. "Where are they?" he gasped.

"Gone." Andy pressed his fingers against Donner's throat even though he knew it was a wasted effort. No pulse. Andy felt like throwing up. He'd been trained to check for pulses in critical situations, but he'd never touched a dead man before. He was suddenly dry-mouthed. People screamed in the background, but hardly any of it touched him.

The hostess approached cautiously. Shock masked her face. "Is—is he—"

"Yeah," Andy said. He scanned the ripped seats and bullet-pocked walls. Further back a row of potted plants had been shattered, and dirt and greenery scattered across the tiles. Some of the windows facing the street were heavily starred by bullet holes. "Call 911."

"It's already been done," the hostess said.

Other people started to gather. Two other patrons had been shot, but both appeared to be alive, though in considerable pain. Sirens screamed out on the street.

Solomon pushed himself out of the booth. Andy tried to block him, but Solomon shoved him with both hands and ran for the back door. Andy slipped in Donner's blood and fell. When he got back up, the crimson stained his palms. He ran toward the exit, following Solomon. Andy caught Solomon outside, easily outrunning him.

Solomon took off, jogging away from the restaurant.

Andy sped up and got in front of Solomon, blocking his way.

Solomon came to a reluctant stop. "Get out of my way!" He bunched his fists. "Or I'll take you apart!"

Andy reached for the rage that had been inside him that morning, hoping to fire it up again. He thought he'd have liked nothing more than to finish the fight he'd started with Solomon that morning. But the rage wasn't there. Only the image of Donner lying dead at the table filled his mind.

"You can't leave," Andy said. "The police are going to want to talk to you. Why did those men kill Donner?"

"How should I know?" Solomon tried to look angry or insulted, but mostly he looked scared.

"You know," Andy said.

"Hey," Solomon said, "for all I know those guys went there looking for Donner."

"Then why didn't they kill you?"

"Because they weren't after me."

"They shot two other people in there," Andy pointed out. "But around you they were really careful. They wanted you alive. They were there for you, Solomon. What have you gotten yourself into?"

"If they were after me," Solomon replied, "it's because of your dad. Because of the dirty little secret the U.S. government made up about him to protect themselves."

"Who?" Andy asked.

Solomon shook his head. "Even if I was sure it was me they were after, I wouldn't tell you." He took a step toward Andy. "Now get out of my way. I've got to get out of here before someone else shows up to finish what they started."

"If they came here looking for you," Andy said, surprised at how empty he felt, "and killed Donner to get to you, they're not going to stop. You won't be safe on your own."

"I've trusted me a lot longer than I've ever trusted anyone else."

Andy looked at Solomon, knowing he wouldn't try to stop him from leaving. Everything had come undone. There was no way now the story about his dad was going to stay hidden. Not with someone like Donner getting killed because of it. He held his hands up, showing Solomon the crimson stains on his palms.

"This is Donner's blood on my hands. It belongs on yours."

"Donner made his own choices," Solomon stated. He walked past Andy.

Andy didn't try to stop him. It was no use. The police would find him soon enough. He watched briefly as Solomon continued down the street, constantly glancing back over his shoulder.

Resigning himself, Andy headed back toward the restaurant, watching as the first police units arrived. It was all over. Or maybe just beginning.

As Matt climbed out of the cab he'd called to take him to the restaurant, he spotted Megan near the front of the building. It had been less than twelve minutes since Andy had called him.

"What are you doing here?" Matt asked as he walked up to her. A stern-faced policeman blocked the doorway.

"Mark called me," Megan answered, wrapping her arms around herself like she was cold. "He thought maybe it would be better if you had someone here with you till Captain Winters arrived. I was shopping not far from here."

Matt looked in through the restaurant's windows, but all he could see were more policemen and EMS people. "He's on his way?"

Megan nodded.

"Do you know if Andy's okay?" Matt asked. He hated the helpless feeling that filled him.

"No. I can't get an answer from anybody." Megan glared at the police officer blocking the door. "I heard somebody say maybe two or three people had been killed."

Matt immediately thought of Solomon. And Andy wouldn't have sat idly by watching a murder. He remembered the way the foilpack had gone blank, and knew it had been hit by a stray bullet. Maybe Andy had, too.

Tires screeched out in the street.

At first Matt thought it might be Captain Winters when he saw the luxury model Dodge SUV rocking as it double-parked, but then a thin gray-haired man got out. He wore a neat dark green suit and ran to the front of the restaurant. He unfolded a wallet and shoved it in front of the police officer guarding the door.

"I'm Gerard Walker," the man stated. "City editor for the *Washington Post*."

"I'm sorry, sir. No reporters are allowed." The police officer stood his ground. "We're securing the scene now, and no one's allowed in or out."

"I've got a man in there," Walker said. "A reporter."

Cars out in the street honked at the double-parked Dodge.

"Excuse me," Matt said. "You're talking about Keith Donner, right?"

Walker eyed him. "You're from Bradford?"

"Yes, sir."

"Were you the boy he was meeting?"

"No, sir. I just got here, but I know Donner was shot. I saw it happen. From what I saw, I'm afraid it looked pretty bad."

Walker's mouth formed a grim line, and he looked as if he'd been hit.

"You saw the shooting?" the police officer asked.

Matt nodded.

"You weren't inside this building."

"No, sir. I watched it over a vid-equipped phone."

The police officer tapped the ear/throat comm headset he wore and spoke briefly, asking for Detective Gray. He told Gray about Matt and Walker, and listened to the response, then gave a quick, "Yes, sir." He looked at Matt. "You're going inside." He pointed at Walker. "You, too."

"I'm here with a friend," Matt said, indicating Megan.

"No friends," the officer said. "I'll keep an eye on her for you."

Megan touched Matt's shoulder. "It's okay. Someone should stay out here to meet Captain Winters."

Matt nodded, knowing she was right. "If I find out anything about Andy, I'll let you know." He followed Walker into the restaurant. He smelled the blood and cordite at once. The scent was something that wasn't easily forgotten.

Somewhere, someone was crying. Voices rumbled throughout the restaurant, but the normal sounds of cooking and utensils banging was missing. The absence of the usual noises made the restaurant's interior sound hollow, cavelike.

"How did you happen to see Keith?" Walker asked. He strode through the restaurant, toward the back rooms.

"I was talking to a friend here at the restaurant."

"Was he meeting with Keith?"

"No." Matt spotted the EMS techs ahead. They were working on a woman about his mom's age. Her blouse had been cut away enough to reveal her side. The EMS techs were trying to staunch the bleeding from a wound below her ribs. Matt didn't think it was life-threatening.

Walker's gaze drifted up to the corners where the walls met the ceiling.

Matt knew the *Washington Post* editor was searching for security vids. He felt slow-witted. If he'd been thinking, he could have asked Mark to hack into the restaurant's security archives and get copies of what had happened. With McDouglas and Tomlinson involved, there was no doubt that Donner's killing tied back into the attempts at Bradford.

Walker approached the booth where Donner lay. Matt knew at once the reporter was dead. His wounds were all centered in his chest, and no EMS techs were working on him.

"Keith," Walker said raggedly.

There was no sign of Andy or Solomon.

"Matt Hunter," a deep voice boomed.

Matt turned as Detective Gray approached him. The big detective didn't look anywhere close to happy.

"You're going to tell me what's going on," Gray stated, "and you're not going to leave anything out." He dropped a big hand heavily on Matt's shoulder, bringing him along.

Together, they skirted the shooting area. Forensics people were nearly finished shooting flatfilm and holo of the scene. They left the expended brass, weapons, and dead men where they were. Those would be gathered and identified later. When it was all over, Matt knew the forensic teams would make vee-yars of the crime scene that detectives, attorneys, and even juries could walk through as it became necessary. He'd been through some of the ones in the FBI labs in Quantico himself as a Net Force Explorer.

Matt talked, holding nothing back. Finally, with relief, he spotted Andy at the back of the room being interviewed by a uniformed police officer. Andy's face was pale and wan, and he looked right through Matt.

"You don't know what Solomon Weist was doing talking to this reporter, Donner?" Gray asked when Matt finished.

"No, sir." Matt figured that was as close to the truth as he could get. Andy had thought Solomon was there to talk to Donner about his dad, but wasn't sure. Matt decided not to mention it. That was Andy's call.

"Is this Weist kid a hacker?" Gray asked.

"He had the skills," Matt answered. "What he'd been up to, though, I couldn't say."

Gray nodded and pointed at a booth by the window. "Sit down. I'll get back to you."

Matt did. He put a call into Megan, telling her that Andy was all right. Then he sat there watching the forensic people at work. They were good, thorough, and functioned well in the middle of the chaos that was scattered all around them. And he couldn't help looking at the corpses of McDouglas and Tomlinson. They'd been alive yesterday, Thursday, and threatening him. Somehow it seemed unbelievable.

"Detective Gray," one of the forensic people called out. He was working under the table where Donner's body was.

Gray approached. "Yeah?"

The forensics man opened his glove-encased palm to reveal a device smaller than a button. Matt recognized it as a miniaturized transceiver. He knew exactly what it meant. Someone had stuck it underneath the table and listened in on Donner's conversation with Solomon. The people who hired McDouglas and Tomlinson?

Gray hunkered down beside the bodies of the Irish terrorists, and called over a forensics man. After a brief discussion the tech took a similar button-sized device from McDouglas's ear canal.

"They were the ones listening to Donner?" Detective Gray asked.

The forensics man examined the tiny machine and shook his head. "Different channel set up. Your shooters were listening to someone else."

But who? Matt wondered.

Solomon stood in a candy store across the street from the restaurant. He had a clear view of the business and the police activity from where he stood.

His stomach rumbled. He hadn't had the chance to eat before Donner had gotten shot, and now he was standing in a candy store and was afraid to use his swipe card. The police would have his name, and they'd check all the electronic data on him, and he didn't want them to know he'd stood across the street watching them.

He knew he should go. But he still couldn't believe that Donner had gotten killed right in front of him. His hands trembled and his knees quivered when he thought about it. The killers had walked up so quietly, like it was nothing, and just shot him.

Solomon had never seen anything like it outside veeyar or holos. Acid burned at the back of his throat, and he thought for a minute he was going to be sick. He swallowed hard.

Why would anyone want to kill Donner? he wondered. *It can't be because of me, because of what I know. That's not worth killing over, is it?* Suddenly he wasn't so sure.

Maybe Donner's death was directly linked to his own presence there. *They could have killed Donner at any time. He wasn't that hard to get to. They got Donner and worked real hard to spare me. I caused this.*

He watched the uniformed police officers working to push the crowd of spectators from the front of the restaurant. They took red-and-white striped sawhorses from the backs of their cars and positioned them, linking them with yellow crime scene tape. The crowd moved back reluctantly. Three more media vehicles parked in the blocked street as well, disgorging reporters.

Solomon remembered what it was like looking down the barrels of the killers' weapons. He was never going to do anything like that again. He touched his broken nose. Andy might fight him, might even hurt him, but Solomon was certain Andy would never kill him.

But people like the two men who'd killed Donner, they would. Killing was as simple as breathing to men like that.

Suddenly Solomon had a hard time breathing himself, thinking about how deeply he might be involved. What had he done? Who was behind it? The American government wouldn't do something like that. Net Force might arrest him for hacking, but they wouldn't send assassins.

That leaves the South African government.

Icicles of fear pricked his spine, doing a quick tap dance all the way up to the bottom of his skull, so cold it made his teeth ache. But the South African government hadn't traced him, had they? If they had, he'd have been in trouble before now, wouldn't he?

Unless they hadn't known who he was until he arranged the meeting with Donner.

That thought started Solomon trembling again. *There's a way out of this,* he told himself. *There has to be. And I'm smart enough to figure it out.*

Despite all the attention on the restaurant across the street, he suddenly felt as if he was being watched. He glanced around the candy store, but no one seemed to be taking any interest in him. Still, he couldn't shake the feeling.

He left the candy store and headed out to the side street. He flagged down the first cab he saw. He had enough cash on him to pay for a ride out of the immediate area.

The feeling he was being watched was still with him when he settled into the cab's backseat. Feeling foolish, he turned and looked back over his shoulder.

A blue sedan pulled away from the curb, pacing the cab exactly. Two men sat in front.

Solomon almost threw up. He turned back around, breathing hard. It wasn't just paranoia. He *was* being followed!

18

"So do you want to tell me again why you were here?"

Andy looked at Detective Gray—it was Detective Gray now, not David's dad. Mr. Gray had a definite way of separating those two entities. If he hadn't already been through so much in the past few days and in the last few minutes, Andy figured he'd probably be pretty intimidated by Detective Gray.

"I thought I'd grab something to eat." Andy was hoping to keep the story about his father quiet. At least until he could get home and tell his mom about it. He wasn't hiding anything really. At least, nothing that mattered to the murder investigation.

"Here?" Detective Gray asked. His voice didn't exactly drip with sarcasm, but it was there.

"Yeah." Andy didn't back down.

Detective Gray looked at his audiocorder as if to make sure the chip hadn't miraculously filled in the few minutes they'd been talking. That was sarcastic, too. "You come here often?"

"I did today," Andy said. "I guess it was a mistake."

"Do you know who Donner was talking to?"

"Solomon Weist."

"And how do you know Weist?"

"He goes to school at Bradford. David's probably mentioned him."

If his son had, Detective Gray's face didn't show it. "Do you know what they were talking about?"

"They didn't have much time to talk," Andy said. "Those guys started shooting pretty quick." The corpses remained in the restaurant, but the wounded were gone. They'd been taken to hospitals.

"Hey, Martin."

Detective Gray looked up at his partner.

"We got the shooters. They turned up at the ER," the other detective said. "They were Terrence Sullivan's bodyguards."

"The lobbyist?"

"Right. Sullivan's in the parking lot in his limo—his guys got him out of here when the shooting started. He was here on business. When the gunplay started, two of his bodyguards put these guys down. They all say it was self-defense, and Sullivan and the witnesses here back them up. One of the shooters was pretty badly injured. He's headed into surgery. He was conscious when he arrived at the hospital, and was able to give a quick preliminary statement to a uniformed cop. Our guys at the hospital say that it was touch-and-go there for a while. The other shooter is heading to the precinct house now to give a full statement."

"Tell him the sooner the better." Detective Gray flicked his gaze back to Andy. "How do you know Weist and Donner didn't have much time to talk?"

Andy thought quickly, not wanting to give up the fact that he'd been following Solomon. "Solomon's not exactly fond of me. I keep an eye on him whenever he's around me."

Detective Gray nodded and made a notation in his notepad.

Andy had already learned to hate the notepad. Gray didn't write down answers there, he'd noticed. The detective wrote down questions. Andy braced himself for another round, knowing Gray's curiosity hadn't been satisfied.

"I don't think Donner set up a meeting with a Bradford student," Gray said. "I kind of get the feeling Weist set up the meeting with Donner. Have you got any idea why a *Washington Post* reporter would take a meeting with a Bradford student?"

"Maybe he was going to complain about the food in the

cafeteria?" Andy quipped. "But that's been done before."

Gray's eyes hardened.

"Detective Gray."

Recognizing the voice, Andy looked over at Captain Winters. The Net Force Explorers liaison crossed the floor, taking in the scene in a glance. Andy knew Winters would be able to accurately describe the scene later.

"Captain Winters," Gray said, standing. Although the two men were friends, Andy didn't have to be a detective to spot the animosity between them now. "I didn't know you could walk right through a police cordon."

"I think we've got overlapping interests," Captain Winters said.

"I've got three bodies, an attempted kidnapping, and an attempted murder in five days," Gray said. "What have you got?"

Winters didn't flinch from the question. "A high-security clearance." He paused to let that sink in. "And a Net Force Explorer who was almost in harm's way today. I came to check on him."

"Did you just happen to be in the neighborhood?"

Winters smiled. "Mark called me. If I'd been in the neighborhood, this wouldn't have happened."

Gray grudgingly nodded. "I don't want the kids involved in this."

"Neither do I."

Gray looked at him. "They aren't, are they?"

"Not at my request," Winters replied. "Matt certainly is, though, since he was nearly run down on Monday, and he's your kidnap attempt yesterday."

"How involved is he?"

"I don't know. I'm going to ask."

"And you'll let me know."

"You have my word on it," Winters agreed. "Can I get Andy out of here? He doesn't need to spend any more time around this."

"I was just asking him why Solomon Weist would have a meeting with a *Washington Post* reporter," Gray said.

"Can it wait?" Winters asked. "The boy's been through a lot."

"It can't wait long. The body count's too high."

"Wouldn't it be more useful to find Wiest and ask him?"

Gray nodded but looked at Andy. "If anything else comes

up I think I should know about, I know where you live. We'll go through this again when matters are a little more settled."

"Yes, sir." Andy got up from the table. He was vaguely curious about Captain Winters showing up there, but none of it seemed to matter anymore. What was he going to tell his mom?

"Do you know Solomon Weist?"

Matt looked at Gerard Walker and nodded. They stood near the back of the dining room near the main wait station. The smell of fresh coffee brewing drowned out some of the stink of gunpowder and blood. "He goes to school with me at Bradford."

The editor nodded, watching the forensics people move around the room. "From what I gather from the police officers, he seems to be missing. And he was sitting with Keith when he was killed." His sharp eyes stared into Matt's.

Matt remained silent. Trouble never seemed to get as big if he kept his mouth shut.

"You look like a smart boy," Walker said. "Would you be interested in finding Weist and talking to him? Finding out if he's interested in talking to me?"

"Why?"

"I'll pay you," the editor offered quietly.

Matt shook his head. "I don't think so."

The lines in Walker's face showed hurt from the loss he'd suffered. "Look, Keith was more than just a reporter to me. He was a friend. A good friend. We spent a lot of years together, covered a lot of stories, some big, some small. But they were all ours. I don't know if you can understand that."

"I think I can," Matt said, feeling guilty for not telling Walker what little he did know. But if he did, he might be making more trouble. And there'd been enough trouble to go around already.

"Keith gave his life for this story," Walker said.

Knowing he had the editor at a disadvantage, Matt felt a stab of guilt when he asked, "What story?"

Walker looked at him but remained silent.

"If I talk to Weist," Matt pressed, "I'll need to know what to ask him about."

"You're right." Walker shook his head. "Secrecy's second

nature in this business. I don't know the exact story Keith was working on, but I know it had something to do with South Africa."

At mention of the country, Matt's stomach tightened. Solomon had implicated Andy's dad in using the plague bomb. What if the story *was* true? *It can't be true. Not Andy's dad.* "What about South Africa?"

"Keith found out there was some kind of cover-up during the war. He didn't believe his source at first. After all, it was a Bradford high school student. Barely born before the war ended. Really didn't even remember it. But Keith started checking around based on some of the information the kid had gotten. Doors in Washington closed to him. Even doors that would normally be open because of his past history in reporting that war. Nobody was saying anything."

Matt knew that from Andy's own search. If a soldier's son or daughter started asking questions, even about ops that weren't quite in the public domain yet, there were ways of getting information to them. No one had even offered in Andy's case.

Walker took a card out of his jacket pocket. "If you find out anything, this is my personal number at the office and at home. Call me."

"Sure." Matt took the card and put it into a pocket. He glanced over at Captain Winters and saw him get Andy free of Detective Gray's interview. Since Solomon had been identified, the police would have no problem picking him up. Matt really felt sorry for Andy. Everything would come out then. Solomon would do anything to save his own skin.

Solomon fought the panic that threatened to pull him under. He stared at the cab's rearview mirror and tried to see if the blue sedan was still following them.

He cleared his throat. "Driver, I've changed my mind about the destination." He'd given the man his home address, but he didn't worry about that. Now that whoever was following him knew who he was, finding out the address would be no problem. So he couldn't go home anyway.

"Where to, pal?" the man asked tiredly. He definitely wasn't somebody in love with his job.

"Take a left at the light," Solomon said. "I'll let you know."

"Just so you don't let me know too late," the driver warned. "This cranky old beast don't stop on a dime."

"I won't." Solomon glanced out at the neighborhood. This was his home turf. The men trailing him wouldn't know the area nearly as well.

The cab made the light just as it turned green and cruised through the intersection. Solomon looked behind them.

The blue sedan made the left turn behind them, maintaining the same distance.

Sweat covered Solomon's face, and he had trouble breathing. But his mind worked quickly. The problem was he knew his mind was the quickest thing about him. Still, they were on turf he knew, turf he'd had practice running on before. He glanced at the trip meter. $9.12 already. He palmed a ten-dollar bill from his pocket.

He leaned forward, unsnapping the seat belt and setting off the alarm.

"Hey!" the driver protested.

"Pull over there." Solomon pointed to the right, in front of a small, family-owned convenience store. He'd known the Tran family most of his life.

The driver pulled over quickly and bumped up against the curb.

Solomon slipped the ten through the pay slot in the glass separating him from the driver. The driver managed one sarcastic comment about what a big tipper he was, then Solomon was out of the vehicle.

Solomon charged across the sidewalk and up the short flight of stairs leading into the convenience store. He spotted the blue sedan in the reflection of the plate-glass window under the faded red awning that faced the street. Three men got out of the sedan and took up pursuit.

It was Friday, and Solomon knew Mr. Tran would be checking the fresh fruit and vegetable crates he'd gotten in for the weekend. Mr. Tran ordered conservatively when it came to perishables. When Solomon had worked there in the summers, Mr. Tran had constantly explained that aspect of his business. No waste meant bigger profit, even if he had to pay more for more frequent deliveries.

"Solomon!" Mr. Tran cried out as Solomon whipped by. "Don't be running in my store!"

"In a hurry," Solomon apologized. "Sorry." He was breathing rapidly. He'd never been a long-distance runner. He sprinted through the convenience store, weaved through the aisles, and zipped toward the back room.

Three doors led out of the back room—one to the bathroom, one to the alley, and one to the room where Mr. Tran kept his guard dogs. Solomon unlatched the door to the guard dogs, opened it slightly, then slapped on it. The dogs barked and lunged. They ran into the stockroom just as Solomon slipped through the alley door and closed it behind him.

He turned to the right and ran down the alley, hoping the wooden fence to Mrs. Conda's backyard was still missing the planks it had been missing last summer. Luck was with him, or Mrs. Conda's procrastination. The planks hadn't been replaced. He squeezed through as the dogs growled and men shouted hoarsely. Gunfire cut through the neighborhood.

Solomon felt sorry for the dogs. But only for a moment. He wanted to live more than he wanted them to live. He ran through the unkempt backyard, dodged the clotheslines hanging from the drunken posts, and sped past the house.

Gasping, almost out of breath, Solomon ran across the next side street and went two blocks farther on. Black spots swam in his vision by the time he reached the Pulpmaster. The bookstore had started life as a two-bedroom house a hundred years ago, but for the last dozen years it had been a bookstore. The books had started out in the garage, but as Mr. Myers had kept trading two-for-one or half-price for cash, his book supply had grown. Now books swamped every room in the house except for the single bedroom Mr. Myers kept to himself.

Solomon ran toward the open mouth of the garage door. Shelves lined the walls, filling the room with the stink of old paper. Handmade bookshelves filled the center area. None of them were taller than a man sitting down could reach.

"Hey, Solly." Mr. Myers rolled out of the darkness between the stacks in his wheelchair. He was a big bear of a man with octagon-shaped glasses and big hands. He was a veteran of the South African War who'd lost his legs over there. But for the last handful of years, he'd been the guy who'd opened Solomon's mind to all the possible worlds in books, navigating him through dog-eared copies of science fiction and fantasy. "You running again?"

Breathlessly Solomon nodded. During those years, Mr. My-ers had also been his guardian. With his loud voice and an ax handle he kept on hand for people who made the mistake of trying to rob him, he'd chased off the other kids who'd intended to beat Solomon.

"Go on in the house," Mr. Myers said, flipping his ax handle from the wall and into his lap with practiced ease. "I've got some OJ in the fridge. Help yourself. If these guys show up, I'll chase 'em." He rolled himself forward, sitting just inside the garage entrance.

Solomon went on into the house, trying to slow his pounding heart. *Oh man, if those guys catch me, they're going to kill me.* He shook his head, still not believing it. *Over a stupid war no one should even care about anymore.*

He stopped in the cramped little kitchen, avoiding the book-shelves and taking a glass from the dish drainer by the sink. Mr. Myers did his own dishes, so everything stayed within reach. He filled the glass and struggled to think clearly.

Despite all his plans to really tear Andy Moore down with the story about his father, Solomon knew he didn't have a choice. For whatever reason, the South Africans were willing to kill him over those files he'd hacked. He only hoped they'd agree to leave him alone when he offered to give them back.

Andy rode out the gentle ocean swells on the pirate ship in his veeyar, watching the sun set. In the real world, it was late. His mom had gone to bed. So far Solomon's story hadn't hit HoloNet. However, Solomon hadn't been found.

And Andy hadn't found the guts to tell his mom what was really going on, either. Before bed he'd tried twice. He just didn't know how he was going to do it.

He had a window to the HoloNet in the veeyar, and for some reason it kept attracting the virtual pirates. They sat on barrels in front of it, watching. That surprised him. Only the first mate was programmed to let him know as soon as any stories about Solomon or South Africa broke.

Andy watched the curve of the water and tried to think of a plan. He'd talked briefly to Matt and Megan after Captain Win-ters had picked them up, but he hadn't been especially chatty. Thankfully they'd left him alone.

Another piece of luck was the fact that Captain Winters

didn't seem to be aware of the fight between Solomon and him. Or maybe he had something else on his mind. The Net Force Explorers' liaison definitely wasn't as attentive as he usually was. At least, that's what Matt and Megan had said later. Andy hadn't noticed.

"Cap'n."

Andy turned to the first mate.

"There's someone to see you, sir."

Andy walked back to the stern castle and touched the Net icon. A window opened up, revealing Mark in his cybernetic crashsuit. It looked more daunting than ever, filled with sharp planes now instead of rounded surfaces. Mark floated in the black sea that filled the Net.

"What's up?" Andy asked.

Mark grinned, floating weightlessly. "Going to crash a party. Want to join me?"

"I don't much feel like parties," Andy responded. "Maybe another time."

"Oh, I think you'll go to this ball, Cinderella."

Mark's flippant remark irked Andy. "Look, I really don't feel much like—"

"—like raiding the South African archives?" Mark asked. "I understand. Maybe another time." He saluted and started to drift away.

"What?" Andy exploded. "Wait a minute! Get back here!"

Mark turned toward him again, completely guileless.

"Since when did you decide to raid South African files?" Andy demanded.

"Since Matt and I turned up a lead that may take us there." Mark quickly explained about the janitor they'd spotted in the "borrowed" security vid archives.

Andy's excitement grew despite the fact that he hadn't slept well in almost a week. "How long have you guys been working on this?"

"Today."

"Why didn't you tell me?" Andy reached for the window in his veeyar and pulled himself through.

"When?" Mark asked. "While you were beating up Solomon in the hall? Or while you were getting yelled at in the principal's office? Or how about while you were busy getting shot at and interrogated by the police?"

"You've got a point," Andy admitted.

"And we didn't even know if the attempts on the hackers were related to what Solomon was doing. Not until we came up with the possible South African tie. We could still be wrong. But since I was going to be in the neighborhood anyway, I thought maybe you'd like to run with me."

"Sure." Andy heaved himself through the window opening onto Mark's veeyar and hurled himself off into the Net. He touched Mark's outstretched glove and saw the tiny spark of contact. Immediately a crashsuit like Mark's spread over him like an incoming tide. Andy felt around in the gloves, finding the suit controls in the left hand and the programming panel for the built-in safeguards and programs in the right. He'd made runs with Mark before, so the crashsuit was familiar to him. "How do you plan on getting in?"

"By knocking." Mark grinned. "Follow me." He jetted forward.

Andy pulled his arms tight against his sides and rocketed along behind him. The cyber towers of business, government, and religion stabbed up beneath him. When Mark aimed for the BelTelComm building in downtown Washington, D.C., Andy knew they were about to take electronic wing.

"Why didn't Matt go with you?" Andy asked. "This seems like the kind of thing you'd invite him to."

"I'm here." Matt's voice echoed inside Andy's helmet.

"Matt's our knocker," Mark said.

Andy was hot on Mark's heels when they rammed through the BelTelComm. Their trajectory changed at once as they sped through the telephone maze. They shot upward, blasting toward the sat-link infrastructure beginning six miles out. Andy lost count of how many times they circulated within the lines, following the path Mark blazed. The circuitry snapped and popped as he worked his way through it. The edged surface of the crashsuit allowed him to dig in.

Then they were streaking again, faster than ever. The Atlantic Ocean's representation stayed mostly a ruddy black, punctuated by the umbrella cones of brightness from sat-link units on the station that denoted Net-accessible points on ships at sea. The world blurred around them. In seconds they were in South Africa.

19

Andy wouldn't have known they'd arrived in South Africa without Mark telling him. In the Net, Mandelatown looked like just another metropolitan area. They passed through the South African comm-relays and streaked across the city representation. They halted just outside the tallest building in the city.

"The archives?" Andy asked.

"The government building," Mark corrected. "The archives are inside. I checked."

"So are we going in?"

"When Matt calls them," Mark said, "we're going to try."

"Try?"

"Hey, nothing's guaranteed. Worst case scenario, we get bumped and have to log off."

"How's Matt going to get us in?"

"He's going to call the South African government here and tell them he knows where the stuff is they've had their people looking for."

"Does he?"

"No." Mark's attention was locked on the building. "But they'll try to do a trace-back on his call."

"Where's he calling from?"

"A public booth downtown. Even if they manage the trace-back, they won't get anything useful."

Andy considered that, but it left one question. "You haven't said how we're going to get in."

"We're going to ride the bounce off the trace-back utility," Mark said. "We probably can't penetrate on our own without drawing a lot of attention immediately, but if we mask ourselves as part of the trace-back, we should get in."

"Guys," Matt called. "Ready?"

"Go for it," Mark said. He turned to Andy. "Stay with me or you'll never make it in."

Andy nodded. He heard the sound of a phone connection being made, then someone at the South African government offices answered. Matt launched into his spiel, demanding to talk to the man in charge of the American operation. The South African operator acted ignorant of any such operation, but when Matt threatened to hang up, the man handed the phone link along quickly enough.

A line of electric blue shot from the South African comm-relay to the government building.

"There's the phone signal," Mark said. He flew over to the line. Then he pointed as an amorphous dark blue mass nearly hidden in the electric blue shot out of the government building. "And there's the trace-back."

Andy watched the trace-back whip past him, accelerating so fast that he almost lost it.

"I'm locked on to it," Mark said. "Lock on to me."

Andy flipped the controls in his left glove, locking his crash-suit to Mark's.

"When it comes back by," Mark warned, "we'll be sucked into it and things will happen quick."

"I'm ready."

The blue trace-back returned almost immediately. And it seemed it now possessed a gravity field about ten times as great as anything Andy had ever felt. A momentary quiver of fear ran through him when he realized he had no control over his own movements. Instinct told him to log off, but he kept the urge at bay.

He and Mark dropped into the phone connection. Now it seemed like a tunnel nearly twenty feet wide. They stopped just short of the trace-back's surface as the rest of the Net blurred out of visibility.

"Heads up!" Mark warned. "There's the first of the security programs!" He shoved his hands forward and purple lasers burned into the small shapes that shot toward them.

To Andy the security programming looked like a school of gleaming metallic piranha. Their jaws opened, their serrated teeth caught blue points of light. He opened fire, using the crashsuit's onboard targeting systems. The lasers touched the piranha, and they vanished in wisps of foul-smelling smoke that somehow penetrated the crashsuit's defenses.

It looked neat. But the programming was actually more about stealth than about brute force—this was all just Mark's way of conveying visually what was happening electronically. The piranha imagery represented the computer's security program questioning their presence in this system. The lasers were streams of data that convinced the computer that they were normal traffic, packets of regular internal communications that the security program should allow through without question. It appeared to be working so far.

"Wow," Mark said appreciatively. "Now, that was interesting. Some kind of afterburn security. I'm downloading all this to look at later. It's something I haven't seen before. If the programming I used to make these crashsuits wasn't as good as it is, that could have been nasty."

Andy didn't even want to know how nasty. And all the piranha weren't gone. Three of them had slipped past his lasers and sunk their fangs into the crashsuit.

"Get them off!" Mark shouted. He was flailing at some of the metallic creatures that clung to him. "They'll eat their way through the suit! And if they do that, we're history in this system."

Andy slapped at the piranha, but they remained dug in. He tried pulling at them, but their sharp metal fins left deep cuts in his gloves. Thinking quickly, he slammed his hands together on one of them. Fracture lines showed in the piranha's steel-hard skin. He slammed them together twice more and watched all the fish spill away in parts. Bite marks scored his crashsuit.

In the background he could hear Matt's conversation with a South African man. Their voices were strangely distorted.

"Shield-grid!" Mark shouted. "Look out!"

Andy reached for the controls in his right glove and looked up just in time to see the glowing yellow square appear in front of them. The shield-grid was evidently the second line of defense. He only hoped Mark's programming was up to the task. He triggered the icon just before the trace-back swept through the shield-grid and they crashed into it.

A tingling vibration ran through Andy when he hit the shield-grid. If Mark's programming hadn't worked, if the machine hadn't thought they belonged there, their crashsuits would have unraveled and they'd have been thrown out of the Net. Instead, they seemed to burst apart into a cloud of bloodred atoms that peppered through atom-sized holes in the shield-grid. If even one of them hadn't lined up perfectly, they wouldn't have made it through.

The piranha clinging to Mark's crashsuit imploded with thunderous crashes. Thanks to clever programming, their host machine thought the piranha were the invaders, not them. And it had destroyed them—just as it would Mark and Andy, if it got the chance.

Andy reformed on the other side, and Mark was just slightly ahead of him. They remained locked on to the trace-back. Then it disappeared from view. For an instant Andy thought something had gone wrong, and in the next instant the world went away.

He blinked, realizing he was standing now. He gazed around at the small office around him.

"We're in," Mark said beside him. "Let's go." He took off at once, running for the door. "But we're not where I wanted us to be." He touched the doorknob, and white fog boiled up, turning into a demonic face. "Personal security on the office." He sounded totally cool as he touched the face. Ruby sparks shot out from the contact, and the face went way. Mark opened the door and walked through it.

Out in the hallway Mark conjured up a map of the building. How had he gotten *that*?

"We're not far," Mark said, closing the chestplate. He took the lead, sprinting down the hallway.

Andy ran after him, listening as Matt broke the connection. Klaxons suddenly screamed, echoing through the hallway.

"They know we're inside their system," Mark said. "But they don't know where. Yet." He ran to the end of the hallway and pushed open the elevator doors. "Now they know where we are—so let's move!" He didn't hesitate before dropping into the empty shaft as the car lumbered up from far below.

Andy jumped in after him, using the crashsuit's propulsion to stop his fall two stories down. The elevator doors there glowed. Mark touched the light, and it vanished, then the doors opened.

They ran down the next hallway and took the first right. Vaulted doors blocked their access. Mark slapped both hands on either side of the electronic lock holding them closed. Blue fire pulsed through his gloves, and the digital readout suddenly spun through itself in a series of at least a dozen numbers.

The doors ratcheted open. Mark's program had worked.

Mark plunged inside. The archive room seemed to be made of pure obsidian and was filled with towers that reflected neon colors.

Andy almost lost it when he saw how many vaults were in the archives. *How are we supposed to find anything in that in time?*

Wordlessly Mark stretched out a hand. Glowing red and white striped triangles tumbled from his palm and sped through the air. They attacked the archives at once, zipping through the files.

"Strainer program," Mark said. "One of the best I've ever designed."

The doors behind them suddenly whipped open with crashing booms. Andy wheeled around and saw the monstrous shape that filled the doorway.

It looked nine feet tall and at least that broad. It had a leathery lizard hide, but there was no mistaking the mechanical aspects of its internal structure and the gliding way it moved. Sharp fins stuck out everywhere.

"Now, that," Mark breathed, "is *ugly*."

And it was also quick. It slapped out a huge paw and knocked Mark reeling in a sudden storm of green sparks. Then living lightning seemed to wrap around Mark's crashsuit.

The creature turned its attention to Andy. Glassy, reptilian eyes fixed on him.

"Get the data!" Mark ordered. He grabbed the lightning in his gloved hands and yanked, breaking it loose. As soon as the current was broken, the lightning faded from view.

Andy glanced up at the archive towers and spotted winking strainer program triangles halfway up two separate towers. He leaped up and kicked in the crashsuit's propulsion system, lifting off just as the creature's talons screeched along the crashsuit's armor.

Mark wheeled toward him and threw his gloves out. Bands of three-hued green leaped from his hands and snared the creature, trapping it. But they didn't hold. The thing was too big and too strong. Angrily it launched itself at Mark.

"Get the files!" Mark yelled. "We have to get out of here! They're tracing our signature!"

Andy flew up to the two indicated vaults. He shoved his hand into the first one and triggered an upload program. His right arm seemed to become a huge-mouthed vacuum duct. Data fed into the crashsuit. He repeated the process with the other vault.

Mark's crashsuit came apart, crushed in the grip of the monster security program, and Mark was gone. Then the creature turned toward Andy. It leaped a dozen feet and more straight up, digging its talons into the sides of the vault tower. It swiftly climbed straight at him.

Andy finished copying the data just as it reached him. With relief he logged off the Net.

"There's a unit in the back you can use."

Solomon thanked the clerk, then turned from the counter and walked through the rows of computer-link chairs in the cyberbar. The bar was long and narrow, nearly all of the room taken up by the computer-link chair rental units. Neon tubing formed game characters, symbols, and design trademarks on the high walls. It was after midnight, but nearly all of the chairs were taken.

He dropped into the computer-link chair and swiped his Universal Credit Card through the reader. Even though people could track him through it, he didn't intend to stay on-line long enough for them to get to him.

Once the reader enabled the computer-link chair's systems, he slipped the datascrip he had with him into the slot. He leaned his head back and let his implants boot up. By the time he took his next breath, he was on-line. He wore his cyberhybrid proxy, and that gave him a little extra confidence.

The veeyar he'd constructed at Mr. Myers's was simple, consisting of an image taken from an ancient cartoon. He stood at the edge of a cartoon canyon, the colors bright and vibrant under the eternal noonday sun. A road led up to the edge of the canyon though he never could imagine why anyone would build a road there.

Solomon pointed at a nearby cactus, and it became a phone kiosk. He stepped inside and punched in the number for the South African government offices. When a woman's voice answered the call politely, he asked for the general's office. The woman hesitated for just an instant, letting him know that such a call through public channels probably wasn't an everyday occurrence.

Staring out at the broken land around him, at the canyons and mesa striped in cartoon stratas, Solomon tried not to think about how scared he was. Even going to a public place like the cyberbar had almost been too much. In the distance he spotted a whirling dust storm coming down the road.

"Hello," a deep voice replied in British English.

"Is this General Nkosi?" Solomon asked, knowing it wouldn't be. The South African military chief wouldn't be available to just anyone. But Solomon knew that the people he wanted to talk to would be listening in on the line. He tapped the phone, and a digital clock appeared on the face, the second hand sweeping around.

"No, I'm afraid the general is busy. I am Captain Mbeki. May I help you?"

"I wanted to speak to the general," Solomon replied. "I've got some information for him."

"May I inquire as to what?" the captain asked.

"About what's going on in Washington, D.C.," Solomon said, watching the clock. "And if you ask any more questions, I'm off here."

"I'll take care of this, Mbeki," a man said. The voice was smooth, uninflected and unaccented, someone who'd have no trouble crossing regions or countries and not standing out. "What information do you have?"

"Who am I talking to?" Solomon asked.

"Someone who has the general's ear," the man stated. "And I think that was what you were after all along."

Solomon grinned, feeling like the spy he played at being in

his own veeyar. And a successful spy at that. "Yeah," he said, "that's what I was after."

"What information do you have?"

"I think we both know I don't have any information," Solomon told him. "I'm the guy your people are looking for over here."

"Go on."

"Instead of information, I'm willing to make a deal."

"I'm listening."

"I hacked into your systems," Solomon said. "I'm willing to give back what I took."

"It may be too late for that," the man told him.

Too late? It can't be too late! Solomon flinched. "Then I can go to Net Force."

"Why haven't you already?"

"They don't know who I am. If I went to them, they'd want to know who I was. I think you'll deal with me as long as you get your stuff back."

"Perhaps."

Solomon stared at the clock. "I'm wasting time here, and you're wasting time trying to trace me. Even if you found out where I'm at, I won't be there by the time you get someone here."

There was a momentary pause. "Of course. What is your deal?"

"Let me give you the files back," Solomon said. "Then General Nkosi can order everybody to forget about me."

"How do we know you won't copy the files?"

"Because if I did, I'm sure you guys would find out about it and come looking for me again. I don't want that."

"Fine," the man said. "Send our files back to us, and we'll consider the matter dropped."

Exhilaration flared through Solomon. "I can't get to them now."

"When?" The voice had a distinctly unhappy edge to it.

Solomon got the impression the man only let him hear the emotion because he wanted to. "Tuesday. It'll take me till Tuesday to get everything set up." He wanted the extra time to hide and watch to see what happened. And he still wasn't entirely comfortable giving back the only leverage he had.

"When Tuesday?"

"Tuesday afternoon."

"We'll look forward to hearing from you," the man said. "I'll give you a number you can contact." He read it off.

Solomon made a pretense at writing the number down. There was no way he was going to use it. That line would probably be filled with all kinds of trace-backs and traps. They might even be able to triangulate his position before he could log off the Net.

"This is," the man said, "what do you call it there? A one-time opportunity. Don't waste it." He broke the connection.

Solomon looked at the dead handset, stunned. He couldn't believe the guy had hung up on him. That was what he was supposed to do, recognizing the guy was trying to hold him on the line. The people he was blackmailing weren't supposed to hang up on him. He got angry, but it quickly went away, replaced by cold fear. They were confident enough to hang up, and that was the bottom line.

The dust storm he'd spotted earlier came whirling by. Solomon recognized the familiar figure in the center of it as a roadrunner. The bird ran toward the edge of the cliff. Behind it, the coyote sat astride a blazing rocket, reaching for the roadrunner. Incredibly, the roadrunner stopped at the very edge of the canyon. The rocket spluttered and died a few feet past the edge. The coyote managed one heartsick look of disappointment before it started the long fall to the ground.

Solomon longed to stay in veeyar—not in the cartoon landscape but in a place he enjoyed. He knew that would be a mistake, though. He was certain that the man had unleashed a team to get him. Having him in hand was better than having to deal with him.

Far down below, the coyote *PLOPPED* against the hard sun-baked earth.

The sound echoed over the still land. Solomon knew he had to make sure he didn't meet the same fate. There was always another cartoon for the coyote. Solomon didn't have that opportunity. Tired and hungry, he logged off the Net.

Andy, Matt, and Mark stood in the shadows of the stand of trees around Site 43, waiting tensely. They'd searched through the hacked files after they'd returned to Andy's veeyar until they'd found the file dealing with the area.

When he'd seen the file marked so distinctly, Andy's hopes fell. He, Matt, and Mark hadn't talked as they'd loaded it into the veeyar.

Only a few minutes later the soldiers came into view wearing night-black. When they closed in on them, the weapons were definitely American. Even then, Andy didn't completely give up. He tried to see through the night's shadows but couldn't. Even if he could, he felt it would only be an exercise in futility.

It's all going to happen again, he thought.

The events unraveled. The lone figure in the protective suit crept forward to the plague bomb and set the timer. Then he tried to run back across the river only to be pinned down by fire from the enemy. The plague bomb went off. The figure went down, then checked his suit as the deadly gas rolled over him. A moment later the light revealed his face through the faceplate.

Andy recognized his dad, knowing the face even better after spending all the time in veeyar with Bob. "It was him," Andy said bitterly. "My dad did set off the plague bomb. Solomon called it right."

"Something's wrong," Matt said. "If the South African Nationalists had this, why didn't they use it when it would have made a difference in the war?"

Andy was beyond caring. "It doesn't matter, does it? They didn't. Maybe Solomon called it right when he said the Nationalists used it as bargaining leverage to stay in power after the war. What matters is that my dad was responsible for killing all those people." He thought again of his mom.

"The Nationalists wouldn't have held back," Matt told him. "Andy, I'm telling you this isn't right. We're missing something."

Andy spun on him, venting his anger and frustration. "We're missing nothing! It's all right here! You've seen it for yourself! From two separate sources!"

"From one," Matt stated.

"You don't know that Solomon didn't get his copy of the footage from someone else," Andy said.

"Then where else?" Matt demanded.

"I don't know." Andy watched the American Special Forces unit leave, running through the jungle. "It doesn't matter."

"It does matter. Don't give up on your dad, Andy."

Tears ran down Andy's cheeks before he could stop them, making him even angrier. "God, Matt, I can't hang on to the hope that he was innocent. Don't you see how stupid that is? He did it. He killed those people. All of them. And then he died himself a day later. I can't just sit here and deny it."

"You don't know this is the truth."

"And you don't know that it isn't."

Matt didn't say anything. He swapped glances with Mark, but Mark didn't have any help to offer.

"I never knew him," Andy said. "Neither did you." They stood in the epicenter of the swirling plague death. "Maybe it was better that way." He logged off before Matt could say anything else.

In his room Andy pushed up out of the computer-link chair. He retreated to his bed, sitting on it with his back against the wall. He put his forearms on his knees and pulled his head forward on them.

There in the silence of his room, he prayed that once in his life he could give up. It was stupid to think his dad was innocent. But his mom believed, so for her sake he had to go on.

Andy had always believed in his mom.

He was conflicted. It was one thing for him to give up, but how could he expect his mom to? And if she did, how much of her would be left?

20

Matt pushed away thoughts of fatigue as he trudged through the South African jungle. It was almost six o'clock on Tuesday morning. He'd fallen asleep last night at eight, prompting a worried flurry of questions from his mom about whether or not he was sick.

Then he'd woken at three, unable to sleep anymore. He'd gone to the computer-link chair, knowing his body would at least get a little more rest that way since his mind was going to stay active.

Over the weekend the Explorers had combed Washington, D.C., looking for Solomon Weist, who still hadn't been found. According to David Gray, the police were looking, too. They'd also questioned Bradford's hacker population, but that had been a blind alley, too.

At least nothing else bad had happened at Bradford.

Matt guessed maybe McDouglas's and Tomlinson's deaths might have something to do with it. Maybe whoever had hired them hadn't found someone else to hire, or maybe *it* had been found and returned.

Thinking like that made Solomon's disappearance even more interesting.

Matt's mind kept turning to the footage from August 12,

2014. Andy wasn't being sociable, and trying to talk to him about the footage came near to provoking a fight. Everyone had quickly given up trying. Matt felt bad for Andy, but he knew forcing the issue wouldn't help.

Instead, Matt focused on the footage. It was the only clue they had left that they could pursue. Mcgan and Maj were going over it as well.

He ran through the heat with the other members of the covert team. Sweat drenched him and made the BDUs stick to his skin. He carried an M-16, running just behind Colonel Moore after they'd jumped from the deuce-and-a-half.

Matt had been over the route a dozen times and more. The footage didn't show how the covert team had gotten into the area, but he assumed it had been by helo.

Except that didn't account for how the team had come up with the deuce-and-a-half. He'd tried pulling at that loose end but hadn't been able to go anywhere with it.

The crated bomb was left on the riverbank again, then quickly pried open. Matt was so tired that when he finally saw the discrepancy for the first time, he thought it was just his tiredness showing.

"Computer, freeze current program. Remain three-dee." After the computer shut the program down, turning the world to still life around him, Matt walked over to the crate. He'd been so intent on watching Colonel Moore that he hadn't paid too much attention to the other men.

Two men stood on either side of the crate, their pry bars locked in place.

One worked left-handed and the other worked right-handed. And they were in perfect synchronization with each other.

Matt had seen military teams that worked to develop that synchronicity, but none of them had ever hit it this exactly. He glanced at their faces and found their features weren't sharply defined. And they looked enough alike to be brothers.

"Computer," Matt called. "Identify subjects through military and civilian records." He waited impatiently, looking around at the faces of the other men and saw almost the same features. He tried not to get too excited. Maybe the program had been set simply to reproduce men without getting as exact as it had with Colonel Moore.

But the program had been built from the flatfilm, right? The men would have had real features. Or they would have had none if the camera couldn't identify them. The black camouflage cosmetic they wore on their faces would have thrown most people off.

"Unable to identify," the computer reported.

Matt wasn't surprised. He checked the time and found it was 6:20. Megan would be up by now, though probably not on-line yet. He gave her a call.

She picked up on the fifth ring but didn't include vid. "Matt? What are you doing calling so early?"

"I've been up for hours," Matt replied. "I need a favor."

"If it's not too impossible." She yawned, and the sound traveled over the connection.

"I need a copy of the report Solomon Weist turned in to Dr. Dobbs."

"Why? I thought you and Mark and Andy got the original."

"Yeah," Matt said, staring at the mannequin men around him. "I thought we did, too. But I want to check something."

"What did you find?" Excitement sounded in Megan's voice.

"You're welcome to come take a look."

"Give me a minute to brush my teeth and my hair, and throw something on."

"You could always wear a proxy," Matt offered. "I wouldn't know you were actually standing there out of whatever it is you're not wearing."

"You must be tired," Megan said. "One, for *ever* making a suggestive remark like that to me. And two, for ever thinking I would go somewhere and not be the best I could be. I'm uploading Solomon's report to you now."

Megan's *minute* actually turned out to be seven. By that time Matt had the second file running as well. He set up two veeyars, one for each version. By the time Megan arrived, he'd already confirmed his hunch.

"So what's up?" Megan crossed her arms, looking around the bush. "This place really creeps me out."

"Hang on while it gets creepier," Matt told her. He took her through the file Mark had hacked from the South Africans first. He showed her the same-face men who couldn't be identified. "I noticed them when I started paying attention to their movements."

Megan shrugged. "So what? Lots of programs produce stuff

like this. Sometimes details so far removed from the actual presentation would only get in the way of everything else."

"Yeah, I thought about that, too. But check this out." Matt opened a window in the veeyar and climbed into the other one. "This is Solomon's version." He guided her down the hill where he'd frozen the men into place with the crate.

"They've got faces," Megan said, seeing the difference at once. Understanding dawned in her eyes. "Solomon altered the files?"

"Evidently," Matt said. "Because if he took a copy from the South Africans, the men should look the same. I'll show you something else. Count how many men are around this crate."

Megan did. "Seven."

"Now check this out." Matt led her back into the South African version.

"Six," Megan said. "That's a big discrepancy."

Matt nodded. "Especially for someone like Solomon who's so anal retentive. He wouldn't have blown that."

"Wait, what are you saying?"

Matt bit his lip for a moment, hesitating to say his suspicion out loud. "I guess what I'm saying is that I think both these versions are false."

Megan brushed her hair back out of her face. She took a short walk down the hill, staring at the men. "That's a lot to say."

"I've got something else." Matt opened a window and stepped into Solomon's version of Site 43 again. Megan followed him. He walked back up the hill, away from the riverbank, and stood by one of the frozen men.

The man was thin and wiry, with Hispanic features.

"Computer," Matt said, "identify." He touched the three-dee man.

"This is Sergeant Diego Royo, assigned to special top-secret unit under Colonel Robert Moore in South Africa," the computer replied.

Matt smiled at Megan's questioning look. "Computer, can you tell me what happened to Sergeant Diego Royo?"

"Sergeant Diego Royo died in action in the South African War on August 3, 2014."

Megan's eyes widened as she looked at the man's holo. "Nine days before this. Then he couldn't have been here."

"Yeah."

"Maybe Solomon retouched the faces of the other men," Megan suggested, "working from past references, and he missed the news report about Royo."

"I'd buy that," Matt said, "except for the discrepancy of men around the crate. If Solomon had done that, I think it would have matched exactly. He's too careful about the things he does."

"Then how did the South Africans get their version?"

Matt drew a deep breath. "This is all speculation, but it's the best I've been able to come up with. I think Solomon hacked the South African computers and stole files that have to do with what really went on at Site 43. He used them to make up his own scenario."

"Why?"

Matt shrugged. "He and Andy had a history of bad blood long before this happened. I think he could have done it to get at Andy. After all, where the plague bomb came from has always been the biggest mystery of the South African War."

"So he hangs it on Andy's dad, who died over there." Megan shook her head. "That's so spiteful."

"Yeah, well, you know Solomon. He lives on spite."

Megan's brow knitted. "Where did the South African version come from?"

"I think they made it themselves," Matt replied. "They knew they'd been hacked. Maybe they knew Solomon did it. Or only that someone at Bradford had."

"And that's why those guys came after the hackers? And you?"

"It scans," Matt told her. "Only they couldn't find Solomon or didn't figure out who did it for sure. But they stayed close enough to the school to hear something about Solomon's report. Or maybe they picked it up from the conversation between Donner and Solomon."

"The listening device at the table."

Matt nodded. "So the South Africans created their own version of Andy's dad setting off the plague bomb."

"You think they want Solomon back so they can make sure the versions match."

"I think it's even bigger than that," Matt answered. "I think the South African government wants the files back because Solomon has footage of what really did happen that night."

Megan's eyes narrowed. "If you're right, Solomon's in a lot of danger. Maybe you should go to Captain Winters with this."

Matt shook his head. "Every time I've tried to talk to him about the situation at the school, I've gotten brushed aside. Either Winters doesn't believe something is going on, or he's all over it and can't talk about it. At any rate, I've got the feeling he wants us out of it."

"And we're the people who could help most," Megan said.

"That's what I think." Matt checked the time. "Hey, it's getting late for both of us if we're going to be ready for school on time."

"So what are we going to do?"

"I think we've got to find Solomon," Matt said. "Before the South Africans do."

Andy only answered the door because the knocking wouldn't stop. He had a headache that made his teeth ache, and was seriously considering staying home. When he was younger, he'd hated being sick because it meant staying home, and staying home during clinic hours had meant staying alone. When he had been sick, his mom wouldn't let him come to the clinic. He'd had way too much latch-key time in his life already.

He turned the peep panel translucent, saw Matt standing on the porch, and said, "Go away."

"Andy," Matt said, "we need to talk."

"Can't talk." Andy coughed into his hand. "Sick. Contagious. Probably lethal."

"Open up and I'll take my chances."

"They're bringing a quarantine tent over in a few minutes. You don't want to be there when they get back." Andy opaqued the peep panel again.

"C'mon," Matt said. "We don't have much time."

Andy checked his watch. "You're going to be late to school."

"Not if we hurry. You may as well let me in. I'm not leaving."

Resigned to his fate, Andy opened the door. But he only opened it a little. He blocked the way in. "What?"

"We need to talk about that footage Solomon showed the strategic analysis class."

"I don't." Andy didn't move.

"All right," Matt said, "I'll talk and you listen. Did you look at the South African version much?"

"Now you're involving me in the talking. I only agreed to listen. Actually, I didn't even do that."

"Did you look at it?"

"That one time you were here," Andy replied. "I've seen it enough."

"No, you haven't." Quickly Matt pointed out the discrepancies he'd seen and explained his theory about the two versions.

Andy listened and tried to believe. But he couldn't. "You're reaching too far. Why would the South African government have kept quiet about the plague bomb, anyway?"

"They did," Matt pointed out.

"Look," Andy said, "I appreciate you coming out here all this way—"

"Only because you wouldn't answer your phone." For once Matt seemed put out.

Andy didn't really care. It was hard to find anything to care about right now. "—but you've just wasted your time."

Matt shook his head. "Man, you're stubborn."

"You say that like it's a bad thing."

Matt checked his watch. "I've got to go or I'm not going to make it." He spotted an autobus coming down the street and started for the curb to meet it. "Check out the South African version, Andy. That's all I'm asking. You'll see it's a fake."

Andy stood in the doorway and watched as Matt boarded the autobus. When it drove down the street, he sat in the doorway, still dressed in his pajama pants, and tried not to feel alone. The morning breeze was chill enough to prickle the skin on his bare back.

Matt, I wish I could believe. I really do. But he was just so empty. He sat in the door for a long time, letting the street noises into the house because it didn't feel as lonely that way. Finally he got up and shut the world outside.

Matt arrived late to class, something he hardly ever did and totally hated. Then he spent class time chafing, waiting till he had the opportunity to talk to people who had dealings with Solomon Weist. Solomon didn't have any friends, which, despite everything, made Matt feel kind of bad for Solomon.

It wasn't until lunch, when he was talking to Nathan Griff, one of the school's crypto-geek crowd, that Matt heard about Lewis Winston.

"You want to know about Solomon?" Nathan asked. He was thin to the point of emaciation with a mop of thick brown hair. "Go ask Lewis Winston."

"Why?" Matt asked as they walked through the school parking lot. He'd had lunch with the other Explorers to compare notes. No one had turned anything up, and Solomon still hadn't shown up at school.

"Because Lewis had a sister that Solomon wanted to go out with two years ago," Nathan said. "She didn't like him, so there was no way that was going to happen. Solomon got mad at her and hacked the school computer. He changed all her grades at the end of that semester and flunked her in every class. It got her in trouble with her parents big-time. Lewis went after Solomon and made him fix everything. And Solomon never messed with either of them again."

"How did Lewis do it?" Matt vaguely knew Lewis Winston.

Nathan shrugged. "Nobody ever found out."

Andy stood in the jungle with Bob at Site 43. Pain gripped Andy's chest tightly. He'd promised himself that he wouldn't go through the agony of watching Bob anymore. But he'd made that same promise on Saturday, Sunday, and Monday as well.

Now, here it was Tuesday, and he was with Bob again. And if nothing changed, he was going to blame Matt. Andy had really thought he could manage one day without Bob in it.

Over the weekend he'd gone through other aspects of his dad's past. He'd gone through part of boot camp with Bob, through a few of the offices' candidate school classes, and through missions his dad had been on that weren't classified. There weren't many, and most of the ones that were public had become public at the time.

Everything Andy had seen had pointed to his dad being exactly the kind of man his mom had fallen in love with. But he still couldn't see past his own pain where his feelings for his dad were concerned. Colonel Robert Moore had chosen dying for his country over coming home to his wife and son. Andy just couldn't do the math on that one.

"Computer," Andy called out, "bring up the Site Forty-three two-point-oh program."

The terrain around them shimmered as the veeyar integrated the other program.

"What are we doing here, sir?" Bob asked.

"We're trying to understand what happened here."

"Part of your questions for your debrief, sir?"

"Yes," Andy snapped, scanning the village and the Nationalist tanks.

"I didn't mean to intrude on your thoughts, sir."

Looking up at the holo of his dad, Andy had a sudden attack of guilt. All weekend he'd been hard on the near-AI, badgering him every chance he'd gotten, demanding to know why he'd done everything he'd done. During those times, Bob had calmly called him sir, maintaining a professional air. He couldn't stand it any longer.

If Matt was right, Andy thought grimly, *I was totally out of line while I was doing that.*

"Computer," he said. "Adjust the personality and relationship parameters within subprogram Bob. Redefine as father-son. Execute."

A shimmer passed through Bob.

"Hello, Andy." Bob appeared more relaxed and more animated.

"Hello, Bob."

Bob nodded toward the bush beyond. "Want to explain what we're doing here?"

"Watching film footage of the plague bomb's delivery at Site Forty-three. Do you remember it?"

"No. Only what I saw in the news." Part of Bob's programming had included the media stories about the war, including the bomb. Since no personal memories had been available there was no way he could remember his part in it.

"Watch," Andy urged.

The team rushed from their positions and across the riverbed like they did every time. The crate was opened and the bomb armed. Then the firefight, the explosion, and Colonel Robert Moore's face revealed. But in this version it wasn't the breaking up of cloud cover that lit the scene. It was a spotter light mounted on one of the tanks.

Matt didn't catch that one, Andy thought.

"Andy," Bob said, "this is wrong. I didn't do that."

Andy looked at him. "This is proof that you did."

"No," Bob protested hoarsely. "That plague killed five thousand men, women, and children. Almost all of them innocent civilians. I couldn't do that."

The Special Forces group disappeared into the bush, leaving Andy and Bob standing in the spreading plague cloud that had no effect on them. "This is proof that you did," Andy repeated.

"Why would I do something like that?" Bob asked.

"Because you were ordered to. You told me yourself that would be the only way you'd do this."

"Yes, I told you that. And at the same time I told you that the U.S. government, the government that serves the country I've loved all my life, would never order me to do something like that."

"But what if they did?" Andy pressed. "What if you were ordered to set off that plague bomb?"

"They wouldn't do that."

"What if orders were somehow sent, maybe even faked, that you received?"

"Even in covert ops," Bob replied, "there are sources we can check. If I thought something was wrong, I'd check it out. All it would take is one *no* to halt a mission. Andy, what you're talking about, it just couldn't happen."

"But if they did?" Andy asked. "What if you were ordered?"

"There was no reason for them to order me to do that. We were winning the war."

"The plague bomb ended things earlier," Andy said. "It saved time."

"It didn't save lives," Bob pointed out.

"It might have saved American lives," Andy agreed. "As well as the lives of any of the soldiers the Western powers had in the area. Their lives were saved when the war ended early."

"They wouldn't do that," Bob repeated.

"It was war," Andy said. "Anything goes in war."

"No. That's why we have rules. That's why honor is so important in war."

"Honor?" Andy lost it. There'd been too many images of his dad, too much evidence of all that his dad had thrown away for them by making his selfish decision. "Was that what kept you on that bridge near Mandelatown when you died? Honor?"

Bob looked at him with his dad's eyes. "Yes, Andy, it was."

"Honor for yourself is pretty selfish, don't you think?" Hot tears fell on Andy's cheeks. "You made that decision, and Mom and I didn't get a vote."

"You'd have had me come home?" Bob asked quietly.

"Yes."

"Knowing I'd left some of my boys behind to die?"

"You *died*!" Andy shouted. The existence of the two versions of what had happened at Site 43, neither of which slotted into the events the day his dad died, left him feeling even more confused than ever.

"And how do you think the men under my command felt, Andy? Do you think they felt good about my dying?"

Andy didn't have an answer.

"If I had come home, if I'd decided to look out for my own neck instead, what kind of man do you think I'd have been? You can't live in the shadow of honor, Andy. It's too thin and cold. If you're going to live, it's got to be *with* honor. That's how I've always lived. And that's how I died. What do you want from me?"

Andy struggled to speak. "I just want to know that you thought about me, that somehow I mattered."

"I did think about you, Andy." Bob's eyes glistened wetly. He stepped forward and put his arms around Andy, hugging him tight. "I thought about you then, and every time I relived that night again and again in this veeyar."

Andy resisted at first, trying to keep himself distant from the sim, then threw his arms around Bob and held him tight. He felt sorry for Bob, for all the things he'd made the near-AI do in the veeyar. Bob wasn't human, but in the veeyar he experienced feelings like a person.

Andy also realized that the hug he was getting now came from Bob, not his dad. He gently broke out of the hold and stepped back. "I know you thought about me, Bob, but I still don't know if my dad did."

"Of course he did." Bob stood in the shadows, and even the darkness didn't hide his pain.

"I hope he did," Andy said softly. "Computer, erase subprogram Bob."

"Are you sure?" the computer asked.

Andy looked at Bob. Neither one of them needed to go

through the sims again. It was too hard for both of them. And he had all the answers he was going to have. "I'm sure."

The veeyar shimmered as it started to dissolve. Bob waved. Andy logged off before the holo actually disappeared, unable to watch it happen.

21

"Hey, Lewis, wait up," Matt called. Bradford's halls were filled with students headed for their sixth-hour class. Only two more periods and school would be over for the day.

Matt felt pressured. He was certain Solomon's house had been searched by the South Africans, so if the files they were looking for had been there, they had to be gone now. The next most likely place Matt felt Solomon might have hidden them would be at the school. It made sense—Solomon used the school's computer facilities a lot, and he was the sort of guy who'd want his little trophies handy to gloat over.

Lewis Winston turned around. "Hey, Matt." He was short and athletic, with curly blond hair and brown eyes.

"I've got a question to ask you." Matt maneuvered them over to the side of the hallway where they could talk.

"Sure."

"I found out today what Solomon Weist did to your sister by hacking into the school's computer," Matt said.

An angry look filled Lewis's face. "Who's been talking? That story wasn't supposed to be getting around, and it's old news. Tina doesn't need to hear anything more about it. Has Solomon been talking?"

"No," Matt answered. "This is important. The guy who told

me did it in confidence. I'm not going anywhere with it."

"I should have kicked Solomon's butt back then. Tina was devastated. She works really hard for her grades. Solomon knew that. He knew she'd figure she'd just blown it, and my parents did, too. Until I found out what was going on."

"That's what I need to know," Matt said. Students continued to flow around them, totally wrapped up in their own worlds. "How did you find out, and how did you stop him?"

"I didn't figure it out at first," Lewis admitted. "I thought maybe Tina had blown it, too. See, Solomon had been asking her out, but she'd turned him down. Then she started dating another guy, got a real crush on him. It made Solomon even madder, and it really got Tina's head out of the books maybe more than it should have. That's why everybody thought Tina had just messed up."

"But you found out different," Matt said, aware that the bell was going to go off at any minute. And he was so close.

Lewis nodded. "Once I thought maybe Solomon was behind it, I started following him around. He's a really sneaky guy."

"I know," Matt said.

"I hate creeps like that," Lewis said. "Anyway, I knew that pounding Solomon probably wasn't the answer. Over these past years, he's learned how to take a beating and still be stubborn about it. I think he'd rather die than give in to somebody."

"The bell's going to ring in a minute."

"Yeah. Anyway, I knew I needed something on Solomon if I was going to get him to back off. So I was following him, and one day I followed him down to the school's boiler room. He didn't know I was there. But he had a datascrip with him that he didn't have when he came out."

Mark nodded, feeling his heart rate increase.

"So I went inside, did a little checking around, and found this hiding place he has."

"Where?"

"There's a vent at the top of the north wall. Evidently they reconfigured the vent system at one time because there's an orphan duct about a foot back. It's shut off at the other end and just kind of there, so it's protected. I found the datascrip in there and checked through the files. I found Tina's real grades and copied them. Then I put the datascrip back and told Solomon I'd hacked the school's off-site backup computer—

which has got to be impossible even if you could find it—and found the real grades. I told him to fix it or I'd go to the admin office and have his butt fried."

"Why didn't you do that anyway?"

Lewis shrugged. "You know what a creep Solomon is. You heard what he did to Andy Moore, about his dad?"

Matt nodded, remembering how bad Andy had looked that morning.

"It was better to leave Solomon hanging, knowing that at any moment I could make him take the fall. It felt good just to watch that creep squirm," Lewis said. "Now Solomon stays completely away from Tina and me. If I'd let the admin office deal with him, he'd have been looking to get even. That's just the way he is. This way I'm one up on him and he has to leave me alone."

"Thanks, Lewis." Matt turned to go, his mind already flying.

"Hey," Lewis protested, "you never did say why you needed to know that."

"Tell you later," Matt promised. "Gotta go." He moved quickly through the hall, just below a sprint that would have drawn teachers' wrath. He caught David Gray before he entered his sixth-period class. "I need to borrow your laptop. I'll give it back to you after school."

Even though David did most of his work on the Net from a computer-link chair, David also did a lot of programming while he took the autobus to and from school, and during rides to the swim meets he attended. During swim season he made sure his programming skills stayed sharp. The laptop was awkward for anyone used to the Net, but Matt knew it would be good enough for his purposes.

"Find something?" David asked as he passed the laptop computer over.

"If I did," Matt told him, "you'll be the next person to know." He said goodbye, then headed for the school's boiler room as the last bell rang.

The afternoon crowd in the cyberbar was thin, confined to die-hard on-line gamers prowling the Net. Solomon took a seat in the back and fed in some of the cash he'd gotten from selling some hacker programs he'd devised to people he knew.

His programs were worth the money, but he seldom sold

them because sometimes Net Force could trace them back to
the originator rather than just the person who used them. The
last thing he wanted was to lose privileges to the Net. Veeyar
and the Net offered him the only life he'd ever really wanted.
But he hadn't had much choice this time. He needed the money.

He laid his head back and felt the buzz of connection as his
implants fired. He used one of the generic veeyars the cyberbar
provided to operate from. After Friday night the South Africans
would know he was hanging out in the city, not using his home
veeyar.

Inside the veeyar he tapped the phone icon and subvocalized
the South African government number he'd used before. The
woman who answered barely had time to say hello before the
man he'd talked to before got on the line.

"You're not calling on the line I requested," the man said.

"I lost the number," Solomon lied. *How can you argue about
irresponsibility with someone who's hacked state secrets?* "So
I called this one."

"Where are the files?"

Solomon drew a deep breath. "Once we're finished here,
that's it. Right? You'll leave me alone."

"There were some who felt that punitive damage should be
dealt to you or your family."

"That would be a big mistake," Solomon said. "I don't have
any family I care about and you would only draw attention to
you and me. And remember that I got into your systems once.
You people aren't Net Force. Last time I took something I
wanted to use. Imagine if I got into your systems on a wilding
spree? Even if you take me out, I can leave behind all kinds
of nasty surprises where you'll never find them, surprises that
will keep your computer systems in chaos for weeks at a time.
And if you mess with me, that's exactly what will happen."

"I don't like threats."

Screwing up his courage, grateful the veeyar gave him the
opportunity to be more in control of himself, Solomon said,
"Don't think of it as a threat. Think of it as a promise."

"Then let me give you a promise," the man said coldly. "If
these files should turn up again, you will be found."

Solomon knew the man didn't have to say anything more.
"Then we have a deal."

"Yes."

"The datascrip with the files is at school. In the boiler room." Solomon told him where.

"Good," the man said. "I'm sending someone there now. If he doesn't find it, I'll make you another promise. My operative has planted a bomb at Bradford. He will set if off and blow up both the school and your classmates. That will be your notice, my friend, that you are next. Now I ask you one last time: Are you sure that's where this datascrip is?"

Stripped of his confidence, Solomon could only answer, "Yes."

All the plans he'd set in motion over the last few days—the money he'd gotten together by selling the programs, the deals he'd negotiated to get him out of Washington, D.C., for a time—were all for nothing. If Bradford Academy blew up, the police would be after him. The South Africans would be after him, too. He'd be alone, running for his life, with none of the bright future he'd always figured would be his ahead of him. It wasn't fair.

"What?" the man said. "I'm afraid the connection isn't too good."

"I said yes. It's there."

"Don't try calling the school. If you do, the bomb will be set off. If we see any sign of students leaving early, the whole place goes up."

"What if they have a fire drill today?" Solomon protested. "They do every now and then. I don't have any control over that."

"Then pity them," the man advised. "But it will be over soon. My operative is already on his way." He broke the connection.

Solomon logged off, totally afraid. He wanted to call the school, but he didn't dare. If he did, everyone could end up dead anyway. And as long as the datascrip was there when the South African operative went for it, it didn't matter anyway. Right?

The datascrip was there. He concentrated on that, then he left the cyberbar in case they had traced the call.

Matt stood on a folding chair and peered into the air duct. He held a penlight in his mouth. He'd found the side duct Lewis had told him about, but it was empty. The penlight's beam shone into the empty cavity. He ran his arm into it to make sure it was as empty as he'd thought. He even checked for false panels.

There was nothing inside except a light layer of dust.

He brushed his arm off. At least the dust meant that no one else had been there, either. He stepped down from the folding chair and switched his penlight off. He glanced around the boiler room.

The boiler was huge, holding a thousand gallons or more of hot water. Even across the room the heat from it brushed against Matt. He heard the hiss of gas feeding the flames under it.

Matt tried to remain calm, but it was frustrating. Still, he reasoned, if the boiler room was a favorite place of Solomon's to hide things, maybe he'd just chosen another hiding place.

Dropping to his hands in push-up position on the cement floor, Matt peered under the boiler. Datascrips could take exposure to heat and cold, and no one would want to stick an arm under the unit with all the heat coming off it. But there was nothing under it except dust bunnies.

Meticulously Matt covered the floor first, looking under the lockers and the stack of folding chairs in the corner. He looked through the cleaning chemicals closet, even checking the open boxes. The ceiling was solid cement, so there were no hiding places there. He used the folding chair again to examine the light fixtures. All his efforts resulted in zilch.

Frustrated, he put the chair away, trying desperately to think of another place. Then, almost lost behind the boiler's bulk, he spotted the four-inch gas main pipe running down the wall. Beside it was an auxiliary light switch.

The light switch caught Matt's eye. The light switch panel was stainless steel, but dozens of scratches marred the surface. He glanced back at the one near the boiler room door. The light switch panel there was almost like new despite being the one probably most often used.

An idea formed in Matt's mind. He returned to the cleaning closet for a Phillips screwdriver in the tool chest he'd spotted. Stepping behind the boiler, he quickly unscrewed the scratched panel, then placed the screwdriver and panel in his back pants pocket.

"Oh, yeah," he breathed when he shone the penlight inside the revealed cavity and spotted the two-inch datascrip cube tucked in behind the black and white electrical wires.

He hooked the datascrip out with a finger and took it from its protective case. He retreated to the door and picked up David's laptop. He switched the unit on and inserted the datascrip, bringing the files up quickly. They were huge.

A footstep dragged on the carpeted stairs leading down to the boiler room.

Matt glanced at his watch, seeing it was almost time for seventh period. He'd searched for almost an hour. The afternoon janitors would be starting their rounds. He looked up, thinking he was going to have to explain himself to one of the school's janitors.

Instead, the night maintenance man he and Mark had noticed on the security vid glanced at him. A spark of recognition glinted in his dark eyes. His hand came out of his overalls pocket with a 9mm pistol that he pointed squarely at Matt's chest.

Andy dropped into a seat in his sixth-period class behind David after giving the teacher his admit slip. He felt better about coming to school. Home wasn't fun right now.

"Nice to see you could make it," David whispered dryly.

"Better late than never. Is Solomon here today?" After seeing the South African version of Site 43, Andy had decided no matter what it took—even expulsion from Bradford—he was going to beat the truth out of Solomon.

David shook his head. "MIA again. It's not like him."

The bell rang and all the students lurched up from their seats.

"What about Matt?"

"I saw him before class when he came and borrowed my laptop."

"Why'd he do that?" Andy followed David through the press of students and out into the hall.

"He didn't say. Told me he'd get back to me if he found anything out."

"Do you know what he has this period?" Andy knew David kept up with who was where much better than he did. David and Matt sometimes studied together.

"Psych. At the end of the hall. Lewis Winston has that class, too. I saw Matt talking to Lewis in the hall before he borrowed my laptop. If you find Lewis, you might find Matt."

Andy said thanks and sped off, weaving through the crowd easily. When he got to the psych class, Matt wasn't there, which wasn't like Matt at all. Andy glanced back in the hall and spotted Lewis. "Hey, Lewis. I want to talk to you a minute."

"What?" Lewis asked, walking beside a pretty redhead. "I'm kind of busy walking Nan to class."

Now there's a polite way of telling somebody to butt out. Andy fell in beside Lewis anyway. "I'll only take a minute. I'm looking for Matt."

"Matt Hunter?" the redhead asked. "He wasn't in last period. Maybe he went home."

A warning tingle shivered through Andy. He shook his head. *Not after borrowing David's laptop.* He pinned Lewis with his gaze. "We need to talk."

"I'm busy."

"Lewis," Andy pleaded, "I'm serious. I need to know whatever you talked to Matt about. This is important." He stepped in front of Lewis.

Lewis clearly didn't look happy.

"Talk to him," the redhead said. "I'll see you after school."

Lewis watched her walk away. "Man, Andy—"

"I'll get you tickets to a holo this weekend to make up for this minute or two," Andy promised. "Now tell me."

"You have the datascrip?" the night maintenance man asked after the period bell finished ringing.

The bell had sounded so unexpectedly that Matt had almost jumped out of his skin. "I don't know what you're talking about."

"Yes, you do," the man said. "You don't lie very good." He waved the pistol slightly. "Put the laptop down. Turn around and face the wall. Place your palms against the wall. I'll use this if I have to."

Having no choice, Matt did as he was told. "You're from South Africa, aren't you?"

"Yes. And since you know that, you know I'm more than willing to kill you." The man was a professional. He stayed well clear of any quick move Matt might make, and kept the pistol aimed right at his target.

Glancing over his shoulder, Matt watched the man look at

the files displayed on the screen, then take the datascrip from the laptop.

The man put the datascrip in a protector, then in his pocket. He slid the laptop away with a foot. "If you move from the wall, I'll shoot you, then destroy the datascrip. I'll take my chances with school security. Understand?"

Matt nodded.

"Good." The South African agent crossed to the boiler. He took something from inside his overalls and reached behind the boiler. "Come here, boy. Slowly."

Matt turned, keeping his hands up. He looked for an opening, but there wasn't one. The South African was very cautious.

"Look behind the boiler. I want you to know what the stakes are going to be in this little game we are going to play."

Matt peered behind the boiler. He spotted the rectangular shape beside the gas main pipe immediately. The top of it looked extremely sophisticated and had a computer comm-link jack on it. The blank digital readout suddenly flared into motion, starting at 15:00 in black numerals on a gray field, then changed immediately to 14:59. The countdown continued.

"That's an explosive," the South African told Matt. "Two separate charges. A small one first, to break the pipe. Then, after the room fills with gas, another to ignite the gas." His face never changed expression. "From what I'm told, it will level this entire building."

"You can't do that," Matt protested as the full impact of what the bomb could do filled him with horror.

"It's already done. If I'm not out front in that time, the bomb will go off. If anything happens to me before the time runs out, the team outside will detonate the bomb themselves. I'm carrying a dead man's switch on a remote control, so I can set the bomb off at any time, if I'm not happy with the way things are going. If somebody hurts or kills me, or even if I just loosen my grip on the switch, the bomb will go off. It'll blow if anyone attempts to pull the explosive from the gas main." He paused. "All that matters is getting this datascrip out of the building and back to my country, or destroying it. Your friends don't have to die to see that done. We can disarm the bomb if you play ball."

"What do you want me to do?" Matt asked.

"You, my young friend, are going to help me get out of the

building. Without being stopped. Do you understand?"

Matt nodded, feeling beaten.

"Good. They told me you were smart. Now let's go. We're wasting what little time your classmates have left." The man gestured toward the door with his pistol.

Having no choice and no time for argument, Matt went. As he started to go up the stairs, he felt the light switch panel in his back pants pocket. He palmed it while taking a look back at his captor.

"Keep moving," the man ordered.

Matt went up the carpeted steps, as slowly as he could. Near the top of the steps the man's attention swept across the students still in the halls between classes.

"If you run away from me," the man warned, "I'll shoot you and anyone else who tries to get in my way. It'll be on your head."

"I won't run," Matt said. He waited till the man moved up beside him.

The South African shoved the pistol's blunt snout into his side, keeping it hidden behind Matt's arm. "Even if you succeed in taking the pistol from me, I still have the bomb." He showed it in his cupped hand. "Now let's go."

As they started forward, Matt dropped the light switch panel to the carpeted steps. It wasn't much of a clue, but it was all he could do.

Andy jogged through the halls, dodging people, then turned toward the boiler room. As he started down the steps leading to the basement, his foot shot out from under him. He fell, bruising himself on the steps and knocking the breath from his lungs.

A metallic clink sounded below.

Groaning, Andy pushed himself up again and started back down the steps. A silvery gleam caught his eye in front of the door. He leaned down and picked up the metal rectangle, discovering it was a light switch panel.

Man, how did that get down here? He took it with him, figuring he'd throw it away inside the boiler room. He opened the door, glad to find that it was unlocked. For Matt to have been gone for an hour, he had to have found something.

"Matt?" Andy gazed around the empty room. "Matt?" Thinking maybe Matt had already come and gone, Andy was about to turn around and go back up the steps when he spotted David's laptop in the corner of the room.

No way would Andy leave that here. Andy crossed to the laptop and scooped it from the floor. He felt it vibrate in his hands as the hard drive whirred through an auto-save. He opened it and saw gibberish strung across the screen. *And there's no way he'd leave it running, either. He knows how David is about his stuff.*

Puzzled, but certain something was wrong, Andy looked around the boiler room. If Matt hadn't left on his own, someone had forced him to.

Andy glanced up at the vent Lewis had told him about. The vent plate showed streaks where the accumulated dust had been knocked away. *Matt had time to raid the hiding place and put the vent plate on, but he didn't have time to take David's laptop with him?*

It didn't make sense.

Andy gazed back at the light switch panel in his hand. Then he looked at the doorway and spotted the one there. *Okay, this had to come from somewhere.* He gazed around the room slowly, walking to get a better look at the walls.

He spotted the open light switch cavity a moment later. *If that's where it came from, why did Matt leave in such a hurry?*

Andy moved closer for a better look. Flickering digital numbers caught his eye, pulling it to the rectangular shape beside the gas main.

9:12.

Oh, man, Matt. Did you go for help? Andy dismissed that idea at once. Matt had a foilpack. He'd have called Winters. There'd be Net Force agents everywhere down here. Andy reached into his own back pocket, digging out the foilpack he'd replaced on Saturday after his had been shot on Friday. He punched in Winters's number and asked for the captain when the secretary answered.

"I'm sorry," she told him officiously, "but Captain Winters is in a meeting."

Andy ran his fingers over the bomb's surface, quivering inside. "Then get him out of it!" he demanded. "This is Andy Moore, one of the Net Force Explorers! Tell him I'm looking at a bomb that's attached to the gas main at Bradford Academy and it's set to blow in less than nine minutes! I need help!"

22

By the time the second bell rang, the hallways had cleared. Matt stayed close to the South African agent, feeling the pistol barrel digging into his side.

"If someone sees me out here," Matt said as they walked by the trophy cases toward the west side exit, "they're going to ask questions."

"You're sick," the South African said. "I'm helping you out-side." The pistol pressed harder into his side. "And you'd better act sick."

Matt scanned the empty hall and hoped that no one stopped them. "What's on the datascrip?"

"None of your business."

"It's about Site Forty-three, isn't it?" Matt asked. "Someone hacked into the government archives and found out what really happened there."

"Shut up." The South African showed him the remote con-trol.

"Or what?" Matt asked. "You'll blow us up just because I'm asking questions?"

"Silence."

Matt shook his head. "No. You want to get out of here alive. Otherwise you'd have blown us up down in the basement." He continued pressing the man, knowing the South African had to be afraid, too.

The man blinked rapidly and perspiration streaked his face.

"But while they were trashing the archives in South Africa, your net security teams tracked them back to Bradford Academy," Matt said, thinking it through. The hack had to be done from the school. Otherwise they'd have traced it back to Solomon's house. "But who did it here at the academy? Man, that must have been a nightmare for your security chief. How to find the guilty party in the whole student body here?"

The man said nothing.

"So they started with the hackers last week," Matt went on. "Only they didn't use their own people because they were afraid of setting off more alarms. They hired McDouglas and Tomlinson to do the heavy work."

"You don't know what you're talking about," the man insisted as he yanked Matt around the corner.

"McDouglas and Tomlinson weren't effective enough," Matt said. "Even after they kidnapped me. So the South African recovery team razed the hacker veeyar, putting more pressure on whoever had the files. You've had security teams around the Academy. That's how you found out about the meeting between Solomon and Donner. Or was it Donner's sudden interest in the South African War? Did you have surveillance on the media around the city? Or just on the Net where those archives were? Or maybe Donner was doing research through the archives down in South Africa?"

The man didn't answer.

"You had to have known something," Matt said, knowing it made sense. "That's how McDouglas and Tomlinson were there, and how they'd put a listening device at Donner's table."

Unexpectedly the South African slammed Matt up against the wall. No one was in the hallway.

"You will shut up," the man ordered. He held the remote in his hand. "You have just cost your friends a lot of time." He pressed one of the buttons on the remote. Matt watched in horror as the digital readout changed from 8:13 to 4:06.

"Winters."

"Captain, this is Andy Moore." Andy got closer to the bomb

on the gas line. Quickly he described the situation and the bomb, then added his thoughts about Matt.

"I agree," Winters said when Andy had finished. "Matt wouldn't have left without calling. We'll find him."

Andy remembered Matt's story about the janitors who moved and acted like Net Force agents. "You have people on-site here at the campus?"

"Yes, and they've been notified. How much time is left on the bomb?"

"Eight minutes, thirty-two seconds," Andy said. He heard Winters growling orders off the phone connection.

"I've got a team en route," Winters told him. "I've had a security net around the campus for days. What I want you to do is leave the boiler room."

"Meaning no disrespect, Captain," Andy said, "but I'm not going to be a whole lot safer up there. And down here I can make sure nobody else bothers this."

Winters evidently didn't feel like arguing. "I'll have a team there in minutes."

"What about evacuating the school?" Andy asked. "We could get everyone out."

"I'm calling the school administration on a secure line now," Winters said. "One of my agents will get a phone to the principal. We'll take care of it."

The digital readout suddenly froze, blanked, and reappeared with 4:06 showing. Andy tried to remain calm while he told Winters.

Resignation sounded in the man's voice. "Get out of there, Andy. There's no time to get a bomb team down there."

"Sir," Andy said, "you can't evacuate this building in four minutes. Not and get everyone far enough away to keep them from getting hurt."

"Andy, after what just happened, we can't evacuate the building at all until we make sure the people who took Matt have gotten clear. If we sound a fire alarm, they may blow the building anyway. Get out of there."

Andy wanted to. The last thing he wanted was to be in the boiler room when the bomb blew. At least, that's what he told himself. But he knew he couldn't leave. "I can't," he said.

"Get out of there, son."

"I can't," Andy repeated. 3:57. "If you can't get a bomb team

SHADOW OF HONOR191

down here, walk me through it. Let me see if I can disarm it."

"No. I can't take that kind of chance."

"Captain," Andy said soberly, "that chance is all the people in this building have."

The South African agent fisted Matt's shirt and yanked him from the wall.

Matt felt like throwing up. He couldn't see the timer anymore. *How much time is left?* He tried to figure it out by counting down himself, but it was hard to keep up with the numbers and pay attention to his captor at the same time.

He listened to the quietness out in the hall, to the *chuffing* of his feet hitting the floor, and to his heartbeat.

"No more wise ideas," the South African said. "You've already cost your friends four minutes of their lives."

Four minutes of their lives? Matt thought about the choice of words and realized the man intended to set off the explosive anyway. Trying to keep his panic in check, he lost count of the time remaining.

He walked forward, feeling the pistol in his side, trying to figure out what he could do. They were only fifty or sixty feet from the exit.

Footsteps echoed from the hallway to the right.

Matt glanced in that direction, spotting a janitor approaching them. He immediately identified him as one of the two men he and Mark had thought might be Net Force agents.

"Hey, buddy," the Net Force janitor called out. "Do you know anything about those vacuums?" He hooked a thumb over his shoulder back the way he'd come. "I've got one that won't start in the chemistry lab. You want to give me a hand?"

The South African didn't say a word. He jerked Matt forward and raised the pistol to fire.

"Can I just yank it off the wall and get it away from the gas main?" Andy asked. He didn't see any wires attaching the explosive to the pipe.

"No," Winters replied. "There's probably a contact-sensitive plate on that type of bomb. Once it's activated, it can't be moved."

Andy watched the digital numbers flicking through the countdown. Time was relentless. "It looks like there's a computer-link on the front."

"That's what it is, but a foilpack phone doesn't have the proper connections to link with it."

Remembering David's laptop on the floor, Andy dashed back for it. "Wait a minute. I've got a laptop right here."

"Andy, you've got to get out of there. There's no time."

"You're wasting what little time we have." Andy wanted to scream. He flipped the laptop open, then checked the compartment under the keyboard. A direct-connect for an implant rig was there. He took it out and shoved the end into the computer socket, then slapped the other end across the implants at the base of his skull.

"A laptop won't be enough," Winters argued.

3:17.

"I've got my foilpack. I can get into veeyar with the laptop. You can walk me through this with the audio input from foil-pack. David has a feed for that inlaid into his veeyar setup, so I'll be able to hear you and you'll be able to hear me."

"Andy."

"Captain Winters, we don't have much time."

"Son, if you can't shut that bomb down, it's going to be too late to get out."

"Okay," Andy said, acting nonchalant but taking a shudder-ing breath, "so it's all or nothing."

"Do you want to tell me what I'm supposed to tell your mother?"

Andy faltered for just a moment. His dad hadn't come back from the war, and he'd seen what that had done to his mom. What would it do to her if something happened to him as well? Because he chose not to walk away? His dad had been a warrior serving his country, and he'd made her aware of the sacrifices he was prepared to make before they'd ever married. What right did Andy have to make those choices before she knew he was prepared to make them?

Who lived and who died?

He was making a decision that would affect her before she even knew he might have to. That was even more unfair to her than his dad's death had been. He shook, almost lost in himself amid the fear and the confusion.

You can't live in the shadow of honor, Andy.

Bob's words—his dad's words in all probability—came to Andy then. He pushed the fear away as much as he could and connected the foilpack to the bomb.

2:43.

"Tell her that I love her," Andy said in a hoarse voice that cracked. "And tell her that I'm proud of my dad. That maybe after all these years I understand, and that I hope I turned out to be somebody he could be proud of."

He punched the Net access button on the laptop. The back of his neck burned as the implant-rig jerked him into cyber-space.

As the South African shoved his pistol forward, Matt grabbed for the man's hand holding the dead man's switch, lacing his fingers around the man's fist and pulling. He knew he'd left himself exposed to the man's weapon, but there wasn't any other way.

"Gun!" he yelled, the way he'd been trained to in Net Force Explorer courses.

The shot echoed down the hall. The bullet dug into the wall. Matt's actions had thrown the South African's aim off.

Matt hung on to the hand desperately.

The Net Force agent drew a silenced pistol from his overalls and squared off automatically in a Weaver's stance. The South African screamed and tried to shake Matt free of his hand. Matt dropped to his knees, dragging the man down with him. He watched helplessly as the South African aimed the pistol into his face. The barrel suddenly looked impossibly wide.

Then two bright red dots materialized on the South African's shirt, less than an inch apart and right over his heart. The pistol dropped from the man's nerveless fingers as he stumbled back and fell.

"You okay?" the Net Force agent asked, rushing forward.

"Yeah." Matt hung on fiercely. "I'm Matt Hunter. I'm a—"

"I know who you are and what you are." The Net Force agent fitted an ear/throat rig in place. "Eagle, this is Bluebird One. I have our loose cannon secured."

Matt looked up at the man, still holding on to the South African's lax hand. "Dead man's switch," he explained.

The agent nodded. "Can you hang on to that just another

couple minutes? One way or the other, this will be over by then."

Matt nodded, trying not to think how shaky he was and how much force it actually took to hold someone else's limp hand closed.

Andy blazed through the Net. As soon as he'd entered the simple veeyar in David's laptop, he'd dialed Mark's computer number. Mark always left a door open to all his friends so they could check in or borrow select programs he'd developed.

Plunging into Mark's closet of program-busters, Andy picked out one he was familiar with. In a heartbeat the familiar crash-suit he'd worn on the raid to South Africa covered him.

He zipped back to Bradford on the Net, then opened a channel to his foilpack number. "Captain Winters."

"I'm here, son."

"I don't have the digital counter in here. I don't know how much time is left." Andy dropped through Bradford's virtual representation and dived deep into the basement.

"One minute fifty-two seconds," Winters replied. "Andy, I've got Lieutenant Scobie on the phone with us. He's the best demolitions man I know."

Andy examined the bomb. In veeyar the complexity of it was daunting. He looked into the security lock and felt like he was looking into one of those endless mirror-reflecting-mirror effects.

"Hi, Andy," Lieutenant Scobie said. "We're going to have to work fast. The best time I've ever beaten that type of bomb in was thirty-eight seconds, so we don't have much leeway for mistakes."

"Yes, sir," Andy replied.

"I also want you to know I've never lost a man on my squad, and you're not going to be my first."

"No, sir."

"Touch the bomb," Scobie said. "When you make contact from the Net, you're going to feel like you've been sucked into it."

Andy did, and the sensation was exactly that.

"That's because the bomb has its own veeyar systems on the Net. Now, when it clears, you're going to see a maze in front of you. Tell me what it looks like."

Andy stared at the cubed maze of revolving mirrors and described it as best as he could.

"Go inside," Scobie said. "Have you got any stealth utilities?"

"Locked and loaded," Andy said. "I borrowed some stuff from Mark Gridley's computer."

"Hey," Scobie said confidently, "the way I hear it, we're in good hands. Enter the maze."

Armored up in the crashsuit, Andy flew forward. He saw his own image reflected hundreds of times in the surrounding mirrors.

"Not too fast," Scobie coaxed. "Try to keep from touching the sides, top, or bottom."

"How much time?" Andy asked.

"Andy," Winters said, "you'll know when you run out. Concentrate on getting the job done."

"Yes, sir."

"Call out the turns you see ahead of you."

"Left and right juncture." Scobie directed him to the right, calling out a series of left, right, up, and down turns that took Andy deeper and deeper into the maze.

"Ease off," the lieutenant said after the last one. "Here's one of the deciding points to figure out which version you're in. Tell me what you see."

Andy stared ahead. "It's a four-way."

"That's no help. You're looking for one of the tunnels that has two reversed reflections of you."

Andy grew frustrated. "There must be a thousand reflections in each one."

"One of them will have those two reflections. I know it's hard to see."

Andy stared harder, trying to see clearly through the reflections. A clock seemed to be ticking in the back of his head. Images of his dad blowing up on the bridge haunted him. "The center one."

"Go."

Andy flew forward. No sooner had he passed the entrance than a klaxon screamed to life. "I picked wrong! I picked wrong!"

"It's okay, Andy. It'll be the one on the left. Get going because the lock has sent out an IFF-program. If it catches you and you don't have the password, it'll report back to the bomb's main program."

Andy sped forward. "I've got more tunnels ahead of me."

Calmly Scobie called out the necessary twists and turns. Without warning a purple sun dawned behind Andy and started coming up quick.

"The IFF's on my tail," Andy said.

"Stay away from it," Scobie directed. "Do you have a mask routine?"

"Yeah. I'm bringing it on-line." Andy triggered the mask program and saw the crashsuit change to a purple that almost matched the IFF program. He continued following the lieutenant's directions.

The IFF caught Andy after a few more turns. A strong electrical current raced through him. Immediately the IFF program turned and headed back the way it had come.

"It didn't buy it," Andy said. "It knows I'm intruding."

Scobie remained calm, continuing to call out the turns. In the next heartbeat all the lights inside the maze went out, leaving Andy totally in the dark. He crashed into the dead end ahead of him. Immediately something grabbed him from the walls and floor.

Triggering the programs built into the crashsuit's architecture, Andy turned on an exterior light. Vines representing antivirus coding snaked around him, trying to hold him fast.

"A purge program's probably on its way," Scobie advised. "You've got to get out of there."

Andy cut his way free of the antivirus coding with bright red flames that represented the Trojan horse coding Mark had written to destroy most antivirus programs. The vines burned and blackened and turned to ash.

Leaping into the air, Andy flew to the left, following Scobie's directions again.

"I've got the make now," Scobie said. "Get there ahead of the purge program, and we're home free."

Andy flew through the maze, taking all the turns the lieutenant called out. But he spotted a radiant green glow catching up to him quickly from behind. He made two more turns, then the maze opened up into a miniature galaxy with double suns, one orange and one blue.

"What do you see?" Scobie asked.

If time was running out, Andy couldn't tell it from the man's voice. He described the galaxy as he plunged toward the heart of the suns.

"Fly through the suns," Scobie directed. "When you're inside them, unload every worm program you've got stacked in that deck. Then let's hope it's enough."

Before Andy was halfway there, the purge program overtook him. The green glow completely enveloped him. The heat was incredible. As he watched, the purge coding started eating away the crashsuit, chipping it in small flakes that burst into fire and were consumed.

Andy screamed out from the pain. All he had to do was log off and it would be gone, leaving no permanent marks. But how many seconds remained before the bomb blew? It was too late to run.

By the time he reached the orange and blue double sun, he was a flaming comet himself. The orange sun swelled into view, filling his vision. He held himself together and willed the suit to stay together, too. His faceplate was melting as he flew into the heart of the sun. The fiery plasma flowed in toward his face, burning his skin.

He unleashed every worm program he had access to in the crashsuit. Then he logged off.

Gasping, trembling, and terribly afraid, Andy stripped off the implant rig and glanced up at the bomb.

:18
:17
:16
:15
. . .

The numbers froze.

"Hey," Scobie called over the foilpack, "you did it, ace!"

Covered in sweat and feeling as if he'd just run a marathon, Andy pushed himself up to his knees. He was alive. They were all alive.

"Andy."

Turning, Andy spotted Matt flying down the stairs into the boiler room. Matt glanced at the bomb, saw that the numbers weren't advancing, and let out a whoop that filled the boiler room. He helped Andy up from the floor, and they hugged each other fiercely.

"Enough," Andy said breathlessly. "I've got an image to uphold."

"C'mon," Matt said. "Let's go upstairs and watch Net Force do their thing." He led the way upstairs, passing a team of Net Force agents dressed in demolitions gear and carrying a bomb-proof box.

A moment later, standing at the large windows overlooking the main street, Andy watched as Net Force descended en mass over Bradford Academy. Three helicopter gunships patrolled the section of sky that Andy could see, and the parking lot was suddenly filled with fast-attack vehicles.

"Man," Andy said, watching the agents deploy, "Winters sure didn't spare the muscle."

Matt shook his head. "The captain never does once he identifies the target." He glanced at Andy. "You took a big chance back there."

Andy shook his head. "I just did what I had to. Any less and I couldn't have lived with myself. Did I ever tell you about my dad, Matt?"

"No."

Watching the men securing the area, Andy nodded. "Well, I'm going to. He was a real hero, you know."

"Yeah," Matt said. "I've heard that."

Epilogue

"Matt had most of it right," Captain Winters said.

Andy sat in the veeyar of the captain's office Wednesday for the debrief. "You mean about the South Africans knowing who'd really set off the plague bomb?"

Winters nodded. "It's all becoming public knowledge as of five o'clock this evening. The *Washington Post* is releasing a statement then."

"About who set off the bomb?" Andy asked. He was still washed out from the last several days and was having to work to achieve any kind of focus.

"Yes."

"Who?"

"The South African Nationalists did," Winters replied.

"They used it against their own people?" Andy couldn't believe it. But then, it made perfect sense. Why else would the South Africans be so adamant about keeping everything secret?

"Yes. And against the Patriots, don't forget." Winters pushed back in his chair. "It was war, and they were determined to win it. At any cost. They were convinced that it would turn the Patriots against the Western powers and draw more international sympathy."

"But our military knew what was going on," Andy said.

"Right," Winters told him. "We knew."

"Then why not tell them?"

"It was the easiest way to end the war and get what was needed without losing more lives," Winters said. "The Nationalists agreed to do business the way the majority of their population wanted, and we agreed not to release the story."

"What happens now?"

Winters grinned coldly. "Personally, I think there might be a few new faces in the South African political scene. Those men won't stay in office."

"Yeah, but won't the U.S. get kind of tarnished for their role in the lie when all this comes out?"

"Andy, those were the terms of the cease-fire. We'll be able to show how many lives we saved by agreeing to it. We'll still come out okay. No war is good, but we made the right decisions in that one."

Andy figured the captain was probably right. "What about my dad? Why did the South Africans try to frame him? Or was that just something Solomon did?"

Winters hesitated. "Your father was involved in that mission, Andy. Beyond that, I can't say anything. The military still has to keep some of its secrets."

That evening when Andy answered the knock on his door, he found Solomon Weist standing there. A white adhesive bandage still covered his swollen nose. He looked uncomfortable. A cab waited at the curb.

"I bet I'm probably the last person you'd ever expect to see over here," Solomon said.

Andy nodded, not trusting himself to say anything. Solomon's immature feud with Andy and his irresponsibility online had almost cost the lives of every student at Bradford.

"I only came over here to give you this." Solomon held out a datascrip.

Andy made no move to take it.

"It's not a peace offering," Solomon explained. "I know you're probably going to hate me forever. This is for you. Something you deserve."

Andy still didn't take the cube.

"It's a copy of everything I hacked from the South Africans. There's a file on there about your dad. When I saw HoloNet tonight, I noticed they didn't release the story about him, so I figured they were still holding on to that one."

"If this is another trick . . ." Andy began.

"No. I swear." Solomon looked at him. "Andy, you saved the whole school yesterday. You're a hero. And heroes deserve a lot."

Andy felt uncomfortable. Solomon didn't ooze praise . . . ever.

"I don't know if they told you about your dad," Solomon said. "He was on a covert mission. It was him and his team that shut down the supply of plague bombs headed into South Africa. The Nationalists were going to use them against the Western powers, and against the Patriots. If your dad hadn't taken out the suppliers and the diamonds the Nationalists had paid for them, there could have been a lot more plague deaths. Maybe even all over Africa. Your dad's a hero, Andy, even bigger than what they're telling you. That one plague bomb had already been delivered, but your dad and his team stopped all the others."

Andy didn't know what to say. He reached for the datascrip.

"It's all on there," Solomon said. "You can see it for yourself."

Andy held the datascrip in his hand and his throat felt thick. "Thanks, Solomon. They hadn't told me."

Solomon nodded. "Well, then, I'm glad I could be the one." He turned to go.

"Hey, Solomon," Andy said.

Solomon glanced back at him.

"I'm sorry about your nose."

Solomon grinned. "Yeah, me, too. But I got off light. At least no one wants to kill me anymore. Internationally, I mean. Net Force still wants a bit of my blood."

"There's always tomorrow," Andy cracked.

Solomon laughed and walked to the cab.

Andy watched him leave, then went back to his room to the computer-link chair.

Thursday morning Andy stood high on a hill in Arlington Cemetery. He knew the white stone cross in front of him well; knew the name, rank, birth, and death carved into the stone.

It was the first time he'd ever gone there alone.

He knelt at the foot of the grave, feeling the emotion balling up in his throat and threatening to choke him. He'd dressed in some of his best clothes, even worn a tie.

He touched the grass covering the grave, running his fingers through it gently. His father's body hadn't been recovered from South Africa, so Andy knew he really wasn't in the grave. But it was the best place where he could go visit him.

"Hi, Dad," he said hoarsely. "I wanted to come out here today because this is where Mom always says she feels closest to you. I guess I kind of wanted to feel that way, too."

The wind blew gently across the hill, taking the tears from his cheeks.

"I wish things had been different. I guess you know what I did yesterday. When Mom found out, she about freaked. But it taught me one thing, Dad. If I really want to know you, all I've got to do is get to know myself." He cleared his throat, waiting till he could speak again. "And I wanted to tell you that I miss you and how much I love you." He glanced at his watch. "Got school today, so I don't have much time, but I'll talk to you again. Soon."

Andy stood and walked back down the hill. And somehow along the way, the sun seemed warmer on his face than it had all morning.